RELICS

She stiffened, her body quivering almost imperceptibly as if a high voltage charge were being pumped through it. She sucked in a breath but it seemed to stick in her throat, and for terrifying seconds she found she couldn't breathe. The skin on her face and hands puckered into goose-pimples and a numbing chill enveloped her. A small gasp escaped her as she actually felt her hair rising, standing up like a cat's hackles. She swayed uncertainly for a moment as the feeling seemed to spread through her whole body, through her very soul, and Kim clenched her teeth together, convinced she was going to faint. On the verge of panic, she screwed up her eyes until white stars danced before her. Her throat felt constricted, as though some invisible hand were gradually tightening around it. Her head seemed to be swelling, expanding to enormous proportions until it seemed it must burst.

And somewhere, perhaps in her imagination, she thought, she heard a sound. A noise which froze her blood as it throbbed in her ears.

Also by Shaun Hutson

SPAWN
SLUGS
SHADOWS
EREBUS
BREEDING GROUND

RELICS

Shaun Hutson

A STAR BOOK
published by
the Paperback Division of
W.H. ALLEN & CO. Plc

A Star Book
Published in 1987
by the Paperback Divison of
W. H. Allen & Co. Plc
44 Hill Street, London W1X 8LB

Reprinted 1987

First published in Great Britain
by W. H. Allen & Co. Plc in 1986

Copyright © Shaun Hutson, 1986

Printed and bound in Great Britain by
Anchor Brendon Ltd, Tiptree, Essex

ISBN 0 352 31797 3

Acknowledgements

To anyone and everyone who helped with this book I offer my thanks. Special thanks to Niki who helped me revive something that wasn't just dead but was buried and starting to smell a bit. To everybody at W.H.Allen who, as usual, did the *hard* work. To John Willsher (Who wants to eat in a carvery anyway?).

For different reasons I would also like to thank John, the Manager, and his staff, at the Bletchley Studio cinema. Also Dave 'Divine' Holmes at Andromeda (sorry I couldn't rip your teeth out . . .), Jon Gower at BBC Wales (yes, I may be crazy but it's fun), and finally, as ever, Belinda (Burn rubber and look out for that brick wall . . .).

Shaun Hutson

FOR MUM AND DAD
WHO ASKED FOR NOTHING
BUT GAVE ME EVERYTHING
(except that Batman outfit I wanted when I was six . . .)

THIS IS FOR YOU
WITH LOVE AND THANKS

'The oldest and strongest emotion of mankind is fear, and the oldest and strongest kind of fear is fear of the unknown.'

H.P.Lovecraft

PART ONE

'Beware of night, for we all know he's loose again . . . '

Queensrÿche

One

The knife felt cold against her flesh.

As if some icy finger were tracing a pattern over her skin, the girl felt the blade being drawn softly across her cheek.

The point brushed her lips, nudging against them for a moment as if seeking access to the warm moistness beyond. She opened her mouth slightly and, for fleeting seconds, she tasted steel. Then the knife was gone.

The girl's eyes were closed, but as she felt the point gliding down towards the hollow of her throat she finally allowed herself to gaze upon the one who wielded the blade.

He was almost invisible in the darkness but she knew that, like her, he was naked.

As were the others who stood close by, little more than pale outlines beneath the dense canopy of trees whose gnarled branches twisted and curled together, rattled by the chill October wind which whistled tunelessly through the wood. It also ruffled the girl's long dark hair, causing the silky tresses to writhe like reptilian tails.

She was barely seventeen but her body was shapely and belied her youth. Her breasts in particular seemed over-developed, the nipples coaxed to stiffness by the cold air. She shuddered involuntarily as she felt the knife being moved in a circular pattern around her aureola, brushing the puckered skin for a moment before prodding the nipple. This time she felt not only the needle-sharp point of the blade but the actual cutting edge too as it rested against the swollen bud of flesh. She closed her eyes again as the same movements were repeated on her other breast.

The pressure increased and she gritted her teeth, waiting for the cut.

But she felt only an icy tickle as the cold blade was drawn between her breasts, down to her navel and then towards the dark bush of hair between her legs. It parted the tightly curled down, guided with unfaltering skill by the powerful hand which grasped it.

She let out a low sigh, her breath clouding in the cold air, as the knife was pressed slightly harder against that most sensitive area. She opened her legs wider, as if to welcome the blade like some kind of steel penis.

For what seemed an eternity it remained there; then she exhaled slowly as it was eased aside.

Opening her eyes once more, she saw the one who held the blade turn slightly, until he was facing a youth no more than a few months older than herself. He was powerfully built, his head supported by a thick bull neck which he offered willingly to the wielder of the knife. The cutting edge left an almost invisible white mark as it was pressed against the boy's throat. But after a second the pressure eased and the blade found its way to his chest before plunging deeper towards his limp penis. He tensed as the cold steel brushed his organ, tracing the course of the thick veins before gliding over his contracted testicles.

A moment later it was withdrawn and now both the girl and the youth knelt, fallen leaves crunching beneath them. They were close, within arm's length.

Suddenly they caught the powerful smell which drifted on the wind.

A goat was being led towards them by a rope tied around its neck.

Another thick length of hemp had been wrapped tightly around its jaws so the only sound it could make was a low mewling deep in its throat.

The young couple lay face down on the carpet of leaves as the goat was coaxed between them. It was held firmly by the man who gripped the knife. He now moved behind the creature and straddled it, holding the blade before his chest in one strong hand. With the other he gripped the horns of the goat and yanked its head back so savagely he almost broke its neck.

The knife flashed forward, shearing through the animal's throat, slicing effortlessly through muscle and sinew.

Huge gouts of blood erupted from the massive wound, spraying into the air with the force of a high pressure hose. The crimson fluid splattered the young couple as the goat bucked madly between the man's legs, its body jerking uncontrollably. The knife-wielder watched the white clouds of vapour rising into the air as the hot blood continued to fountain from the ruptured arteries.

From either side, figures approached, all of them men. All of them naked.

They lifted the goat into the air, its struggles now becoming more feeble as its life fluid gushed away. It suddenly re-doubled its efforts as the knife-wielder thrust his blade into its exposed belly, slicing open the fleshy sac with one powerful movement.

Intestines burst from the wound like the bloodied arms of an octopus, huge thick lengths falling to the ground with a loud, liquid splat. Steam rose from the spilling entrails, the pungent odour now mingling with the reek of excrement as the goat's sphincter muscle loosened and a stream of liquid and solid waste pumped from its writhing body.

Still no one spoke, but as if a signal had been given, the young couple rolled over to face each other.

The girl closed her eyes and rolled again, allowing herself to slide into the thick mass of viscera. She felt its warmth surround her, felt the slippery wetness of the pulsing organs beneath her buttocks. She spread her legs and waited for the boy to join her. His penis was already swollen and he found no difficulty penetrating her, for she was as eager as he. They writhed amidst the blood and internal organs, now oblivious to the choking smells which surrounded them and the crimson fluid which coated their bodies. They were aware only of the pleasure which they both felt.

The man with the knife watched impassively as the frenetic coupling continued.

Blood ran down his hand from the blade of the weapon

and he gazed at the crimson droplets in fascination as one fell onto his own rigid penis, staining the head bright red.

He chuckled.

So much blood.

And there would be more.

He looked around at the other naked bodies in the clearing.

Much more blood.

Two

It was getting difficult to breathe inside the tent. The air was full of dust and the small structure was definitely too small to adequately accommodate three people. Nevertheless, Kim Nichols looked on with rapt attention as the piece of hard stone was broken open.

A fragment came free as the tracer was worked slowly around it, exposing the encased relic.

Charles Cooper picked up the small hammer which lay on the table before him and tapped the wooden end of the tracer. The chisel-like implement shaved off some more stone and the article within became more easily visible.

'It looks like a currency bar,' Phillip Swanson said quietly as Cooper prised away the last of the clinging rock. He swept the metal ingot with a small brush, then laid the rusted artifact on the white cloth before him. A number of other articles already lay on view there, including coins, a couple of arrow-heads, a brooch and a roughly hewn figurine shaped like a phallus.

'It's strange,' Kim observed, picking up the metal ingot and turning it carefully between her thumb and forefinger. 'Coins *and* currency bars used by the same tribe. The Celts usually kept to one form of currency, didn't they?'

'Don't forget there was trade with other tribes,' Cooper reminded her. '*Atrebates* like the Iceni and the Trinovantes would still have traded with *Demetae* such as the Brigantes and the Cronovii.' He prodded the other slim metal bars with his index finger.

'A tribe that used both forms of currency,' Swanson mused. 'It must have been a large settlement from the amount of stuff we've found.'

'Then why haven't we found any bones?' asked Kim, but she received no answer from either of her colleagues. Cooper merely sat back in his chair and ran a hand over his hairless head. It was a feature which made him look older than his thirty-five years. Apart from the tufts over his ears and at the back of his head he was completely bald. Even his eyebrows appeared to be thinning. His sad, baleful eyes looked as though they had seen all the worries of the world and still carried their imprint. It was Cooper who had initiated this particular dig.

Builders working on a nearby site had unearthed a number of artifacts and Cooper had been notified. He'd ordered an electro-magnetic search of the area which had revealed a large ancient settlement of unknown origin. Subsequent aerial sweeps had confirmed the presence of a Celtic settlement which covered an area almost a quarter of a mile square.

Kim, who worked at the museum three miles away in Longfield, the nearest town, had joined his team of twenty archaeologists and their work had so far revealed a positive treasure trove of relics. A profusion of gold torcs and other neck rings had convinced Cooper and his team that this particular site had been home to one of the most powerful Celtic tribes of the time. Slave chains and shackles had also been discovered, suggesting that the tribe, unlike their contemporaries, had used forced labour.

Bones were the only thing missing.

Shields, weapons, currency, pottery and sculpture had all been unearthed during the past two weeks. Some of the finds were not only valuable in a financial sense but priceless in their archaeological worth. All these artifacts confirmed that the settlement had been very large indeed, yet still no physical remains of the tribe who'd created the horde had been found.

Kim looked down at the relics laid out before her.

What the hell had happened to the tribe?

Three

The air was turning blue.

A thick haze of diesel fumes hung over the men and machines like a man-made fog bank. Thick and noxious.

The roar of powerful engines mingled with the screech of caterpillar tracks as a number of large earth-movers rumbled across the landscape, flattening or digging according to their individual function.

Frank King watched approvingly as a JCB was manoeuvred into position, its great metal arm swinging down to scoop up a mound of earth which it then dumped into the back of a waiting lorry. The driver was sitting contentedly in the cab smoking and he waved to King as the foreman passed, unable to hear King's comment about 'not straining himself' because of the roar of machinery.

Away to his right, King could see a group of men laying tarmac. Despite the chill in the air they worked in shirt-sleeves. Sweat was soaking through their clothes from the heat given off by the red-hot tar.

The Leisure Centre itself was all but finished. An 'E' shaped two storey building, it looked like something a child might fashion from plastic blocks. Painters still swarmed over it like so many overall-clad termites, only these termites were busy applying coats of weather-proof paint.

King stood a moment longer surveying the activity, then

turned and headed towards the yellow Portakabin close by. On entering he moved across to the welcoming warmth of a calor-gas heater and held his hands over it, meanwhile trying to catch the tail end of the phone conversation one of his colleagues was engaged in.

John Kirkland was nodding as he held the phone, his mouth opening and closing like a goldfish as he struggled to get a word in. Finally he held the receiver slightly away from his ear and cupped a hand over the mouthpiece. He looked up at King and shook his head as if signalling defeat. The other foreman smiled. Another three or four minutes and Kirkland replaced the phone.

'Jesus,' he muttered.

'Cutler?' King asked, grinning.

'Who else do you know who can talk non-stop for twenty minutes flat?' Kirkland said, picking up his mug of tea. He sipped it, wincing when he found that it was cold.

'What did he want?'

'The usual. "Is everything going according to schedule? Are we going to be finished on time?" I don't know why he doesn't move his fucking desk out here so he can sit and watch, at least it'd save him ringing up so often.'

Frank King chuckled and poured his colleague a hot mug of tea, repeating the action for himself.

'I don't know what he's worried about,' Kirkland said. 'We're ahead of schedule if anything.' He sipped some tea. 'Anyway, Cutler reckons he's coming out here this afternoon to have a look for himself. He said something about flattening that wood.' Kirkland tapped the map which lay on the table before him. 'He wants to build on the land, extend the project.'

King peered through the window of the portakabin, rubbing some grime away with his index finger. He could see the wood that Kirkland meant. It was a mile or so to the east of the main site, on a slight rise.

'It's more work, John,' he said. 'None of us can turn our noses up at that.'

'I'm not arguing with you, but things are going to get a bit crowded around here soon,' he said, taking a sip of his tea.

'I mean, there's that archaeological dig going on over there.' He motioned to his left, to the west. 'They've been at it for a while too. Knowing Cutler, I'm surprised he hasn't offered to build them a bloody museum.'

King laughed, his eyes drawn once more to the dark outcrop of trees which grew so thickly to the east.

The wood looked like a stain against the green of the hills.

Four

It was Kim who felt the tremor first.

She felt a slight vibration beneath her feet and for a moment she paused, looking up at Phillip Swanson, who seemed not to have noticed the movement. He was more concerned with unearthing a gold receptacle from the floor of the trench in which they both crouched. Kim waited a second longer, then began to help Swanson.

'It's gold,' he said excitedly. 'Some kind of ornamental bowl.'

They had uncovered the top half of the container when the second tremor came.

'Did you feel that?' Kim asked, pressing the palm of one hand to the earth.

Swanson nodded distractedly, apparently uninterested.

No more than ten yards away from them, a small rift opened in the earth.

Loose dirt and gravel immediately began to tumble into the crack, which was widening with alarming speed and extending lengthwise along the trench they were working in.

It was now less than six yards from them.

Swanson dug carefully beneath the bowl, freeing it from the last clods of earth which held it captive.

The crack in the ground was widening, yawning a full six feet across now and still lengthening.

There was another vibration, so violent it rocked Kim on her heels, causing her to overbalance. As she fell to one side she saw the rent in the earth, now only two or three feet from them.

She shouted a warning to Swanson but it was too late.

It was as if the bottom of the trench had simply fallen away. The crack opened like a hungry mouth and Kim realized with horror that she was falling.

Swanson too began slipping into the crack, which was now a gaping wound across the land.

Kim clutched frantically at the side of the trench, digging her fingers into the earth in a desperate effort not to fall. There was nothing beneath her feet and she gritted her teeth, trying to force from her mind thoughts of how deep the hole might be. Swanson also grabbed onto the ledge of hard ground and felt his feet dangling in empty air. An icy cold blast of wind erupted from below them and Kim sucked in an almost painful breath, fearing that the sudden uprush might cause her to lose her grip.

But now others were running to their aid. She saw Cooper sprinting toward the side of the trench. He dropped to his knees and thrust a hand down to her. Beside him another man, whom she didn't recognize, was shining a torch past her down into the hole, trying to see just how deep it was.

The light was swallowed up by the impenetrable blackness.

The rift which had opened was obviously much deeper than anyone could have guessed.

'Take my hand,' Cooper urged, but Kim dared not release her grip on the earth ledge for fear of falling. Her boots dug into the sides of the hole but only succeeded in dislodging some pieces of rock. From the amount of time they took to hit the bottom it was painfully obvious that the hole was deep enough to cause serious injury, if not death, should either she or Swanson fall.

'Somebody get a rope,' yelled Cooper, straining to reach Kim's hand.

She felt his powerful hand close over her wrist, and with lightning speed she gripped his forearm and clung tightly. He tried to pull her up, two of his colleagues holding onto him to prevent him from toppling head first into the black chasm.

The veins on his forehead bulged as he used all his strength to haul her up, inch by inch.

The wall of the trench started to collapse.

Just small pieces of earth at first, then great lumps of it began to fall past Kim, some of the fragments striking her as they disappeared into the gaping maw which had now opened out into an almost circular pit.

Cooper almost overbalanced, his grip on Kim's wrist loosening for an instant.

She screamed as she slipped an inch or two, but Cooper regained his grip and began once more to haul her up the crumbling wall of the trench.

Behind her, Swanson was muttering to himself, struggling to retain a hand-hold on earth that was crumbling beneath his frantic fingers.

A spade was lowered to him and someone shouted to him to grab the handle but he was afraid to release his hold on the ledge. His heart was hammering against his ribs, the perspiration running in great salty rivulets down his face. He closed his eyes tightly for a moment, screwing them up until pain began to gnaw at his forehead.

A lump of earth the size of a fist came loose and hit him on the top of the head.

He lost his grip.

A woman standing on the side of the trench screamed as the archaeologist flailed with one hand, trying desperately to regain his hold.

Kim heard his shout of terror as he sensed he was slipping away. She tightened her grip on Cooper's hand as he slowly dragged her upper body clear of the hole, aware that the trench wall would not hold out much longer.

His foot slipped and he almost overbalanced, but strong arms held him upright and he continued to drag Kim out.

Her legs finally cleared the hole and with one last surge of strength, Cooper pulled her completely clear. Both of them fell back onto the earth, which was still crumbling beneath them. They rolled away, seeking firmer footing. Kim could hardly get her breath but she clambered to her feet and looked round.

'Help me!' shrieked Swanson, now clutching at the spade which was offered to him. He closed one desperate hand over the wooden shaft and clung on, knowing that his life depended on it.

His would-be rescuers kept trying to drag him up but his full weight, now dangling helplessly over the pit, was too much for them.

'Where's that bloody rope?' shouted Cooper, running to get it from one of his colleagues. He fashioned it into a makeshift loop, then lowered it towards Swanson.

'Put your arm through the loop,' he bellowed as the other end was secured to a tree stump.

Swanson did as he was told, though he hardly needed prompting. He grabbed the rope and tried to haul himself up.

Kim watched helplessly as three of the archaeologists pulled on the rope. Slowly, inch by inch, they started dragging Swanson clear.

Picking up a torch, Kim shone it into the pit and saw that the hole was cylindrical, a tube of earth with smooth sides. She daren't guess how deep it was.

Swanson was more than half clear of the pit when the rope began to fray.

At first a handful of strands sprang from the hemp, then more.

Swanson heard a creak as it unravelled quickly.

'No!' he shrieked as the final strands came undone.

The men holding the rope tried to pull him up faster and flailing hands tried to catch him, but it was too late.

With a scream of fear he plummetted from sight into the pit, his shout reverberating inside the shaft.

Kim closed her eyes, waiting for the thud as he hit the bottom.

It never came.

Instead, everyone near the pit froze as Swanson's shout suddenly changed into a bellow of unimaginable agony. The sound, amplified by the shaft, was like a slap in the face.

'Oh, God!' murmured Kim, peering down into the darkness. But she could see nothing.

The darkness of the pit hid his body from sight.

Had he broken his back? Shattered his legs? Perhaps his skull had been pulped by the fall?

Stunned by that roar of agony, the other archaeologists, too, stood gazing helplessly into the enveloping blackness.

Now they all felt an icy breeze which seemed to rise from the pit. With it came a choking smell, a pungent odour of decay which made Kim cover her nose and mouth. She looked at Cooper, but he could only shake his head, wondering, like the others, what fate had befallen Swanson.

Had he known the truth he would have been glad that he could not see the body.

Five

The lights on the two police cars and the ambulance turned silently, casting red and blue splashes of colour onto the faces of the people gathered around the deadly pit.

No one spoke, and the whole scene reminded Kim of an extract from a silent film. She stood close to Cooper, a mug of tea cradled in her hands, but the warm fluid was doing little to drive the chill from her bones. What she was feeling was not induced by the cold wind. It was the icy embrace of fear and shock, and it gripped her tighter every time she looked at the hole into which Swanson had fallen.

A couple of policemen were busy constructing a winch beside the pit, watched by the crowd of onlookers. Kim brushed a strand of blonde hair from her face, noticing that her hand was still shaking.

Cooper placed an arm around her shoulders and pulled her close in a gesture which suggested concern rather than affection.

She took another sip of her tea and glanced across the open ground towards a grey Sierra which was bouncing awkwardly over the dips and gulleys in the earth as it approached the other vehicles. Kim watched as it came to a halt and the driver climbed out.

He was tall, dressed in a suit which was stretched almost too tightly across his broad chest and back. His dark hair was uncombed and he ran a hand through it as he slammed the car door. A uniformed man approached the car and said something which Kim couldn't hear, but he motioned in her direction and the newcomer nodded and headed towards her, casting a momentary glance past her towards the pit where the winch had been all but secured.

'Inspector Stephen Wallace,' said the man in the suit, flipping open a slim leather wallet which he took from his inside pocket.

Kim looked at the photo on the I.D. card, thinking it did the policeman scant justice. He was powerfully built, and his shirt collar looked painfully tight around his thick neck. As if reading her mind, he reached up and undid the top button, relaxing slightly as he did so. He smiled reassuringly at Kim, who despite her condition found herself returning the gesture.

'I already know what happened,' he told Cooper. 'One of my men informed me over the radio. I'm sorry about Mr Swanson.'

Cooper nodded.

Wallace moved as close to the edge of the pit as he felt prudent, staring down into a seemingly bottomless maw.

'Did you know this site was unstable?' he asked.

'Certainly not,' Cooper snapped, 'or we wouldn't have started work here.'

'Just asking,' Wallace murmured quietly.

The uniformed man beside the winch gave a thumbs-up and the inspector walked around the shaft, guessing that the hole must be at least twelve feet in diameter. He pulled off his jacket, handing it to another of the waiting constables, then turned to the ambulanceman.

'I'll go down first,' he said. 'Check it out.' He took a torch from one of his constables and held out his hand again. 'Let me have that two-way.'

The harness which dangled from the winch was a piece of rope tied into a loop at the bottom. Wallace put one foot into it, gripping the hemp securely with his free hand, and lowered himself the first few feet into the darkness. He flicked on the torch, playing the powerful beam around the walls of the shaft. The rope creaked ominously as he was lowered.

A foul stench filled his nostrils. A fusty, cloying odour which made him gasp for air. It was cold too, and the policeman shivered involuntarily, pointing the torch down every now and then in the hope of illuminating the bottom of the shaft. The beam was quickly swallowed by the gloom.

He was lowered further. Slowly, evenly.

The smell was growing worse and Wallace coughed, trying to breathe through his mouth to minimize its effects. The stench was making him light-headed.

Fifty feet and still no sign of the bottom of the shaft.

'Anything yet, guv?'

The voice on the two-way belonged to sergeant Bill Dayton and Wallace recognized it immediately.

'Nothing,' he said and coughed again.

Seventy feet.

Wallace was beginning to wonder if his men had enough rope. Just how deep *was* this bloody hole? The cold, like the smell, seemed to be intensifying, so much so that the inspector was now shivering uncontrollably. And yet there

24

was no breeze. The air was unmoving, like stagnant water in a blocked well.

Eighty feet.

He shone the torch beneath him once more and, this time, it picked something out.

A few feet below, something was glistening.

'Nearly there,' Wallace said into the two-way.

'Can you see Swanson?' asked Cooper.

'Not yet . . .' He snapped his jaws together, cutting off the sentence.

There were sounds of movement from below.

Faint rustling sounds, almost imperceptible but nevertheless present. Like . . .

Like what, Wallace thought?

He swallowed hard and shone the torch down once more.

'Oh, Jesus!' he exclaimed.

Another couple of feet and he'd reached the bottom of the shaft. Wallace stepped out of the harness and shone his torch forward, waving a hand in front of his nose to waft away the nauseating stench that filled his nostrils. He wished he could wipe away what he saw, too.

There was a wooden spike in the centre of the pit, placed with almost mathematical precision so it was in the very middle. The stake was fully fifteen feet tall, tipped by a razor-sharp point unblunted by the passage of time.

Impaled on this spike, like an insect on a board, was Phillip Swanson.

The spike had penetrated his back just above the left scapula, tearing through his body before erupting from it at the junction of his right thigh and torso. He had landed on the spike with such momentum that his body was almost touching the ground. Blood had sprayed everywhere. It had run in thick rivulets from his nose and mouth, gushed freely from his shattered groin and pumped in huge gouts from his stomach which was torn open to reveal a tangle of internal organs which looked on the point of breaking loose. Thick spurts of odorous green bile from the pulverized gall bladder had mingled with the blood which was now caked thickly all over the corpse and the base of the sharpened pole. There were fragments of broken bone scattered about, and Swanson's arms dangled limply on either side of him, one of them attached only by the merest thread of skin and ligament. Smashed bone glistened whitely amidst the pulped mess of flesh and blood.

Wallace knelt close to the dangling head, hearing that strange rustling once more. It took him a second to realize that it was wind hissing through Swanson's punctured lungs. Wallace frowned. For that to be happening the man had to be alive but surely that was impossible.

He lifted the head gently, looking at the bloodied face.

Swanson's eyes snapped open.

In that split second Wallace fell back, dropping the torch, stumbling in the darkness.

He heard a thick, throaty gurgle and realized that it was Swanson's death rattle.

'Shit,' muttered the policeman, his heart thudding madly against his ribs. He wiped his face with one shaking hand, gradually regaining his composure.

Somehow Swanson had clung to life for over an hour while skewered on the stake.

Wallace didn't even attempt to imagine the suffering he'd gone through. The inspector regained his torch and shone it on the archaeologist's face once more, seeing that the eyes were now staring wide, the pupils hugely dilated. The soft rustling sound had stopped.

'Wallace, are you all right?'

He recognized Cooper's voice and found his radio.

'Terrific,' he said, wearily. 'Dayton, can you hear me? Clear everybody away from the pit, then get a stretcher down here.'

'On its way, guv,' the sergeant told him.

Wallace shone his torch around the base of the shaft, looking at the objects which were scattered in all directions. Coins, weapons, jewellery.

And bones. So many bones.

As the beam fell on Swanson again he quickly moved it away, playing it over the walls. He reached for the two-way, his eyes fixed ahead.

26

'Cooper, you still there?' he said.

A crackle of static, then the archaeologist answered.

'What is it?'

'When the body's removed you'd better come down here,' the policeman said, the torch wavering slightly as he shone it ahead. The beam flickered for a second.

'There's something I think you should see.'

Six

He didn't time it, but Wallace guessed that it took him and the ambulanceman almost twenty minutes to remove Phillip Swanson's body from the wooden stake. As the body was finally pulled free, the left arm came loose and fell with a dull thud. The ambulanceman laid it alongside the body, then carefully wrapped the remains in a thick blanket and secured the whole grisly package to a stretcher with rope. On Wallace's order the corpse was winched up, along with the ambulanceman.

The two of them had spoken little during their vile task. The ambulanceman in particular seemed glad to be away from the cloying blackness of the pit and, as he was winched up towards the light again, he did not look down.

Now the policeman stood alone wishing he had a cigarette, partly to calm his nerves, but also to mask the rancid stench which filled the shaft. He rummaged in his trouser pockets and found half a stick of chewing gum. It would have to do for now. He shone the torch over the floor of the pit, realizing at last how many strange objects lay around him. To his untrained eye it reminded him of some ancient rubbish tip. Articles of all shapes and sizes were scattered in all directions around the base of the stake.

The roving beam illuminated a skull, the jaws open in a soundless scream. There was a large hole in it just above the crown. Another lay beside it. And another. All bore jagged cracks or hollows.

But it was beyond the mounds of bones and relics that Wallace finally allowed the torch beam to rest.

What would Cooper and the others make of this?

He chewed his gum thoughtfully and glanced up. The pit's depth prevented any natural light from reaching the bottom and it also cut out any sounds from above. The combination of deathly silence and unyielding darkness was a formidable one. And there was the ever-present smell, too. An odour of decay which clutched at Wallace's throat like an invisible spectre.

A few feet above him he heard something move. He aimed his torch up into the gloom.

Cooper was descending on the winch and with him was the young woman Wallace knew as Kim Nichols.

She had a firm hold on the rope and looked unperturbed by the sight which faced her. Even when she glanced at the bloodied wooden stake she didn't flinch. Wallace watched her for a moment, offering his hand as she stepped out of the harness. There was a warmth in her touch which contrasted sharply with the bone-numbing cold in the shaft.

'You don't need an explanation, do you?' said Wallace, motioning towards the stake.

Cooper shook his head.

Kim shuddered and looked away, thinking how easily she could have been the one to suffer Swanson's agonizing death. But that thought was pushed aside as she saw the piles of artifacts before her. Cooper too was staring in awe at the array which faced him. He bent and picked up a short sword, the blade dulled but still remarkably well preserved considering its age. Flecks of rust had formed around the tip, but apart from that the weapon looked surprisingly sturdy.

Kim found a number of large bowls, some gold, some iron. But she was more interested in the bones. Skulls, femurs, tibias, pelvic bones, and here and there complete skeletons. The place was carpeted with them.

'It's a sacrificial well,' said Cooper excitedly.

Wallace continued chewing slowly, watching the two archaeologists.

'That would explain the bones,' Kim added.

'I don't get it,' Wallace said.

'This shaft and the wooden stake were put here by a Celtic tribe thousands of years ago,' explained Cooper.

'Offerings like these coins and weapons,' added Kim, 'were thrown in to please their gods. So were human beings. Prisoners of war, lunatics and sacrificial victims from the tribe were all thrown down here in the hope of gaining favour with whichever deity was being worshipped.'

'I'm sure Phillip Swanson would have been pleased to hear that,' Wallace said acidly.

'You don't understand the importance of this find, Wallace,' Cooper snapped. 'It's unfortunate that Swanson is dead but it was an accident. What do you expect us to do? Close the site as a mark of respect?' There was scorn in his voice.

Wallace turned away, pointing the torch at the far wall of the pit.

'What do you make of that?'

Cooper, who had been crouching close to the wooden stake, looked up. His jaw dropped open. He got slowly to his feet and wandered across to join the policeman, closely followed by Kim.

The three of them stood mesmerized by the sight that faced them.

Two large, almost perfectly circular stones were propped against the smooth wall of the shaft. Spreadeagled on each one was a skeleton. Iron spikes fully ten inches long had been driven through the wrists and feet of each one. The mouths were open as if the skeletons were still screaming. More of the iron spikes had been driven through the eye sockets of each one, nailing the head to the stone behind it.

'Were *they* thrown in here like that?' Wallace asked. 'Because if they weren't, then whoever nailed them up died down here with them.'

'Criminals,' said Cooper, quietly. 'To have suffered punishment like that they must have transgressed against the tribe itself.'

'These stones,' Kim said, poking one finger behind the rock closest to her. 'They're like gates. There's something behind them.' She peered through the narrow gap into the odorous gloom beyond. 'It looks like a tunnel of some kind.'

'I'm going to leave you to it,' said Wallace. 'After all, I'm a copper, not an archaeologist. I've done my bit.'

Cooper nodded perfunctorily, more interested in the finds.

'Thank you,' Kim said as Wallace gripped the harness.

'I may need a statement from you, Miss Nichols,' he said. 'When you've finished.'

She nodded and smiled.

The rope, and Wallace, began to rise.

Seven

Frank King double-checked that the handbrake of the Land Rover would hold on the sharp incline, and then he and John Kirkland clambered out.

From where they stood the building site was clearly visible away to the west.

The wood stood defiantly before them, its trees jammed tightly together as if to form a barrier to any who might wish to enter. As the two men pushed their way through the chest-high bushes which grew on the perimeter, Kirkland cursed the brambles that cut his flesh. One particularly long hawthorn spike dug deeply into the back of his right hand, drawing blood, and he winced in pain.

'Why the bloody hell couldn't Cutler have come up here himself?' he snarled, wiping the crimson droplets away with his handkerchief. 'I mean, if he wants the wood levelled, fair enough. All we have to do is send a dozen blokes up here with chainsaws, then bulldoze the whole lot when they've finished.'

'It seems like such a waste, doesn't it?' said King, looking around at the ancient trees which towered over them like sentinels. 'Flattening this lot.'

'Come on, Frank, don't have a fit of environmental conscience now,' Kirkland said, tugging himself free of a clinging gorse bush.

The foreman smiled.

'There should be a few thousand quids' worth of paper here,' he said, tapping the trunk of one tree.

As the men moved deeper into the wood King noticed how dark it was becoming. Despite the scarcity of leaves on the branches, the trees still seemed to be blocking out a great deal of natural light. King wondered how any of the mosses and lichens which carpeted the floor of the wood managed to grow. He kicked a rotted tree stump aside, stepping back in revulsion as he saw dozens of wood lice spilling from the hulk like maggots from a festering wound. Two or three extremely large ground spiders also scuttled into view. Kirkland crushed one beneath his foot.

Ahead of them was a clearing, perhaps twenty or thirty yards in diameter, and here the ground was covered by a blanket of brown leaves. They crackled noisily as the two men walked over them.

King stopped in the centre of the treeless area, relieved to be free of the dark confines of the dense wood. He was beginning to feel quite claustrophobic.

High above them, the sky was the colour of wet concrete and a gathering of black clouds to the north promised rain.

Kirkland kicked away some of the dead leaves and dug the toe of his boot into the earth, kicking up a large clod.

31

'The foundations are going to have to be laid deep if Cutler wants us to build here,' he said, sucking at the small cut on his hand. He bent down and picked up a handful of the moist topsoil, turning it over in his hand, prodding the dark matter and then finally dropping it.

His palms were stained a deep, rusty red.

The colour of dried blood.

Kirkland rubbed his hands together, trying to wipe away the stain. He smelt a musty odour and coughed. The ground around his feet was also tinged dark red.

The trees rattled noisily in the wind as the two men turned to make their way back.

'The sooner this lot's flattened the better,' said Kirkland, rubbing his hands on his overalls.

As they left the clearing, the gloom closed around them again.

Eight

'What sort of rock is it?' Kim asked, watching as George Perry used a chisel to shave off a piece of the slab.

Perry held the lantern over it and prodded the powdery rock with one finger.

'It looks like limestone,' he said. 'It would have to be reasonably soft to take those nails.' He motioned to the circles of stone with the skeletons spreadeagled on them.

'Then they shouldn't be too difficult to move,' Cooper said excitedly.

The gas lamps cast a dull yellow glow around the base of the pit, illuminating the host of artifacts and bones that littered the sacrificial well. Many of the objects had already been removed for analysis. Three or four of the team were packing them carefully into the back of the Land Rover which would transport them into Longfield.

As yet none of the bones had been touched.

Cooper stepped forward, dug his fingers into the soil behind the edge of one of the circular rocks, grasped the rock and braced his shoulder against it. George Perry added his considerable bulk to the effort and they were joined by a third man, whom Kim recognized as Ian Russell. Perry was a grey-haired individual and despite the chill inside the subterranean chamber, dark rings of sweat were visible beneath his armpits. Kim directed the beam of her powerful torch at the rock and watched as the trio of men braced themselves. At a signal from Cooper they began to tug on the stone.

Gritting his teeth, Cooper pulled as hard as he could, feeling a slight movement.

The other two men also noticed that the stone was beginning to shift and they re-doubled their efforts.

An inch.

Two inches.

The concerted effort was working.

Three inches.

Several small fragments of the rock broke off and fell to the ground, and Perry found that he was losing his handhold. He swiftly dug his hands in behind the stone once more, scraping his palms as he did so.

Six inches.

Kim stepped forward, aiming the torch beam into the blackness behind the monolith.

Eight inches.

Russell grunted in pain as his finger slipped and part of his nail was torn away as far as the cuticle. A dark globule of blood welled up and dripped from the end of the digit.

One foot and still they heaved, trying to clear a gap large enough to squeeze through.

The skeleton suspended on the rock shuddered slightly as the great stone was moved. Two of the fingers broke off and dropped to the ground.

Cooper, his face sheathed in sweat, was finding it

difficult to get his breath. The effort of moving the rock was over-exerting his strength and the cloying atmosphere inside the shaft wasn't helping.

'Stop,' he grunted and the other two men carefully released their hold on the stone.

Reaching into his pocket, Russell pulled out a handkerchief and dabbed at the blood from his injured finger, but he seemed more concerned with what lay behind the rock than with his own discomfort.

Cooper took the torch from Kim and stood by the entrance they had unblocked. The gap was large enough to admit him now but he hesitated, shining the torch beam through the blackness to what lay beyond.

It was a tunnel.

As Cooper stood there he felt the beads of perspiration on his forehead turning cold, as if the icy breeze were freezing them into dozens of crystal beads.

He didn't move.

Kim looked at him and frowned, wondering why the archaeologist did not advance into the tunnel. He had been so eager to discover its secrets that she could not understand why he should hesitate now.

She sucked in a startled breath as the muscles in her body suddenly seemed to spasm, as if some powerful electric current were being pumped through her for long seconds. The feeling passed and then she was aware of a rancid stench, much more powerful than that in the shaft, but it was carried on no breeze; it simply hung in the air like a noxious invisible blanket.

Perry coughed and covered his face with one hand.

For what seemed like an eternity no one moved. Finally, as if suddenly galvanized into action, Cooper eased his way through the gap into the waiting tunnel.

The ground was surprisingly soft beneath his feet, and clay-like in consistency. The walls, too, were porous, almost clammy to the touch.

'There must be a lot of moisture in the soil,' said Kim, following him inside, touching the wall with her fingers.

'It's amazing,' said Perry. 'There don't appear to be any stantions to support the tunnel roof and yet it seems solid.'

'The Celts were very skilled builders and architects,' Cooper reminded him. 'You only have to look at the broch of Midhowe to realize that.'

'The broch?' Russell said.

'It's a stone tower in the Orkneys,' Kim told him, 'said to have been built by the Celts over 2,000 years ago.'

Ahead of her, Cooper found that the tunnel was curving to the right. Less than four feet wide in places, its narrowness forced the archaeologists to walk in single file. Kim touched the wall closest to her and found that in places droplets of moisture were forming and running like dirty tears down the wall.

Cooper stopped.

There was another tunnel leading off to the left.

'Which one do we take?' asked Perry.

'We could split up,' Russell suggested.

'No,' Cooper said. 'There's no telling how deep these networks go or how complex they become. We'll stay together for the time being.'

They moved on.

Kim saw her breath clouding in the air and she shuddered as the numbing cold seemed to penetrate her bones, freezing the marrow until her whole body felt as if it were stiffening. She found it an effort to lift her feet. Ahead of her, she saw that Cooper too was slowing his pace. It was as if they were walking into a high wind, battling against the force of some powerful blast of air. But there was no movement in the air. The atmosphere remained still and as stagnant as filthy pond water. The stench and the cold closed around them like a reeking glove, squeezing more tightly until each of them was gasping for breath.

Cooper stopped and pulled a box of matches from his pocket. He lit one and held it up.

The flame did not move.

Not a flicker either way.

In seconds the match burned out, as if there wasn't

enough oxygen in the foul atmosphere to sustain it.

'Shouldn't one of us go back and tell the others what's happening?' Russell suggested.

Cooper agreed.

'We'll push on and see if we can find the end of the tunnel,' he said. 'You go back.'

Russell nodded, flicked on his torch and retreated down the narrow tunnel. Within seconds the light was enveloped by the blackness and he became invisible to his three colleagues.

'Come on,' Cooper said, noticing that the tunnel turned to the right again, more sharply this time. Kim sensed that it was also getting narrower. She put out her hands and touched both sides with ease, recoiling slightly from the clammy, moist feel of the walls.

'How much further?' Perry murmured wearily. 'We must have come five or six hundred yards already.'

'The Celts didn't usually build labyrinths like this, did they?' said Kim, not sure whether it was a question or a statement.

'Their hill-forts are very complex but I've never seen anything like this *under* the ground,' Cooper confessed.

The tunnel widened slightly, turning an almost ninety degree bend. The three archaeologists came around the corner virtually together.

The sight which met them stopped them in their tracks.

Nine

The skeletons were piled six deep in places.

The bones, blackened by the ages, lay lengthways across the tunnel like a mouldering barrier, preventing the archaeologists from moving any further.

Cooper shone his torch over the macabre find, overawed by the sheer number of ancient forms. Kim took a faltering step forward, kneeling beside the closest one. Cooper joined her, muttering to himself as the torch beam flickered once more.

'This kind of mass burial wasn't normal Celtic practice,' Kim said, quietly, as if reluctant to disturb the unnatural silence around them. Even as she spoke her voice seemed muffled. Stifled by the choking smell and the almost palpable darkness. 'There must be hundreds of them.'

'They look like children's bones,' said George Perry, noticing, like his companions, that not one of the skeletons was more than about three feet in height.

Kim prodded one with the end of a pencil, hearing the lead scrape along the bare bone like fingernails on a blackboard.

Perry looked down at the skeletons, then past them, the beam of his torch catching a larger object.

It was another barrier, this time stone covered with rancid moss, its surface mottled by the few lichens that had managed to survive in such a fetid atmosphere. Perry was about to say something when Cooper stood up and spoke, a note of urgency in his voice.

'We need to examine these bones as soon as possible,' he said. 'We also need some light down here. George, see if you can rig up a generator on the surface. We can run cables down here and fix up some lights so we can see what we're doing.'

Kim had remained silent but now she got slowly to her feet, eyes fixed on the pile of bones before her. When she spoke her voice was low, subdued.

'I think George is right. They are children's skeletons. But where are the heads?'

37

Ten

The dog snarled as the chain was pulled tight around its neck. It wore a heavy muzzle over its jaws and thick white saliva hung like glutinous streamers from its teeth.

The dog was a bull terrier. Small and stockily built but possessing tremendous strength, its black body was slightly more streamlined than average but it lacked none of the musculature which made the breed so powerful. As it tugged on its chain the hair at the back of its neck rose in anticipation.

'Keep still, you bastard,' snapped Rob Hardy, jerking the chain once more, almost pulling the dog over.

As he spoke, Hardy looked past the men near him to where another group of men were gathered, and amongst them he recognized Vic Regis. He was also holding a dog, another terrier, a brindle dog which was slightly smaller than Hardy's but no less ferocious in appearance. It too resembled a spring about to uncoil with tremendous ferocity. The dog was making little noise except for the low breathing which Hardy could hear. It reminded him of damaged bellows.

Another man sat on one of the hay bales which had been used to construct the makeshift arena. He was in his early thirties, tall and thin-faced with a pitted complexion and dark stubble which defied even the sharpest razor. His eyebrows were also thick and bushy and met above the bridge of his nose, giving him the appearance of perpetually frowning. He was holding a thick wad of money in his tattooed hand.

'Vic wants to lay a side-bet of fifty quid,' said Mick

Ferguson, scratching one cheek with the rolled-up cash. 'Just between you and him.'

'I'll cover it,' said Hardy without hesitation. 'I've been training this dog for three months. Even *I'm* scared of him.'

Ferguson laughed and held out his hand for the ten fivers which Hardy pulled from his pocket.

'Are you in for a slice of that too?' Hardy asked.

'What do you think?' Ferguson said. 'I set up these little shows, don't I? I reckon that entitles me to some of the proceeds.' He looked at his watch. 'Come on, let's get started.'

Ferguson got to his feet and walked to the centre of the fighting area. The old barn smelt of damp straw and neglect, mingling with the more pungent odour of sweat from both humans and animals.

He guessed that there were a dozen other men besides himself in the dilapidated barn. Its beams were seething with woodworm and the roof leaked when it rained, but the place was perfect for its present purpose. It was about three miles out of town and half a mile from the nearest road. Motorists driving to and from Longfield came nowhere near it, and anyone who thought of turning into the old dirt track was usually discouraged by the sign on the heavy gate which proclaimed PRIVATE: KEEP OUT.

Ferguson thought how lucky he had been to find this place. Up until then he hadn't dared to stage dog-fights within a twenty-mile radius of Longfield. The coppers in the area knew him well enough already. He'd done a two-year stretch in Strangeways for theft and another six months for receiving. They'd also lifted him for GBH on one occasion, but the case had been dismissed for lack of evidence.

The idea of dog-fighting had come to him after attending a coursing meet one Sunday morning. Two of the greyhounds, after killing the hare, had begun fighting between themselves and one had been blinded in the ensuing battle. It had been only a small step from getting the idea to organizing things properly. He creamed off sixty per cent of the take for himself. The rest was used to pay back bets and give the winning dog owner a few bob. Ferguson had two animals of his own, but he would not unleash them in this arena until he felt the time was right. He'd bred them himself, mating a dog with a bitch from a litter which the dog itself had fathered. This incestuous inter-breeding had spawned another litter of six, four of which had been blind or deformed. Those were useless to Ferguson and he'd taken them straight from their mother, still dripping from the womb, and drowned them in a bucket of water. The other two, though, were savage beyond belief and, as such, perfect for his needs. He kept them in cages in the cellar of his house, feeding them on the best meat he could afford. Training them. Moulding them into perfect killing machines. Soon they would be ready and then he'd clean up with side-bets.

As Ferguson stood in the middle of the barn the spectators scuttled to find the best vantage points. Hay bales not used to construct the fighting area itself were hurriedly employed as seats and a hush descended as Regis and Hardy led their dogs forward.

As they drew closer to each other, the two animals began snarling and straining in their eagerness to fight. Both men removed the restraining muzzles and a cacophony of loud barking filled the barn.

'Let them go,' said Ferguson, quietly.

As the collars were tugged free the dogs hurled themselves at each other, all their pent-up fury now finding vent.

Ferguson, Regis and Hardy vaulted to safety behind the low barrier of hay bales and turned to watch as the two animals locked jaws.

The sound of barking was replaced by a succession of snarls and growls of anger and pain.

The brindle dog gripped the black terrier's bottom jaw and pulled, tearing away a long sliver of skin from its lower lip, but the larger animal pulled loose and lunged at its opponent's head. It snapped off the end of one ear as easily as shears cutting through grass, and the taste of blood seemed to inflame it even more. Like two steam trains crashing head-on the dogs smashed into one another again, and this time the smaller dog succeeded in fastening its jaws on the other's shoulder. Its powerful neck muscles tensed as it pulled the black dog down, ripping a sizeable chunk of skin and fur free. Blood burst from the wound and the larger dog drew back slightly. But the respite was short. The two dogs locked jaws once more, scrabbling with their paws to get a grip on the slippery ground. There was a loud crack as the brindle dog broke a tooth.

Ferguson rolled a cigarette as he watched, apparently oblivious to the shouts of the other men. The thick roll of notes nestled comfortably in his trouser pocket. He lit up the cigarette and drew on it.

The black terrier lunged forward and managed to bury its powerful canine teeth in the back leg of its opponent, but in so doing it exposed its own sleek side to attack and the other animal was not slow to respond. It fastened its jaws firmly into the bigger dog and began shaking its head back and forth.

Blood from both animals began to fly through the air and the ground beneath them turned crimson.

Vic Regis grunted indignantly as several hot red droplets splashed his face. He hurriedly wiped them away.

The brindle terrier drew back an inch or two and then bit down even harder, chewing into the side of its opponent, causing it to loosen its grip. But the bigger dog struck at the other animal's head. Its despairing lunge caught the brindle below an eye, one razor-sharp tooth gouging up through the eyeball, almost ripping it from the fleshy socket. Both dogs drew back and Rob Hardy cursed as he saw a gleaming fragment of bone sticking through the pulped and torn mess that was his dog's side. Each time it exhaled a dribble of thick red foam spilled from its nostrils.

Similarly, Regis saw that his brindle dog had been blinded in one eye, its face a mask of blood and sputum. The savage wound on its back leg was also bleeding profusely.

'Do you want to call it off?' Ferguson said.

'No way,' snapped Regis.

Hardy agreed.

Before either of them could speak again the dogs had joined in battle once more.

Caught on its blind side, the brindle dog saw the charge too late and the other terrier managed to drive its teeth into the fleshy part of its opponent's neck, shaking its head madly back and forth until its teeth sheared through the smaller animal's jugular vein. There was a bright red explosion as the vein was severed. Blood spurted high into the air and soon the smaller dog began to weaken.

The barn stank of blood. The crimson fluid was everywhere. On the floor, the hay bales, the spectators, Even on the walls in one or two places.

'Right, that's it,' shouted Regis. 'Get your fucking dog off.' He glared at Hardy, who smiled and clambered into the makeshift arena. There might have been a slight chance of saving the defeated animal's life, if anyone had been so inclined, but those watching were too busy complaining or rejoicing, depending on which dog they'd backed.

Hardy gripped the black terrier by the back of the neck and pulled it away from the stricken brindle dog, which tried to drag itself upright. But loss of blood had weakened it too much, and with a throaty gurgle it fell back onto its side, its breath coming in sporadic gasps.

'Useless fucker,' snapped Regis, looking down at the dying animal. 'I've lost over a hundred quid because of you.' With a savagery born of anger he kicked the ravaged dog in the stomach.

It raised its head weakly, as if pleading for help, but Regis was unimpressed.

Ferguson joined the two men, stepping over the fatally wounded brindle dog. He handed a bundle of notes to Hardy, who quickly pocketed them. Regis, muttering to himself, stalked off to the far side of the barn and returned a moment later carrying the pitchfork they had used to move the hay bales. He held it above the dying terrier, the twin prongs poised over its heaving chest. Regis hesitated and the dog whimpered forlornly.

Ferguson snatched the lethal implement from Regis and

steadied himself momentarily, then brought it swiftly down. The prongs punctured the dog's body and he forced them down until he felt them strike the ground beneath. A blast of foul smelling air escaped from the animal's punctured lungs and it bucked spasmodically, bloody sputum spilling from its mouth.

Ferguson continued pressing down on the fork until the animal ceased to move. He smelt the pungent stench of excrement as he wrenched the weapon free of the bloodied body. He stuck it into the ground close to Regis, a faint smile on his face.

'Never mind, Vic,' he said, grinning. 'You can't win them all.'

Eleven

It was a child, that much they knew.

Anything else they could only guess at.

The skeleton lay on a piece of plastic sheeting spread carefully over the table inside Cooper's tent.

'Judging from the size,' said Kim, 'the child couldn't have been more than five or six years old. I'll run carbon-14 and nitrogen tests on the bones when I get them back to the museum.'

'If only we knew where the skulls were,' said George Perry.

A moment later the flap of the tent was pulled back and Ian Russell walked in.

'Charles, have you got a minute?' he asked. 'Mr Cutler's here. He says he wants to speak to you.'

Cooper shrugged and got to his feet, following Russell outside. He rubbed his eyes as he stepped out into the dull grey light. He hadn't slept much the previous night; his mind had been too crammed full of the sights which he and his colleagues had seen. Now he saw two men in suits standing beside one of the excavation trenches peering in at a couple of archaeologists who were busy freeing an object from the soil.

Cooper recognized James Cutler. The land developer was tall and wiry, his slim frame topped by a pinched face and thin, bloodless lips. Approaching his fortieth birthday, he was sole owner of Cutler Developments, one of the most successful private businesses in the country. The black Jensen parked on the nearby ridge testified to his material status although it looked out of place amidst the organized chaos of the archaeological paraphenalia which surrounded it.

Beside him stood a man Cooper did not recognize. He guessed that the man was a year or two younger than Cutler although his pale-grey suit was a similar colour to his hair.

Cutler smiled at the archaeologist and the two of them shook hands.

'Mr Cooper, I'd like you to meet Stuart Lawrence,' the land developer said, introducing his companion. 'He's been working as surveyor on my project.'

Lawrence looked at Cooper with ill-disguised distaste. He disliked scruffiness of any kind and this man was positively grubby. He shook hands stiffly, checking his palm to ensure that no dirt or dust had been left on his skin.

'I hope you don't mind us having a look at your little venture,' Cutler said, smiling.

'Not at all,' Cooper told him. 'After all, if it hadn't been for you and your building project we might never have found out about this site.'

'Quite so,' Cutler added. 'By the way, I was sorry to hear about the death of your colleague. As they say, bad news travels fast.' The land developer began walking slowly, Lawrence and Cooper alongside him. 'I'm afraid that I'm a carrier of bad news today, Mr Cooper.'

The archaeologist looked vague.

'My building project is set for expansion in the next few

weeks,' Cutler explained. 'That expansion will more than likely encompass this site.'

Cooper stopped walking.

'Are you trying to say that you might have to close the site down?' he asked.

'I'm afraid so, Mr Cooper.'

'But when? We made an agreement. You said that my team and I could work here.'

'Until I needed the land for my own purposes,' Cutler reminded him.

'What we've unearthed here is one of the most important finds of its type ever. I'm not about to let it be closed down.'

'You don't have any choice,' Lawrence snapped.

'Mr Lawrence is right,' Cutler continued. 'As you yourself said, it's due to me that you and your people are here at all. It was my men who first unearthed the artifacts which led to the discovery of this site. I called you in to investigate it and we both agreed at the time that there would be a time limit on your work.'

'And you're telling me that the time's running out?' snapped Cooper.

'I gave you six weeks,' Cutler said, a note of condescension in his voice. 'When that time is up . . .' He shrugged resignedly.

'You can't do it,' Cooper said.

Cutler smiled humourlessly.

'I'm a businessman, Mr Cooper. This land belongs to me. I own it. I can do what I like with it. You would have been forced to move on eventually anyway. For the moment, you can continue with your work.'

'How very generous,' Cooper sneered.

The land developer smiled again and turned away from Cooper, ushering Lawrence along with him.

'Nice speaking to you,' Cutler said without turning.

Cooper glared at the backs of the two men as they walked to the waiting Jensen.

'Bastard,' he rasped under his breath.

'Can he really stop the dig if he wants to?' asked Perry, joining his colleague.

Cooper watched the car pull away. He sucked in an angry breath, the knot of muscles at the side of his jaw pulsing.

'God help him if he tries.'

Twelve

The dull glow from the television screen provided precious little light and Kim found that she was squinting at the notes before her, so she rose and flicked on the lamp behind her chair.

While she was on her feet she pulled the curtains closed, warding off the impending night. As she returned to her seat she glanced at the three framed photos which stood on top of the record cabinet. Two of them showed her daughter, Clare, as a baby. The other was more recent and in it, the girl was clutching a battered teddy bear, smiling happily at the camera. The picture had been taken a few months before . . .

Kim pushed the thought to one side for a moment. Was it really that painful to think about? Her ex-husband had taken the picture. Photography had always been one of his consuming passions. That and womanizing. It was true to form, Kim thought, that within ten months of becoming a professional photographer he'd run off with one of his models. Walked out on five years of marriage and memories as if he were erasing a tape. She may as well never have existed as far as he was concerned. He hadn't contested custody of Clare at the divorce proceedings, hadn't baulked at paying maintainence (a pittance anyway as far as Kim was concerned). He'd been only too glad to get the case over with and get back to his model. He hadn't even asked for visiting rights where his own child was concerned and that was one of the things which she could not understand, one of the things which made her hate him a little. The other was the blow he'd delivered to her own self-esteem. At twenty-five, Kim Nichols was a very attractive young woman with fresh, natural good looks. The soft air of sexuality she exuded was all the more potent because it was uncontrived.

She had everything that her husband's lover had, so what had made him throw away his settled family life for a fly-by-night tart? It was a question she had asked herself many times and one to which she would probably never know the answer.

She sat down, massaging the bridge of her nose between thumb and forefinger, trying to force the thoughts from her mind. They still hurt, even after two years.

'Mummy, I've finished.'

The call came from upstairs. From the bathroom.

Kim smiled and got to her feet, padding up the stairs in time to see Clare emerging onto the landing, her rabbit-motif dressing gown flapping open, her glistening blonde hair flowing behind her like a diaphanous train, reaching as far as the middle of her back.

'I cleaned my teeth,' Clare said, grinning broadly to show her handiwork.

Kim nodded approvingly and kissed the top of her daughter's head as they walked into the smaller bedroom with its brightly coloured wallpaper and mobiles hung from the ceiling. Clare clambered into bed and pulled the covers up around her neck, looking into her mother's face. Kim leant forward and kissed the child once more, but as she pulled back, Clare touched her cheek, drawing one small index finger through the single tear which had slid down from her mother's eye.

'Why are you sad, Mummy?' she asked.

'I'm not,' Kim whispered. 'People cry when they're happy, too, you know. I'm happy because I've got you and I love you.' She pulled the covers more tightly around her daughter and kissed her on the forehead. 'Now, you go to sleep.'

'Were you thinking about Daddy?'

The question came so unexpectedly that Kim was momentarily speechless. She swallowed hard and then shrugged.

'No,' she lied. 'Why do you ask?'

'I think about him sometimes but I don't miss him. Not as long as you're here. You won't go away, will you, Mummy?'

Kim shook her head and hugged Clare tightly, aware of more tears trickling down her face. She hurriedly wiped them away as she stood up.

'Sleep,' she said, flicking off the bedside light. 'Love you.'

She retreated slowly from the room, pulling the door closed behind her, pausing on the landing for a moment before making her way downstairs. As she reached the hall there was a knock on the door. Kim opened it to find Inspector Wallace standing there. He smiled and reached for his I.D. card, but Kim chuckled.

'It's all right, Inspector,' she said. 'I remember who you are.'

'I did ask you if I could take a statement,' he said, almost apologetically. 'I hope I'm not interrupting anything.'

She ushered him in, through the hall to the living room. He spotted her notes lying beside the chair.

'I won't keep you a minute,' he said. 'Just a few words about what happened yesterday.'

She offered him coffee and he accepted gratefully, watching her as she walked barefoot into the kitchen. She was wearing a pair of tight-fitting jeans and a baggy jumper, the sleeves rolled up as far as the elbows. He sat down on the sofa and loosened his tie as Kim returned with the coffee and settled herself in the chair opposite, one leg drawn up beneath her.

'I'm sorry to bother you at home,' he said, 'but this won't take long.'

He had the questions prepared and as she answered them

he scribbled a few notes down. Just routine, so to speak. Tying up loose ends. All part of the job, Wallace told himself. He closed the notebook again and pocketed it as Kim went to refill the coffee mugs.

'I gather that what you found was important,' he said, sipping his drink. 'At least Mr Cooper gave that impression.'

'Yes, it is important. He thinks it's the biggest site of its kind to have been discovered this century, if you take into account the underground passages. At first we thought there were just two, but it's like a honeycomb down there. Those tunnels could stretch for miles. There's a lot of work to be done. It's a pity we won't have time to finish it.'

Wallace looked puzzled but Kim explained what Cutler had said earlier.

'Charles isn't very happy at the prospect of the dig being closed down. None of us are,' she told him, 'but there's nothing we can do if Cutler makes his mind up.'

'This is going to sound like a cliché,' he said awkwardly, 'but you're not exactly my idea of an archaeologist.'

Kim laughed and the sound seemed to brighten the room. Wallace returned her smile, his eyes held by her attractive pale blue ones.

'What would you say if I told you that you don't look like a policeman?' she said. 'You look too young. And, by the way, the photo on your I.D. card is lousy. It doesn't even look like you.'

It was his turn to laugh.

They sat in silence for a moment, then Wallace got to his feet and announced that he had to go.

'Thanks for the coffee,' he said as Kim led him to the front door. 'And the compliment.' He smiled.

'I hope that next time we talk it'll be for different reasons,' she said, her eyes sparkling in the twilight.

He nodded, thanked her again and walked out to his car.

Wallace heard the door close behind him but he didn't look round. Had he done so he might well have seen the small figure of Clare Nichols standing at one of the bedroom windows looking down at him.

Thirteen

The vein pulsed thickly, looking like a bloated worm nestling beneath the skin. It swelled even more as the youth tugged harder on the piece of material wrapped tightly around the top of his arm. He opened and closed his fist, watching as the bulging vein fattened almost to bursting point.

It was then that he inserted the hypodermic needle.

The steel needle punctured the blood vessel and the lad pushed it deeper, his thumb depressing the plunger of the hypo, forcing the liquid into his body. He drained the last dregs then pulled the needle free, ignoring the small spurt of blood which accompanied its exit from his flesh. He pulled off the tourniquet and clenched his fist, raising his arm up and down from the elbow.

Gary Webb sank back on the leather sofa, his body quivering slightly, but there was a blank smile on his face as he handed the needle to the girl who sat beside him. She watched him for a moment. The veins in his thick bull neck were throbbing and his muscular chest heaved contentedly. He looked at her, watching as she inspected the crook of her own left arm, using her nails to pick away the three or four scabs which had formed there. The pieces of hardened crust came away and Laura Price slapped at the raw part of her arm using the first two fingers of her free hand, watching as the veins began to stand out.

Henry Dexter smiled and closed the door, leaving the two teenagers to their own devices. Out in the corridor he turned to face Mick Ferguson, who was taking a last drag on his cigarette. He dropped the butt onto the polished wood floor of the corridor and shrugged.

'That had better be good stuff,' said Dexter, eyeing the other man suspiciously.

Beside them on a table lay two small bags of white powder.

'It's the best quality heroin you're ever likely to get,' Ferguson said. 'Now, I didn't come here to pass the time of day. You owe me some money.'

Dexter picked up the bags and dropped them into the pocket of his jacket. Then he and Ferguson walked down the corridor to another room. There was an open fire burning in the grate, and the smell of woodsmoke hung in the air.

'Very cosy,' said Ferguson. 'You did well when your old man died. How much did he leave you? Two million, wasn't it? I remember reading something in the paper at the time.'

Dexter passed in front of the fire, the glowing tongues of flame momentarily illuminating his face, deepening the shadows beneath his eyes and chin. He was almost forty-five, slim and athletically built. Dressed in a well-tailored jacket and trousers, his shirt pressed and sparkling white, he looked immaculate.

'Was it two million?' Ferguson persisted.

'What difference does it make to you, Ferguson?' he said, crossing to a large wall safe hidden behind a passable copy of a Goya. It depicted a young witch having intercourse with a demon, the creature's long tongue being used to penetrate her anus. Dexter fiddled with the combination of the safe, pulled the door open and fished out some money. He also carefully placed the heroin alongside the other bags which half filled the cavity.

'It's an expensive habit,' Ferguson said, grinning.

'It is at the prices you charge,' the older man told him.

'Look, most heroin is only 55% pure by the time it hits the streets. The dealers mix it with sugar, brick dust and fucking Vim. That stuff,' he pointed to the safe, 'is 70% pure.'

Dexter nodded and held out a wad of notes.

'It's all there,' he said. 'Five hundred pounds. Count it if you like.'

51

Ferguson grinned and stuffed the money into his pocket.

'I trust you,' he replied, his attention drawn by a large dagger which hung over the fireplace, its blade glinting in the glow of the flames. He reached up and took it down, hefting it before him. On the mantelpiece there was a candlestick shaped like the head of a goat. The eyes were small rubies and the firelight made it look as if they were glowing. 'Do you really believe all this shit about witchcraft?' Ferguson wanted to know.

Dexter didn't answer, he merely fixed the other man with an unblinking stare.

'Or do you think those kids you use believe in it? Have you got one of your little ceremonies coming up again, eh? Is that why you need the heroin? To keep them interested?' He chuckled.

'Why don't you just get out of here, Ferguson?'

'How many of them are underage? Those two in the other room look pretty young'.

Dexter took a step forward but hesitated when he saw Ferguson lower the knife.

'I couldn't care less what you get up to in that wood of yours,' Ferguson said, walking past the older man. 'I don't care how many kids you turn into junkies. It's more money for me. And if that's the only way you can get them to go along with you, then fine, that's your business too.'

He stood by the French doors, gazing out into the darkness, his eyes drawn to the black smudge on the nearby hillside where the wood grew. It lay less than half a mile from the house itself. He ran his thumb slowly along the blade of the dagger, then flipped it into the air, allowing the blade and hilt to spin round before catching it safely. He handed it back to Dexter and headed for the door.

'I'll see myself out,' he said, and Dexter heard his footsteps echoing away down the corridor. He held the dagger before him, then turned and looked up at the mottled sky, where silvery clouds formed a transparent shroud over the moon.

He thought about Ferguson. Arrogant bastard!

He thought about Laura and Gary in the other room, and the others.

His followers.

He smiled crookedly. So what if they only came along for the drugs. They served their purpose. Or at any rate they would. Soon.

Henry Dexter closed and locked the wall safe. Then, replacing the dagger, he wandered off to join his two young companions in the next room.

He could already feel the erection throbbing inside his trousers.

Fourteen

The cellar was large, running beneath the entire house.

As Ferguson descended the stone steps to the lower level a musty odour of urine and straw rose to meet him. The room was empty but for what looked like a set of wall bars in one corner and, against the far wall, two steel cages. The stone floor was a strange rust-red colour. Ferguson paused by the two enclosures and smiled.

Chained inside each one was a dog.

The first was jet black, its coat thick and lustrous, but unable to disguise its powerful, brutish build. The animal was a pit bull terrier. As Ferguson knelt close to the cage it strained against its chain and began barking at him, but it was the animal in the next cage that now claimed his attention.

It was the same breed as its neighbour but much larger, more striking and more fearsome in appearance. The dog was an albino. Its thin coat was brilliant white, in stark contrast to the bloodied pink of its piercing eyes. The offspring of Ferguson's incestuous mating of its sister pup and its own father, the creature was almost insane and that madness showed in the way it launched itself at the man who had come to feed it. But Ferguson merely smiled and looked deep into those watery pink eyes, transfixed by them, still amazed at the ferocity of this particular dog. He went to a small portable fridge in one corner of the room and pulled out two metal trays, both full of raw meat.

'Those bloody dogs eat better than we do.'

He allowed himself only a perfunctory glance in the direction of the voice. Swaying uncertainly at the top of the stairs was his wife, Carol. At twenty-eight, she was four years younger than her husband, but already her face was heavily lined. What make-up she wore was clumsily applied, particularly to her lips. Heavy-breasted and a little too large around the hips, she wore a skirt that was shiny through too much wear and too tight to fasten without strain at the waist.

She watched silently as her husband laid the meat trays in front of the cages. The two dogs, aroused by the smell of food, began barking loudly.

Ferguson took a lump of the dripping raw flesh and tossed it into the albino's cage. The animal snapped it up and chewed hungrily, some of the dark juice dripping from its jaws.

Carol began a faltering journey to the cellar floor, putting out a hand to steady herself.

'What do you want?' Ferguson asked. 'Run out of booze, have you?'

She stood quietly for a moment, watching the ravenous beasts as her husband continued to feed them scraps of meat. The fetid stench of excrement and straw that filled the cellar made her cough.

'It stinks down here,' she mumbled, stepping closer to the cages, her eyes fixed on the dogs.

'Nobody asked you to come down here,' he hissed. 'Go on, piss off back to your bottle.'

'You bastard,' she rasped and tried to hit him, but

Ferguson was too quick for her. He spun round and lashed out, catching her across the face with the back of his hand. The impact of the blow sent her sprawling and, as she scrambled to her feet, she tasted blood in her mouth. The blow had loosened one of her front teeth and she prodded it tentatively with her tongue. The pain galvanized her into action, and with fists flailing she ran at Ferguson.

He grinned, as if her onslaught were some kind of challenge. He ducked under her clumsy swing and grabbed her hair, several tufts coming away in the process.

The dogs were barking madly now, making an unbearable din in the confined space of the cellar. The sound reverberated around the walls until it became deafening.

Carol screamed and struck out at her husband again but he caught her wrist, squeezing tightly, dragging her down to the floor with him. He was smiling insanely as he hauled her across the ground, and her eyes bulged in terror as she saw what he intended to do.

He guided her hand towards the bars of the albino dog's cage, laughing as the ferocious animal barked and snapped at the offered appendage.

Carol shrieked as she felt her hand touch the cold steel of the bars. She made a fist to prevent her husband from pushing the hand through but he slammed it repeatedly against the bars until her knuckles bled and her fingers went limp. The dog, already going mad in its eagerness to reach the hand, became completely frenzied at the sight of the blood which dripped from the gashed knuckles.

Carol could feel its hot breath only inches away from her, and the foul odour of it made her want to vomit.

'It'll have your fucking hand off in five seconds flat,' rasped Ferguson, keeping her pinned helplessly against the bars. 'Want me to show you?' He jerked her hand closer to the foaming jaws of the crazed dog.

Both dogs kept straining violently against their chains, and their barking seemed to grow louder and louder until Carol was aware of nothing else. She felt herself blacking out, but Ferguson pulled her head back and with his free hand tugged her away from the cage. Her blouse ripped and

55

her large breasts were exposed. She could feel his erection pressing against her as they grappled on the floor and his hands squeezed her breasts roughly, leaving red marks around the nipples.

She tried to push him off but he was too heavy for her. She felt his other hand reaching beneath her skirt, tearing at her knickers. He ripped them off with one savage grunt and flung them aside.

'Next time I'm going to let them tear your fucking hand off,' Ferguson said, his breath coming in short gasps. He stared down at Carol and she tried one last time to slither away from him, but he pinned her beneath him with one powerful arm, releasing his bulging organ from his trousers with his free hand and then forcing her legs apart.

The black pit terrier managed to slip its chain and it slammed into the bars only inches from Carol's face, its frenzied barks ringing in her ears, its saliva spattering her.

'Looks like he wants to join us,' laughed Ferguson, and he drove into her savagely, making her shriek with the sudden sharp pain. He leant forward to kiss her and, as he did, she caught his bottom lip between her teeth and bit hard, feeling the fleshy bulge split. Blood filled her mouth and she spat it at him, but Ferguson ignored the discomfort. He pinned both her arms to the filthy floor, wet with dog urine, and pounded into her, his deep grunts of pleasure mingling in her ears with the noise of the animals.

She closed her eyes tightly as she felt him tense, then a moment later she heard his groans as he reached his climax and his thick fluid filled her, some of it spilling out to mix with the reeking mess which coated the floor.

He withdrew almost immediately, rolled off her and pushed his shrinking penis back inside his trousers.

Carol rolled onto her side, the pain from her broken tooth and the taste of blood making her feel sick. Ferguson prodded her with the toe of his boot.

'Now get out,' he chuckled. 'Go on, good dog.' He began to laugh, his raucous guffaws punctuated with threatening snarls from the two dogs.

'You're a bastard,' she grunted.

'Get out,' he rasped.

The dogs continued to bark.

Fifteen

'What is it?' Cooper wondered aloud.

'I don't know,' Perry confessed, 'but I spotted it the day we first found the skeletons.'

Kim approached the slab of stone and touched it cautiously.

'Perhaps it leads into another tunnel,' she suggested. 'Like the others.'

Most of the children's skeletons had been moved away from the slab of rock, and the three archaeologists stood within a few feet of this latest puzzle.

'We've got to move it,' Cooper said. 'At least it looks much lighter than the circular stones at the tunnel entrances.'

As he spoke, the lights in the roof of the tunnel flickered momentarily, dimming until the narrow passage was bathed in sickly yellow, and then glowed brightly once more. Kim stepped back as the two men moved forward to get a good grip on the stone. At a signal from Cooper they wedged their hands behind the rock and simply tipped it forward, surprised at the ease with which it was dislodged. Slivers broke off from the edges as it hit the floor of the tunnel.

Kim picked up one of the gas lamps lying close by and held it above her head, advancing into the yawning blackness behind the slab.

She stiffened, her body quivering almost imperceptibly as if a high voltage charge were being pumped through it. She sucked in a breath but it seemed to stick in her throat, and for terrifying seconds she found that she couldn't breathe. The skin on her face and hands puckered into goose-pimples and a numbing chill enveloped her. A small gasp escaped her as she actually felt her hair rising, standing up like a cat's hackles. She swayed uncertainly for a moment as the feeling seemed to spread through her whole body, through her very soul, and Kim clenched her teeth together, convinced that she was going to faint. On the verge of panic, she screwed up her eyes until white stars danced before her. Her throat felt constricted, as though some invisible hand were gradually tightening around it. Her head seemed to be swelling, expanding to enormous proportions until it seemed it must burst.

And somewhere, perhaps in her imagination, she thought, she heard a sound. A noise which froze her blood as it throbbed in her ears.

A distant wail of inhuman agony which rose swiftly in pitch and volume until it was transformed into something resembling malevolent laughter.

Kim felt her legs weaken and she was suddenly aware of strong arms supporting her.

The lamp fell from her grip and shattered.

Voices rushed in at her from the gloom.

'. . . Kim, can you hear me? . . .'

'. . . What happened to her? . . .'

'. . . Fainted . . .'

Everything swam before her, as if she were looking through a heat haze. Gradually, objects and faces took on a familiar clarity once more.

'Kim, are you all right?' Cooper asked, feeling the deathlike cold which seemed to have penetrated her flesh.

'I must have fainted,' she said. 'Blacked out for a second . . .' Her voice trailed off.

They sat her on the ground for a moment and she rubbed a hand over the back of her neck in an effort to massage away the dull ache which had settled there. After a moment or two it began to disappear.

'I'm sorry,' she said. 'I don't know what happened.' She smiled weakly, almost embarrassed at the little episode. Then, more sombrely, she asked, 'Did you hear that noise?'

'What noise?' asked Perry.

She opened her mouth to speak, to try to describe the keening wail, but then thought better of it. She must have imagined it, or perhaps it had been the sudden outrushing of the air inside the . . .

Inside the what?

What was this place anyway?

As she regained her senses, she, like her two companions, gazed around at their latest discovery.

'What the hell is this?' murmured Perry, playing his torch beam through the gloom.

They were standing inside a chamber of some kind. It was roughly ten feet square, resembling an underground cell. But the walls were completely covered, every square inch of them, with symbols and hieroglyphics. Many were obscured by dirt and grime but they were there nonetheless, carved into the rocks and dirt. But it wasn't the symbols which captured Kim's attention. She swallowed hard, unable to remove her gaze from the sight before her.

The entire room was littered with skulls.

Hundreds of them.

And from their size they obviously belonged to children.

'So this is where they hid them,' Cooper said, his thoughts travelling the same route as Kim's. 'The bodies in the tunnel, the heads in here.'

'It doesn't look like a burial chamber,' Perry offered. 'Besides, what is all this writing on the walls?'

As well as the skulls, the chamber contained a number of swords and spears, a few pots and some other receptacles. But it was a pile of stone tablets which now attracted Kim's attention.

Lying amongst the other relics, each one was about six

inches long, hewn from heavy rock and inscribed with a series of letters, many indistinguishable because of the dirt which caked them. There were a dozen of them.

'This place obviously belonged to the *áes dana*, the wise men of the tribe,' said Cooper. 'Maybe we'll find some answers here.'

'These stone tablets,' Kim said, 'I'd like to take them back to the museum with me, see if I can decipher what's written on them. I'll get a box and load them up.'

'Are you sure you feel OK, Kim?' Perry wanted to know.

She smiled, appreciating his concern.

'I'm fine,' she told him. 'Maybe all this excitement is getting to me.' She laughed humourlessly, rubbing a hand through her blonde hair.

As she did, she noticed that her hand was shaking.

'Charles, could you get someone to load up those tablets so I can get going?' she asked.

Cooper seemed not to hear her. He was gazing at the writing on the wall of the chamber.

'Charles,' Kim called again.

He finally managed to tear his attention from what he was reading, but as he looked at her she saw that his face was pale.

He looked vague for a moment, his thoughts elsewhere.

'Charles, the stone tablets.'

'I'll see to it. You leave now,' Cooper told her, a newly found urgency in his voice.

Kim looked puzzled as, once more, he turned his back on her, his eyes scanning the ancient words before him.

She shuddered involuntarily, feeling as if the horde of skulls were watching her with those gaping eye sockets. A wave of nausea, powerful and unexpected, hit her and she shot out a hand to support herself, her head spinning. She felt her legs weaken, and for a moment wondered if she was going to fall again. Perry put out a hand to steady her, feeling the perspiration that covered her skin. She closed her eyes tightly, fighting back the stomach contractions, gritting her teeth against this new onslaught.

Kim sucked in several shallow breaths and the feeling

began to pass. Perry released his supporting hand, alarmed by the ghostly pallor her skin had taken on, but she waved him away.

'I'm all right,' she said. 'Really.'

Cooper looked on impassively as she turned and made her way back down the tunnel, the light from her torch gradually disappearing.

As she reached the base of the rope ladder she paused again, listening.

Like a long-forgotten memory dredged up from the back of her mind, she heard again that high pitched wail of agony gradually dying away until it sounded like soft, menacing laughter.

Sixteen

There was little traffic on the road leading into Longfield. It was never a busy route, and at this early hour Kim found that she had the road virtually to herself. The clock on the dashboard showed 7:46 a.m.

Rain, which had begun as drizzle, was now pelting down in large droplets which exploded with such force on the windscreen that the wipers had difficulty keeping it clear.

Kim shivered as she drove, telling herself it was the inclement weather that was making her feel so cold. The heater was turned up high and still the chill persisted. She slowed down, reached into the pocket of her jacket and pulled on a pair of woollen gloves.

In the back of the Land Rover the wooden crates were securely tied down. Each one held a precious cargo of relics. She glanced into the rear-view mirror and looked at the two on top of the pile, one carrying some of the bones they'd found in the tunnel, the other filled with the stone tablets. Perry had indeed found twelve of them and each had been carefully packed in the box so that Kim could get them back to the museum in Longfield undamaged.

She drove past a sign which told her that the town was now less than a mile away.

Kim swung the Land Rover around a corner, stepping on the brake when she saw a tractor lumbering towards her, towing a seed distributor. The Massey-Ferguson was about a hundred yards from her, but on such a slippery road, Kim was taking no chances. She pressed down harder on the brake.

Nothing happened.

The Land Rover continued speeding along in top gear, the needle on the speedometer nudging forty-five.

Kim pumped the brake pedal repeatedly, the breath catching in her throat.

Still the vehicle did not slow down.

She was less than seventy yards away from the tractor now.

Kim looked frantically through the misted windscreen, trying to catch a glimpse of the tractor driver, trying to warn him that she was unable to stop. He was just a blur in the rain.

She drove her foot down as hard as she could, feeling the pedal touch the floor.

The Land Rover sped on.

Fifty yards away.

She banged her hooter, trying to warn the farmer to pull off the road, at the same time motioning madly with one hand.

The tractor kept coming.

Forty yards.

She reached for the gear-stick, trying to change down into first, to stop the vehicle that way, but it was useless.

Twenty yards.

If only she could guide the runaway vehicle into one of the banks on either side of the road, she thought, perhaps she could bring it to a halt. But she was travelling too fast and the banks were steep. If she didn't plough straight into one, then the momentum might well send the Land Rover flying into the air, or overturn it. Or . . .

Ten yards, and now the tractor driver was turning his own bulky vehicle, finally aware that a collision was inevitable.

Kim grabbed the handbrake and wrenched it up. Even that did nothing to halt the breakneck progress of the Land Rover. She thought about jumping, but travelling at over forty-five she stood a pretty fair chance of killing herself.

She heard the tractor's hooter blaring out a warning and she crossed her arms on the wheel, waiting for the impact, thrusting her foot one last time down on the brake.

The Land Rover skidded to a halt, its rear end spinning round and coming to rest gently against the radiator grille of the tractor.

For long seconds Kim remained hunched over the wheel, her head bowed. Slowly she straightened up, her heart thudding in her chest.

The driver of the tractor was already out of his cab, scuttling across the rain-lashed road towards her.

She opened her door and stumbled out, her face drained of colour.

'What the hell happened?' he said to her. His anger and fear largely dissipated when he saw how haggard Kim looked.

'My brakes . . .' she murmured, leaning against the bonnet of the Land Rover. A wave of nausea swept over her and her legs almost buckled under her. The tractor driver watched as she gulped down several deep lungfuls of air. 'I'm sorry,' she said, quietly.

'We'd both have been sorry if you hadn't stopped in time,' the driver said.

Kim nodded slowly and wiped some rain from her face.

'How much further have you got to go?' the driver asked.

She told him.

'Will you be all right?'

She was already climbing back into the Land Rover, starting the engine. There was a roar as she stepped on the accelerator.

'I'll be OK,' Kim assured him. She let the vehicle roll forward a few yards and then stepped on the brake.

The vehicle stopped immediately.

She pulled at her bottom lip with one thumb and forefinger, looking first at the speedometer, then at the brake pedal.

'Are the brakes working now?' the farmer asked, his hair plastered to his face by the rain.

Kim nodded abstractedly.

'Yes,' she said in surprise. 'They're working.'

As the farmer watched, the Land Rover pulled away and a moment later it had disappeared around the next bend.

He looked at the dark skid marks on the road before him and shook his head. He found that he too was shaking.

Longfield Museum was a large, modern building that looked more like an office complex than a storehouse for ancient artifacts.

The smoked-glass exterior reflected a mirror-image of the Land Rover as Kim parked close to the main entrance. She switched off the engine and sat silently for a moment, breathing deeply. The rain had eased off somewhat and she had wound down both front windows to let in some fresh air. This had helped to dispel the unpleasant fusty odour inside the vehicle which irritated her throat and nose.

The chill remained.

After a moment or two she climbed out of the Land Rover and strode towards the main entrance. There was a pushbike chained to the bicycle rack with a sticker on it that read SPEED MACHINE.

Kim pushed open the double doors and walked into the almost unnatural silence of the main hall. A large plan of the museum faced her, and on each wall blue signs pointed to various galleries. She turned to the left, heading for the door marked STAFF ONLY. Her heels beat out a loud tattoo on the lino as she walked but the sound was muffled by carpet as she stepped inside the room.

It was a large room with cupboards and filing cabinets

covering the walls on three sides. At the far end was a stainless steel worktop and sink and another door.

The room was empty as Kim walked through it to the door at the other end. She turned the handle, expecting it to be locked, but it opened easily.

It led to a second, smaller room which contained three or four work benches and, in one corner, the pride of the museum, an electron microscope.

On one of the worktops Kim caught sight of a steaming mug of coffee. She'd seen Roger Kelly's bike outside, so the coffee probably belonged to him. Kelly had to be around somewhere. Kim turned and headed back through the staff room, pulling open the door which led out into the main hall.

The figure loomed before her with such suddenness that she jumped back a foot or two, her heart thumping.

'I didn't know I looked that bad first thing in the morning,' Roger Kelly said, grinning.

'I wondered where the hell you were,' Kim told him, sucking in deep breaths, trying to regain her composure.

'You look as if you've seen a ghost,' he told her, noticing how pale she was. 'Are you all right?'

She thought about mentioning the incident with the Land Rover but decided against it.

'I've got some material in the back of the Land Rover,' Kim told him. 'Help me get it inside, will you, Roger?'

He nodded and followed her out to the parked vehicle, watching as she unlocked the back and motioned to the box which contained the stone tablets.

Kelly got a firm grip on the box and lifted, surprised at the weight.

'What have you got in here?' he grunted. 'Gold bars?' Roger Kelly was a powerfully built, muscular young man yet to reach his twenty-third birthday, but the effort of carrying the box appeared to be too much for him. Kim watched anxiously as he stumbled toward the main entrance of the museum, straining under the weight. For a second it looked as though he would drop the box, but after a moment he regained his handhold and struggled on. Kim collected the box containing the skeleton and followed him.

Once inside, they placed both boxes on the worktop. Kelly stood to one side gasping for breath. Kim looked at him, noticing how pale his own face was now, as if all the colour had been sucked from it. After a few moments, she and Kelly returned to the Land Rover to retrieve the remaining boxes, which contained some other relics from the dig.

'We've got to run nitrogen tests on these,' she told him when they were back inside, motioning to the first two boxes. Crossing to the one containing the skeleton, she carefully removed the lid and peered inside.

'Where's the skull?' asked Kelly, puzzled.

Kim explained briefly about the chamber full of skulls, then set about freeing the lid on the other box. Kelly helped, pulling the nails free with a claw hammer. Kim lifted it clear and pulled back the gauze in which the stone tablets had been wrapped.

'We found these with the skulls,' she told him. 'They've got to be dated before we start to decipher this writing.' She indicated the Celtic script which covered each slab of stone.

Kelly nodded and helped her carefully remove each one, laying it on a sheet of plastic which Kim had spread out on the worktop. As he removed the last one Kelly looked down into the box, and once more Kim saw the colour drain from his face. She glanced at him, then down into the box.

The wood on the bottom and sides was scorched almost black.

As if it had been subjected to a powerful source of heat.

Seventeen

Kim sat back on the stool and glanced down at her notepad. Page after page was covered by her neat jottings, some of the phrases underlined.

She sighed and reached up to massage the back of her neck. A dull ache had settled there and threatened to develop into a painful stiffness. She got to her feet and walked up and down for a few minutes, her eyes every so often drawn back to the electron microscope as if by powerful magnets.

The tests were complete. At least those she intended finishing before leaving for home. For nearly nine hours since returning to the museum that morning, she had been working on the relics. Examining the bones, the stone tablets, the coins, the weapons and God knew how many more of the finds. The carbon-14 test had been completed, as had the nitrogen test. The bones were over 2,000 years old, and as far as she could ascertain, they came from the same period as the rest of the relics.

Then there were the tablets.

She'd chipped a tiny fragment of one of them away and ground it up with a pestle and mortar, examining the minute fragments beneath the electron microscope in a test more commonly used on fossils. The petrological microscopy had revealed something which Kim had not expected and it had been nagging at her ever since.

The tablets were much older than the rest of the relics.

All twelve were at least five hundred to a thousand years older than the other artifacts she had examined. It was as if they had been buried by another tribe generations before.

Buried or hidden?

She went to the worktop where the tablets were laid out and prodded one with a small tracer. The chisel-like implement followed a path through the groove which had been fashioned into a letter. She wondered how long it would take her to decipher the writing on the small slabs.

Why the time difference between the tablets and the other relics? she wondered.

As she sat gazing at them there was a knock on the door.

'Come in,' called Kim, turning to see who her visitor was.

Roger Kelly stepped into the room.

'Everyone else has gone home,' he told her. 'I was going to lock up if you'd finished.'

'Yes,' Kim sighed. 'I've finished for today. I don't think I'm going to get any further just staring at all this stuff.' She crossed to the sink and began washing her hands beneath the hot tap. Kelly paused beside the worktop and looked at the stone tablets.

'Have you got any idea what the writings mean?' he asked as Kim dried her hands.

'None at all,' she confessed. 'But I haven't studied them yet.'

'Maybe they're Celtic commandments,' he said, chuckling.

'You could be right,' Kim agreed, also managing a smile.

Kelly began picking up some of the relics and replacing them in a box, being careful not to damage any of the artifacts. He closed the box and carried it toward one of the wall cupboards.

Kim looked across at the tablets once more, wrinkling her nose as she detected a strange smell. Alien and yet somehow familiar. Kelly, preoccupied with putting away the box of fragile relics, seemed not to notice the odour. He reached up to open the cupboard door, but it seemed to be stuck.

The smell, growing stronger, almost made Kim cough. A pungent, nauseating odour like . . . like burnt plastic?

Plastic.

She went to the worktop for a closer look.

68

The sheet of transparent plastic on which the tablets lay was turning a sickly yellowish-brown.

Mouth open in amazement, Kim turned toward Kelly. As she did so, the cupboard door flew open and she saw the bottle of nitric acid topple from the upper shelf.

It hit the young man in the face and shattered.

The corrosive liquid spilled onto his head and face, some of it splashing down his chest.

He dropped the box of relics, both hands clutching at his face, a scream of agony rising from his throat.

Kim ran towards him as he dropped to his knees, wailing helplessly, the deadly fluid puddling around him. But there was nothing she could do.

The action of the liquid was terrifyingly swift. As if someone had thrust a blowtorch at him, Kelly's face was instantly stripped of skin. His eyes rapidly dissolved into seething mush as the acid went to work on them, the pupils and whites merely disappearing. As he screamed in pain the acid trickled into his mouth and ate through his tongue, even dissolving the enamel of his teeth. A purple foam dribbled over lips which were little more than bubbling blisters. All over his face sores rose, then burst as more flesh was stripped away. The lobe of one ear was seared off in the agonizing deluge and his nostrils seemed to widen as his nose was pulped by the acid. Blood burst from exposed veins which, seconds later, were themselves corroded into charcoal.

Kim watched frozen in horror as a thick white plume of smoky vapour rose from Kelly's head. He fell forward, his body jerking uncontrollably, his screams dying away to gurgles as some of the acid slid down his throat and dissolved his vocal chords.

Skin came away in slippery chunks as he clawed at his face with hands now ravaged by a dozen blisters. His clothes and part of his chest were also being attacked by the lethal fluid, but soon Kelly would feel no more pain. His movements quickly grew feeble and then ceased. He was unconscious.

Kim recoiled from the stench of corrupted flesh. She gritted her teeth as she looked at the streaming ruin which had been Kelly's face. Blood mingled with liquescent skin and melting bone to form a reeking gelatinous mask.

She spun round, racing into the other room for the phone. With a trembling hand she jabbed out three nines and managed to blurt out that she needed an ambulance.

As she was about to replace the receiver she heard a sound which froze her blood.

A high-pitched, inhuman wail which drummed in her ears for interminable seconds.

It was identical to the sound she'd heard upon entering the chamber of skulls the previous day.

Had it come across the phone line or had she imagined it?

She dropped the receiver and blundered back into the lab, almost stumbling over the prostrate form of Kelly. She prayed that the ambulance would hurry, that he was still alive.

Her eyes flickered back and forth.

To Kelly.

To the stone tablets.

And to the plastic sheet on which they lay.

Shrivelled and contracted.

As if it had been burned.

Eighteen

'I don't know why we couldn't have stayed in the car,' Sue Hagen said. 'It's freezing out here.'

'Country air is supposed to be good for you,' David Christie reminded her.

A light breeze rustled the trees of the wood, stirring the fallen leaves which already carpeted the ground.

'Anyway,' said David, 'I thought you liked it in the open air.'

'I do when it's a nice sunny day. Not in the middle of the night,' Sue said indignantly.

'Well, I like it anytime,' he told her, grabbing one of her small breasts. 'I'll soon warm you up.'

Sue giggled, then gripped his testicles, squeezing hard. 'You're supposed to be gentle,' she said, smiling.

David winced; his privates were quite sensitive enough without that kind of attention. He yelped in pain and she released her hold.

'How do you know about this place, anyway?' Sue asked as they wandered deeper into the wood.

'I've been out here a couple of times with my mates,' he informed her. 'We used to bring our air rifles here. Got a couple of rabbits once.'

'That's cruel,' she told him, muttering as she snagged her sleeve on a low branch. 'Oh, God, how much further? My clothes will be ruined.'

'How far do you want to go?' he asked, pulling her close to him and stealing a brief kiss. She tasted the warmth of his tongue and wanted more. She gripped the back of his neck and pulled him to her, kissing more deeply. As they pressed together she could feel his erection pushing against her thigh and she reached down to rub it through the material of his trousers. David responded by sliding one hand up inside her short leather skirt, his fingers first gliding over the soft material of her stockings before brushing bare skin. He probed further, eagerly stroking the crutch of her knickers, feeling the coils of pubic hair pressed tightly against the sheer fabric.

'This is far enough, Dave,' she whispered, leaning back against a tree.

They kissed long and hard, each one's tongue deeply probing the other's mouth. Sue let out a slight gasp as she felt him push her long brown hair away from her neck and nip the flesh with his teeth. He repeated the action on the other side of her neck. She slid both hands inside his shirt and massaged his chest and back with firm quick strokes,

71

concentrating on the small of his back and the area just above his belt. After two years together they knew each other's wants and needs perfectly, at least in a physical sense. Both of them had experienced sex before during their twenty years but neither had found it so stimulating with anyone else. Both were unemployed and had plenty of time for sex, but it had not yet lost its novelty value for either of them. In fact, if anything, it was getting better.

As Sue surrendered to the feelings coursing through her, she thought briefly of what her parents would say if they knew she was with David. Neither of them liked him very much, unlike her elder sister's boyfriend. Now he was a 'nice' boy. More their type.

Their type, she thought irritably. It wasn't them who had to spend time with him. But her sister, Barbara, could do no wrong. *She* had a job, and her wonderful bloody boyfriend went to university. It was a match made in heaven as far as her parents were concerned. Barbara hadn't been arrested for smoking pot when she was seventeen. Barbara hadn't cost them three hundred pounds for an abortion when she was nineteen.

Barbara hadn't done anything, had she? It was always Sue.

The vision of her parents faded as Sue felt David's roving tongue flicking its way down between her breasts while his hands skilfully unfastened the buttons of her blouse. She wore no bra and he found her small breasts firm and eager for his touch. He flicked at the swollen nipples, drawing each one in turn between his teeth, rolling his tongue around the stiff cones of flesh.

He knelt on the damp earth, unzipping her skirt, smiling as she wriggled out of it and thrust her pelvis towards him. He nuzzled her mound through her knickers, tasting the moisture which was seeping through the flimsy silk. He pulled the gusset to one side and slipped his tongue into her moist cleft, gripping her hips as she moaned with pleasure and ground herself hard against his face.

After a moment or two he straightened up and released his own throbbing member from his trousers. Sue took it

72

eagerly in one hand, rubbing the swollen shaft, feeling the bloated veins which ran along the top. Then, eager to feel him inside her, she guided his stiffness into her vagina, gasping loudly as he penetrated her. She clasped her hands on his buttocks, urging him into a rhythm which, within minutes, had both of them approaching orgasm.

David felt something wet touch his shoulder.

He pulled his head back slightly and saw that Sue's head was pressed back against the tree, her eyes closed, both her hands fastened around his thrusting buttocks.

He thought that it must be rain.

Sue raised one stocking-clad leg and hooked it around the small of his back, allowing him deeper penetration. Her hands slipped lower, cupping his testicles, kneading the swollen ovoids, trying to coax his semen free. It would not be long now. He felt the unmistakable warm glow beginning to spread through his lower body.

Again he felt a droplet of moisture hit his shoulder, only this time it trickled down his chest, leaving a dark stain.

It took him only a second to realize that it was blood.

Suddenly frightened, David tried to slow his pace, to pull Sue away from beneath the tree, from whatever was dripping blood onto them, but even as a dark globule landed on her left breast she seemed oblivious to his urgency, mistaking it for something else.

Once more he tried to pull away but Sue, her voice a throaty whisper, urged him on.

'Don't stop, please, Dave,' she gasped, grinding harder against him. 'I'm coming!' She threw her head back and cried out her pleasure, her eyes open wide.

At that moment she saw the remains of the goat jammed into the branches above.

Still quivering from the fury of her orgasm, Sue opened her mouth to scream. As she did so, a thick clot of congealed blood dropped from the butchered carcass and splashed between her lips.

Gagging violently, she pulled away from David and dropped to her knees, her stomach contracting until a stream of vomit erupted from her blood-filled mouth.

David too staggered away from the tree, his eyes riveted to the bloodied remains of the animal, his own revulsion now growing.

Sue tried again to scream as she saw the drops of blood on her body and on David but the sound became a gurgle as a fresh wave of sickness swept over her. She saw David overbalance and trip over something hidden beneath a pile of leaves.

His hand sank into something cold and soft and it was his turn to shriek as he withdrew his arm and lifted it into view. His hand was covered in blood and there were pieces of thick, coiled tube hanging from it. It was the intestines of the goat that lay buried beneath the fallen leaves. The blood had blackened and congealed into a treacly mush which coated David's hand. The sight of it made him gag.

Half-naked, Sue and David struggled to their feet and bolted from the clearing, crashing headlong through the tangled undergrowth in their effort to escape the fear and revulsion they felt.

In the inky blackness of the dense wood another shape stirred now. But this one moved quietly, stealthily.

Nineteen

The ground felt soft, almost bog-like, as Inspector Wallace made his way through the trees and bushes, a cigarette dangling from one corner of his mouth. It was unlit. His lighter wasn't working and he'd not been able to find anyone with so much as a match. He chewed on the filter and muttered to himself as he snagged the sleeve of his jacket on a gorse bush.

Even in the light of early morning the wood still cast long, thick shadows, and the dew-soaked leaves which coated the ground squelched beneath his feet as he walked.

Ahead of him, Constable Mark Buchanan moved sure-footedly through the trees, occasionally holding back a branch for his superior. He let go of one a little too early and it swung back and hit Wallace across the chest. The constable apologized but Wallace merely dismissed the incident, smiling when he saw the look of fear on Buchanan's face. The junior man was about twenty-eight, two years younger than Wallace. He was thin and gangling with a pale complexion which made him appear as though he were permanently ill.

'I wouldn't have called you out normally, sir,' he said, apologetically, as they approached the clearing. 'But I think this is important.'

As they reached the clearing, Wallace saw two more uniformed men standing by a gnarled oak tree. He recognized them as Greene and Denton. One of them was holding a large black dustbin bag and looking up into the branches of the tree, his face grim. The other was merely staring into space as if looking at something which only he could see. Both men snapped upright as Wallace entered the clearing.

'So what have you got?' he said to Buchanan, finally taking the unlit cigarette from his mouth.

The constable motioned to the lower branches of the tree and Wallace looked up.

The goat, at least what remained of it, looked little more than an empty husk. The stomach cavity had been slit open and the internal organs removed. Wallace saw those lying in a reeking pile close by. Flies were already feasting on the congealed mess. For a moment, Wallace wondered why the dead animal looked so sickly pink in colour, then he realized with disgust that it had been flayed. Every last piece of fur had been stripped away, exposing the wasted muscles beneath. What drew his attention most was the stump of the neck. A piece of bone shone whitely through the blackened gore.

'Where's the head?' he asked.

Greene stepped forward and opened the dustbin bag, allowing his superior to look inside. The stench which rose from within was unbelievable.

The head lay in the bottom of the bag, one horn broken, the eye sockets choked with thick clots of blood.

Both eyes had been removed.

Wallace coughed, then nodded, and Greene closed the bag.

'It's not the first time this has happened,' Buchanan told him. 'In the last two months we've had reports from two local farmers saying that they've lost livestock, mostly goats and sheep. So far six have turned up, all of them skinned and gutted. Five of those we've found in this wood.'

'Did the others have their eyes torn out like this one?' the inspector asked, hooking a thumb in the direction of the black bag.

The constable nodded.

'It's not just livestock, though,' Buchanan continued. 'A number of household pets like cats and dogs have been reported missing too, but we haven't found any of *them* yet.'

'Could it be kids, Inspector?' asked Greene.

'It's possible,' Wallace said reflectively. 'But I can't think of many kids capable of doing something like this to animals. Not animals as big as goats or sheep anyway.' He sighed. 'Well, one thing's for sure, whoever did it doesn't work for the bloody RSPCA.' He glanced up at the butchered goat once more. 'Were the other carcasses as easy to find as this one? It looks like whoever did it wanted it to be found.'

'They were all found in or around this clearing,' Buchanan told him.

Wallace stroked his chin thoughtfully.

'Bury it,' he said. 'Get rid of the carcass and the head and . . . those.' He nodded in the direction of the intestines, still partially covered with dead leaves. 'Six in two months, eh?' he said, quietly, reaching for his lighter. He tried again to light his cigarette but still could raise only sparks from the recalcitrant flint. He pocketed the lighter again, looking irritably at the unlit cigarette.

'I'm going to drive out to Dexter Grange, have a word with the bloke who owns the place,' the inspector announced. 'He might have seen something. His house is only a mile or so away.'

'Henry Dexter?' said Constable Greene. 'He lives like a hermit. Never leaves the house, I hear.'

'Well, then, a visitor will make a change for him, won't it?' Wallace said, trudging off through the trees. 'Besides,' he muttered to himself, 'he might have a light.'

The inspector put away the cigarette once more and headed for his car.

Twenty

Wallace lit the cigarette from the lighter inside the car. He pushed it between his lips and sucked hard, enjoying the hot, comforting sensation as he swallowed the smoke. He had the front windows open, allowing the breeze to circulate inside the Sierra. It went some way to dispelling the smell of Chinese food left over from the previous night. The fresh-air ball which hung from the rear-view mirror had long since ceased to function.

The trees on the right-hand side of the road gradually gave way to a high stone wall topped at regular intervals by ornate carvings, most of which carried a patina of mould. A lion. A unicorn. And, perched on either side of the main gates, two eagles. Wallace swung the Sierra across the road and guided it up the long drive which led to Dexter Grange.

The house was clearly visible as soon as he passed through the gate, built as it was on a slight rise. It was an imposing place, Wallace had to admit. It reminded him of a stately home. As he drew closer he slowed down, stubbing the cigarette out in the ashtray. There was a large gravelled area in front of the house and the policeman was surprised to see a Jensen parked there. He brought his own car to a halt and climbed out, adjusting his tie and running one hand through his dark hair before approaching the main door. He reached out and banged with the huge brass knocker three times.

He waited a moment, then lifted the intricately carved metal object once more. Before he could knock again, the door opened a fraction.

Wallace found himself facing a rather bewildered-looking young girl.

Laura Price looked him up and down slowly and smiled.

'My name's Wallace,' he said, producing his I.D. card. 'I'd like to speak to Mr Dexter if I can.'

He saw her smile fade as she stepped back into the house. She wore jeans and a voluminous grey sweatshirt with the sleeves pulled up past her elbows.

'Police?' she said, hurriedly tugging the sleeves down over her forearms.

He nodded, frowning as he caught a vague glimpse of the scars on the inside of her left arm.

'Come in,' Laura said, opening the door, careful to avoid his gaze. 'You'll have to wait, though. He's got someone with him.'

The inspector stepped inside the hall, eyeing the girl suspiciously.

The walls were oak-panelled, completely bare, not a single picture or ornament to be seen. The ceiling curved up to a great height, giving the hall the appearance of an immaculately kept mausoleum. The floor, also dark wood, was devoid of carpet. A number of doors, all closed, led off from the corridor along which Laura escorted him.

'What's your name?' he asked.

'I thought you wanted to speak to Mr Dexter,' Laura said curtly.

'I do. I also asked what your name is.'

She told him almost grudgingly, aware of his eyes on her as she led him into a room and invited him to sit down. The room was pleasantly bright, with French windows looking out onto the driveway. There was no carpet here either, but there were paintings on the wall and two or three carvings on the mantel over the marble fireplace.

'How old are you?' he wanted to know.

'Look, have I done something wrong?'

'Just tell me. How old are you?'

'Eighteen,' she lied. 'And before you ask, I've left school. I'm Mr Dexter's friend. I do jobs for him.'

'That sounds cosy,' said Wallace. 'What sort of jobs?'

'Well,' she said guardedly, 'mostly errands and things. I do his shopping. He doesn't like to go into town.'

Wallace crossed to the fireplace and examined one of the carvings there. It was a male figure, the penis erect and disproportionately large. The one next to it was of a woman bending over. There was a large hole hollowed out between the legs. The policeman guessed that both pieces were made from ivory. He didn't attempt to estimate their value.

'Very tasteful,' he said sarcastically, fitting the two figures together. 'I had to make do with Lego when I was a kid.'

'I don't think Mr Dexter would like it if he knew you'd been playing about with those pieces. They're very valuable.' She turned and headed for the door, pausing as she reached it. 'I don't know how long he'll be,' she said, and with that, she was gone.

Wallace stood beside the fireplace a moment longer, then wandered over to the huge bookcase which covered most of the wall to his right. The inspector scanned the titles of some of the volumes, noticing that many were roughly bound, as if Dexter had done the binding himself, with titles handwritten in ink:

SATANISM TODAY

DEMONOLOGY

PAGAN RITES – THE NEW RELIGION

NECROPHILIA AND BESTIALITY

Wallace paused at one in particular and lifted it down from the shelf.

SACRIFICE AND POWER was neatly inscribed on the spine. The policeman flipped open the cover and scanned the closely-written A4 sheets. The volume was at least two inches thick, the words crammed together as if space was at a premium. He wondered how long it had taken Dexter to complete so much work. Wallace glanced through a chapter headed RITUAL SLAUGHTER, then replaced the volume and walked towards the centre of the room, his shoes echoing on the hardwood floor.

He heard voices, low and muffled at first.

Wallace paused, trying to locate the direction from which they came.

He heard the voices again, louder this time, more forceful.

The inspector strode to the door, realizing that the sounds were coming from the room across the corridor. He stood motionless for a moment, then slowly turned the handle, opened the door a crack and peered out.

The corridor was empty.

The sound of raised voices was much clearer now, though. Wallace detected anger in one of them. He crossed the corridor and pressed his ear to the door opposite, trying to make sense of the conversation.

' . . . the land isn't yours, you have no right . . .'

'*You* have no right, Mr Dexter. I have the deeds with me and . . .'

'I don't care about legal documents, that land has always belonged to my family . . .'

'I'm afraid that doesn't entitle you to any claim on it now. If you'd look at these deeds . . .'

Wallace frowned, wondering who Dexter was talking to. He didn't recognize the voice, but whoever it was, he seemed to be growing as angry as Dexter himself.

' . . . the wood will be flattened, with or without your cooperation, Mr Dexter.'

The wood.

Wallace chewed his lip contemplatively. Did they mean *that* wood?

'Get out of my house, Cutler . . .'

The inspector stepped back.

Cutler. The land developer. So that was who Dexter was arguing with. The policeman heard the sounds of footsteps from inside the room. He scuttled back across the corridor, stepping into the library but leaving the door slightly ajar.

A moment later he heard the door on the other side of the corridor burst open and slam back against the wall.

'Get out and take your bloody deeds with you, Cutler.'

The policeman pressed his eye close to the door and caught sight of Cutler and Dexter facing one another.

'I came here to try and talk this situation through reasonably,' the property developer said in a quieter tone. 'It's obvious that I overestimated your ability to hold a sensible conversation.'

'Don't patronize me, Cutler. Get out of here and stay away from my wood,' snarled Dexter.

'It isn't *yours*. It never has been.'

'I'm warning you,' Dexter said, taking a step towards the other man.

Cutler was unimpressed. He merely turned and walked towards the main door, his back to Dexter.

'I'll see myself out,' he said, closing the door gently as Dexter stood glaring angrily after him.

Wallace waited a moment, then stepped out of the room.

'I hope I haven't come at a bad time,' he said, smiling.

'Who the hell are you?' Dexter exclaimed, spinning round.

Wallace introduced himself.

The older man was silent for a moment, running appraising eyes over Wallace, aware that his own face was still flushed with anger from the row with Cutler.

'I'd like a word with you, if it's not inconvenient,' Wallace continued.

Dexter, regaining his composure, ushered the policeman into his study where they sat down opposite one another.

Wallace told him about the discovery of the dead goat and the other animals that had been found in the wood.

'Is that wood part of your land, Mr Dexter?' he asked finally.

'Technically, no, but my family have owned all the other land around this house for hundreds of years, and the wood was always considered part of our property by the local people. That wood is as much mine as the ground out there, if centuries of tradition mean anything. He motioned towards a large expanse of lawn right outside the window. 'Despite what Cutler says,' he added, almost as an afterthought.

'I overheard your disagreement, but coming back to what I said about the slaughtered animals, have you any idea how the carcasses ended up in the wood?'

'You're the policeman, Wallace.'

'What about the girl who lives with you? Might she know?'

Dexter shot the inspector a wary glance.

'No,' he said flatly.

'I hope she's older than she looks, Dexter. She tells me she's eighteen. Do her parents know she's here?'

'She has no parents. I suppose you could say I'm the only family she's got.' He grinned crookedly.

'How touching.'

There was a heavy silence between the two men, finally broken by Wallace.

'Why does that wood mean so much to you?' he wanted to know.

'I don't want builders ruining land less than a mile from my house,' the older man said.

'That doesn't answer my question.'

'It's been part of the landscape for centuries. Cutler has no right to destroy it. It's as simple as that.'

Wallace got to his feet and headed for the study door.

'I hope you're right about that girl's age,' he said cryptically, then closed the door behind him. Dexter listened as the sound of his footsteps echoed down the corridor. A moment later Laura entered.

'What did he want?' she asked.

'He wanted to know if I knew anything about dead animals in the wood. He also was curious about you.'

She looked suddenly afraid.

'Don't worry,' Dexter said reassuringly. 'He doesn't know anything. Besides, it's not the police who are the problem now. It's that bastard Cutler.' He leant back in his seat, his eyes gazing ahead, full of anger.

Twenty-One

The lights flickered, then went out.

In the tunnel, George Perry looked up toward the string of light bulbs, muttering under his breath as he stood enveloped in darkness.

He waited, and a moment later the tunnel was filled with a dull yellow light once more.

'I think that generator's on the blink,' he said, lifting the sword carefully from the earth. He glanced at the hilt, which was fashioned in the shape of a man with arms and legs spread wide. The archaeologists had found many of these anthropomorphic designs on sword and dagger hilts.

Ian Russell shivered, rubbing his exposed forearms briskly.

'It's so bloody cold down here,' he said, making a note of the latest find.

Perry was forced to agree.

'Where's Charles?' he asked.

'In the chamber with the skulls,' Russell told him. 'He's hardly left it since it was discovered.'

'I don't know how he stands it down here for hours at a time,' Russell continued. 'It gets claustrophobic after a while.'

Perry looked at his colleague.

'I've noticed the same thing,' he said. 'Up until a couple of days ago enclosed spaces never bothered me, but working down here . . .' He allowed the sentence to trail off as the lights flickered once more.

This time the power was not restored immediately.

'I'm going to have a look at that blasted generator,' said

Perry, getting to his feet. He rubbed his hands together, removing the dust and dirt. He set off back towards the shaft and started clambering up the rope ladder. As he did so he felt as if his legs were made of lead. Each step up seemed a monumental effort, as if all the strength had been sucked from him. Halfway up he actually groaned aloud and stood still, sucking in lungfuls of air so cold it seared his throat and made him feel as if he were being strangled.

The lights finally came back on, and in the muted glow Perry saw that his hands had turned a vivid shade of blue, as if they were badly bruised all over.

With horror, he realized that he had little feeling left in them.

He began to climb, his progress agonizingly slow, the cold seeping through him all the time until he feared he would simply seize up. It felt as if someone had dipped his hands in iced water and held them there. He managed to hook his numb fingers around each successive rung, but the effort was almost too much.

The thought of that needle-sharp stake at the bottom of the pit made him even more fearful and he closed his eyes, trying to drive away the vision of Phillip Swanson's skewered body as it had been lifted from the shaft what seemed an eternity ago.

He was just over halfway up the ladder now.

Some fifty feet from the bottom of the shaft.

And the stake.

He continued to climb, wondering now if he might be better off going back down. At least if he fell from lower down he ran less risk of badly hurting himself. But from fifty feet, he courted serious injury.

Even death.

Rung by rung he kept on climbing, however, sensing a little more feeling in his hands now. A sudden surge of relief swept through him and he urged himself on, confident now that he would reach the top of the shaft.

Perhaps it was over-confidence which caused him to slip.

He shouted in fear as one foot slipped off a rung.

Clutching the ladder with one hand, Perry desperately

shot out searching fingers and succeeded in closing them around a length of the thick rope which had been suspended by the ladder as a safety precaution.

Above him he could see a vague circle of daylight. He guessed that he had thirty feet or less to climb.

Summoning up his last reserves of strength, he began struggling upward again, soon finding it a little easier. Nevertheless, he moved with an almost robotic rigidity, unable to escape the enveloping chill which squeezed tightly around him like a constricting snake.

Twenty feet to the surface.

His breath was coming in gasps now.

Ten feet.

Daylight washed over him as he emerged from the shaft, perspiration running down his face despite the cold.

Perry slowly straightened up, his entire body shaking. He leant against the generator for a moment, composing himself, thankful that no one asked him what was wrong. The others on the site were too busy with their own work to notice him. He pulled a handkerchief from his pocket and mopped his brow, looking around the site, his expression wrinkling into a frown.

For fifty feet all around the shaft the grass and bushes were blackened and withered, as if they had been sprayed with some deadly poison.

Twenty-Two

Clare Nichols pulled the covers more tightly around herself, trying to keep out the chill which seemed to have filled her bedroom. Each time she exhaled she expected to see her breath clouding in front of her, but this did not happen. Perhaps, she told herself, she was imagining it. Perhaps the room was really warm. Perhaps she was still dreaming.

She put her hand out from beneath the bedding just long enough to feel that the air was, indeed, cold. Clare wondered about calling her mother and asking if she could have more blankets on her bed. The added warmth might at least keep the cold away.

It wouldn't keep the nightmares away, though.

She lay on her back staring blankly at the ceiling, feeling tired but not daring to drop off to sleep again. If she slept, she feared, she would return to the nightmare which had woken her just minutes before. Not with a scream or a cry of terror but with a numbing coldness which seemed to seep through every fibre of her body. Her eyelids flickered closed but she blinked hard, trying to keep herself awake, frightened of what waited for her beyond the boundaries of sleep. Frightened of the creature which crouched in her subconscious and had appeared so unexpectedly for the first time this evening. She'd had nightmares before, although she wasn't quite sure that the dream she'd experienced less than ten minutes before could be classed as a nightmare. But a nightmare was a bad dream, wasn't it? And this had been bad.

In her dream, Clare had been with several other children, none of whom she recognized. It had been dark and they had been as frightened as she because someone or something had been following them. Chasing them through the darkness, drawing closer all the time, until finally they had been unable to run any further and had been forced to turn and face their pursuer. The dark shape had run screaming at *her*, its clawed hands outstretched towards her throat. The worst thing was, she hadn't even been able to see its face.

But despite that, Clare had sensed something horribly familiar about it.

She *knew* this creature from somewhere and it knew her. And wanted her.

Now she lay in bed, her breath coming in short gasps,

trying to keep awake so that the creature couldn't pursue her again and perhaps finally catch her this time.

She heard the sound of soft footfalls on the stairs and pulled the sheet tighter up around her face. The door of her bedroom opened a fraction, light from the landing spilling through the crack, and beyond it she saw a dark shadow.

'Clare.'

She recognized her mother's voice but she didn't relax. She kept the sheets pulled up and screwed tightly between her fists.

'Are you asleep, darling?' her mother asked, but she didn't answer, and after a second or two the door closed again. The room was dark once more. Should she call out? Tell her mother about the nightmare? She decided not to and pulled the sheets up still more, wrapping them around her head until she resembled a nun, with only her face visible.

Her eyes flickered again, and this time she could not fight the part of her mind which wanted sleep. As she drifted into oblivion she had one fleeting thought.

Would the creature come for her again?

And, if it did, would she see its face this time? The face which she felt she already knew . . .

Twenty-Three

The van was parked in the hedgerow with its lights off. So well hidden that Rob Hardy almost drove past it. He stepped on his brakes and brought the Vauxhall 1100 to a halt on the other side of the road. He switched off his lights and his engine.

He turned to see Mick Ferguson clambering out of the

van and heading across the road towards him. Hardy swung himself out from behind the wheel and greeted the other man.

'You took your fucking time,' Ferguson grunted. 'I've been freezing my bollocks off in that van for the last twenty minutes.'

Hardy shrugged.

'Have you got them?' the other man asked, smiling as he saw Hardy reach into the back of his car and grasp a well-secured sack which he dragged free. A chorus of squeals and whines came from inside and Ferguson looked at his companion approvingly. Then his eyes shifted back to the sack, which was twisting and writhing as if it were alive. The two men walked back across the deserted road, satisfied that no more traffic would come this way at such a late hour. It was well past one a.m. and they were more than three miles outside Longfield. No danger of any interference from the law this far out, Ferguson told himself.

They reached the van and he fumbled in his pocket for the keys to unlock the two rear doors, blowing on his hands in an attempt to restore some of the circulation, his breath forming gossamer clouds before him. Hardy, still gripping the sack in one hand, climbed over the nearby fence into the field beyond and trudged about fifty yards through the slippery mud, pulling a torch from his belt. He directed the beam at the sack, watching its frenzied movements and listening to the cacophony of noise from inside which now seemed to be growing to a fever pitch. He jabbed it with his torch and chuckled.

From the direction of the road he heard a loud bark, followed by Ferguson's gruff voice, snarling a command for silence which went virtually unheeded. Hardy turned the torch towards his companion, feeling his own flesh rise into goose-pimples as he caught sight of the dog which Ferguson held securely on a chain as thick as his wrist.

The albino pit bull terrier pulled against the strong links, restrained by a metal collar. The torch light reflected eerily in its pink eyes, turning them the colour of boiling blood. Its lips slid back over huge and savagely sharp teeth. It was the first time Hardy had seen the beast and he was suitably impressed.

When Ferguson was about ten yards away he stopped, flicking off his own torch when the moon emerged from behind a bank of cloud, giving them all the natural light they needed. He held onto the chain with both hands, then nodded to his companion, who untied the sack and reached in, his hand protected by a thick gardening glove.

From within he pulled a spitting, rasping tomcat. Like some malevolent magician, Hardy removed the creature from the sack, gripping it by the neck, ignoring its frenzied attempts to scratch him.

'Now let's see how good this dog really is,' Ferguson said.

Hardy hurled the cat towards him.

No sooner had the cat hit the wet earth than the dog was upon it.

Both men watched fascinated as the terrier's jaws grasped the bewildered cat's right front leg and the dog pulled with all its strength. Most of the cat's limb was torn off in the savage assault and the animal toppled over, blood spraying from the stump, its anger now transformed into terror and pain as the pit bull struck again. This time its teeth closed around the cat's head. The steel-trap jaws crushed the helpless animal's skull into pulp as the dog shook its head madly back and forth, ripping away half of the cat's head. A sticky mass of blood and brain flooded from the massive bite and the terrier, apparently unconcerned that its victim was already dead, savaged the twitching body again, tearing the stomach wall open and ripping several knotted lengths of intestine free. Blood sprayed from them, some of it spattering Hardy, but he seemed barely aware of it. He merely reached into the sack and hauled out another cat.

This one was scarcely more than a kitten and a terrier needed only one savage bite to all but tear the little animal in two.

Ferguson chuckled as he watched the destruction which his mad beast wrought, keeping a firm grip on the chain as the dog tossed one half of the dead kitten into the air.

Hardy needed both hands for the next occupant of the sack.

While the terrier tore what remained of the kitten into blood-soaked confetti, he pulled a small labrador from the mèlée inside the hessian prison. The animal had its jaws firmly bound with strong tape. Hardy seized one end of the tape and tugged mightily. There was a sound like tearing paper as the sticky-backed binding came free, ripping tufts of hair from the dog's muzzle with it. The animal yelped in pain and fear, barking loudly as Hardy kicked it hard in the side, pushing it towards the waiting terrier.

The albino launched itself at the labrador and ripped off one ear with a single bite of its powerful jaws. The stricken dog howled and tried to bite its opponent, but this only seemed to inflame the albino more and it struck upwards at the labrador's belly, its teeth shearing through fur and flesh until it reached the soft entrails. The stomach wall burst open and the terrier pulled several lengths of throbbing intestine free. Blood erupted from the hideous gash and the labrador fell forward onto its front legs, helpless now as the pit bull seized it by the throat, almost severing its head, so awesomely savage was the attack. The spurts of blood looked black in the moonlight and both men watched in awe as the albino, now drenched in the dark fluid, tore ferociously at the body of its newest victim. The smell of slaughter was strong in the air, mingling with the pungent stench of excrement.

The terrier leapt and writhed amidst the carnage it had wrought, inflamed to the point of madness by the blood, until it was exhausted. Only then did Ferguson attempt to grab it by the back of the neck and secure its muzzle. The beast almost twisted from his grasp, its body was so slippery with blood, but he held onto its collar firmly and succeeded in fixing the restrainer over the deadly jaws.

'I'll get rid of these,' said Hardy, prodding the remains of the dead pets with the toe of his shoe. He began lifting the torn remains back into the sack, blood soaking through the coarse material. 'I'll bury them somewhere.'

Ferguson grunted his approval.

'That's a hell of a dog, Mick,' Hardy said, looking at the blood-spattered albino terrier.

'Yeah, that mad fucker's going to make me a lot of money. If you've got any sense you'll have something on him when he fights.'

Hardy nodded.

'Just remember, Rob, I don't want anyone else to know about him, not yet,' Ferguson reminded his companion. He turned and headed back towards his van, dragging the dog with him.

The moon cast a weak, silvery light over the deserted landscape.

The blood which covered the ground glistened blackly in the pale glow.

Twenty-Four

The rabbit was dying.

It lay on its side with its eyes closed, only the barely perceptible movement of its chest signalling that any life still remained.

Kim watched it for a moment, then opened the cage door and lifted the animal out. It was limp in her arms, its head lolling back as if its neck had been broken. She gently drew back its eyelids, noticing how a membranous film was beginning to form over the usually glistening eyes, turning them opaque.

Moving slowly, still holding the rabbit, she walked along the row of cages which housed some of the museum's live subjects. During the summer months the animals were kept outside in a small annexe where they served as an attraction for the smaller children who visited the museum. There were a few more rabbits, some mice and two white rats. Kim noticed that the food trays in every cage were still full, the food untouched. There was an almost unnerving silence too. No squeaking or any other sound came from the animals.

The other rabbits were also lying down. As Kim poked an index finger through the bars of the cage, they glanced helplessly at it, and when one tried to rise it found the effort too great and slumped over once more.

Two of the mice were already dead. They lay in the straw at the bottom of the cage, their limbs stiffening.

Stroking the rabbit she held, as if trying to coax some warmth and movement back into it, Kim gazed into the last cage. The female rat was carrying young. Its belly was bloated and swollen but the rest of its body was disproportionately thin, so much so that the bones which were now visible under its fur looked as if they would tear through. The male wandered aimlessly back and forth, ignoring the food that had been placed there for it.

Kim watched the rodents for a moment longer and then returned the rabbit to its cage, laying it gently on its side, wondering how long it would take to die.

She returned to her seat and sighed wearily, feeling strangely isolated within the museum. With Roger Kelly in hospital, she wondered if she should advertise for a replacement. The building had few enough visitors during the week but she couldn't cope alone forever, and there was also the administrative side to deal with. Normally this was the province of Alec Blane, a retired headmaster who was nominally in charge of the museum. However, he was out of the country enjoying a holiday, so Kim was left alone. She considered her position for a moment, then returned to the work at hand.

Spread out before her on the desk were two of the stone tablets, laid carefully on thick gauze to prevent them sustaining damage. Close by, Kim had placed a bottle of diluted hydrochloric acid with which to remove any particularly stubborn pieces of debris from the small slabs of rock. She tapped her notebook with the end of her pen and studied the lettering, trying to make some sense of what she had already written down:

> WANDERER. THINKER. I AM SO. WITHOUT NEED OR WILL TO BE OF ANY TÚATH. ONE OF THE ÁES DANA. MAN OF KNOWLEDGE LET ME PASS BY THESE YEARS QUICKLY. FOR TIME IS WHAT WE ALL SEEK. AND FREEDOM BUT THAT MAY NOT COME WITHOUT THE KNOWLEDGE. I AM FEARED. SON BORN OF SON BY AEDD MAWR. NONE MAY TOUCH ME. NOT PLEBES. NOT EQUITES. I AM FEARED FOR DAY THAT MUST COME

Kim shook her head, weary from the effort of trying to transcribe what she saw on the tablets into something meaningful.

Whoever had spent so much time creating these tablets, meticulously carving words so small that up to a hundred covered each slab of stone, obviously had been a learned man. One of the *áes dana* as he himself said — the wise men of the tribe. The Celts were insular people, making contact with other tribes usually only for two purposes: trade or war. And yet this man belonged to no tribe.

'I am feared,' Kim read aloud. The Druids were revered and respected by the Celts but not feared as far as she knew. They functioned as law-givers, judges and mediators. Why had this man been feared?

FEARED FOR DAY THAT MUST COME.

Kim sucked in a weary breath, noticing how cold it was in the room. She leant over and touched one of the radiators, recoiling sharply when she found it to be red hot.

And yet the cold persisted.

Puzzled, she got to her feet and walked across to the thermometer.

The mercury was stuck at fifty-one degrees.

Kim shuddered and tapped the instrument.

As she watched, the silver thread which marked the temperature slid even lower on the scale and settled at forty-eight.

She frowned in disbelief, then shrugged and returned to her seat. She glanced over the rest of her notes, blowing on her hands in an effort to restore some warmth.

I CARRY WITH ME THAT WHICH NONE SPEAK OF YET ALL FEAR. WHEN COMES THE TIME THEY SEEK ME THOUGH I KNOW ONLY MY UNDERSTANDING IS WANTED. THEY KNOW NOTHING OF MY WAY BUT FEAR MY PRESENCE NOT KNOWING I AM THEIR ONLY HOPE. YET I ENJOY THE POWER FOR AS LONG AS I AM ITS MASTER. SHOULD HE EVER OVERCOME THESE LAWS THEN MY OWN DEATH WOULD BE THE FIRST. I AM THEIR HOPE AND THEIR FEAR AND THEY KNOW OF HIS DAY. FOR MANY YEARS IT HAS BEEN. FOR MANY YEARS IT WILL BE SO. AFTER ME IF NONE COME THEN MANY WILL FEAR AND MANY WILL DIE BY HIS HAND.

A warrior? A king? Who was *He*? Kim wondered. She was assuming that the man who had engraved the stones was a Druid but whom did he speak of in the strange text? She wondered if the other slabs of rock would give the answers.

Looking up at the clock, she saw that it was almost five-thirty. Time to close the museum. As she got to her feet and walked out into the main hallway it occurred to her that it might be wise to close the museum for a week or two, or at least until she found a replacement for Kelly. She went to the main doors and pulled them shut, then retrieved a large key from the pocket of her jeans and began to lock up. She would leave by a side exit, she decided.

It was as she was turning the key that she heard the noise.

At first she wondered if her ears were playing tricks on her, but then the noise came again.

From above her there were sounds of movement.

Kim realized that someone was still inside the building.

She crossed to the bottom of the staircase which led up to the first floor and cupped one hand around her mouth.

'I've got to lock the doors now,' she called. 'It's five-thirty.'

No answer.

Obviously someone wandering around the galleries had

lost track of time and did not realize that the place was closing, Kim told herself. She walked back over to the main entrance and unlocked it again, then returned to the staircase and made her way up about five or six steps.

'Excuse me,' she said loudly, trying to attract the attention of whoever was up there. 'I'm locking up now.'

Silence.

She thought about calling out again, but instead began climbing the stairs towards the first floor, her heels clicking noisily in the stillness. As she reached the first landing she spoke again but still there was no answer.

Kim frowned. Surely whoever was up there must have heard her by now. She continued up the stairs, aware that the sounds of movement had stopped. Kim stood at the top of the steps and looked around her. Galleries lay in all directions from where she stood. Immediately ahead of her was the one which housed objects of local interest and some specimens of local wildlife and plants. She decided to look in there first. The floor was polished wood. The sound of her footsteps echoed loudly around the building, which seemed almost unnaturally quiet.

Kim paused as she reached the entrance to the gallery, peering in to see if she could see anyone.

A beautifully mounted badger gazed fixedly at her from one of the exhibit cases, and for a moment Kim caught sight of her reflection in its lifeless glass eyes. She moved into the gallery, treading a slow and measured path between the other specimen cases, her ears and eyes alert for the slightest sound or movement.

She heard breathing and spun round, her heart thudding against her ribs.

There was nothing to be seen.

Dozens of sightless eyes bored into her as she stood looking around, wondering where the harsh breathing sound had come from.

She heard it again, and this time a knot of fear began to settle uncomfortably in her stomach.

'Who's there?' she called as she heard the soft hiss once more.

It took her only a second more to realize that the noise was not really breathing, it was the wind rushing through a ventilation duct in the wall.

Kim let out a long, relieved breath, angry with herself for being so jumpy. Satisfied that she was alone in the gallery, she moved on. Perhaps her ears really had been playing tricks.

A new sound came from somewhere up ahead, in the next gallery. Then again, louder.

Kim froze, not sure whether she should continue. She stood listening for a moment, aware that someone was indeed moving about ahead of her. She considered calling out but swiftly decided against it.

Moving much more slowly, she walked on, unconsciously clenching and unclenching her fists, feeling the moisture on the palms of her hands.

She reached the entrance to the gallery and stopped, pausing a moment before taking a step inside.

In the centre of the room was a large sculpture of a mother and baby, the features missing, the limbs long and curving in an abstract way. Although she had seen it countless times, Kim suddenly found it curiously menacing.

She moved towards it, towards the middle of the gallery.

The sculpture was a large, solid object about seven feet tall and three or four feet wide.

Kim was only inches away when she realized that the sounds were coming from the other side of the object.

For long seconds it was as if time had frozen. She tried to stop herself shaking, knowing that any second she was going to confront whoever was hiding behind the sculpture.

They stepped in front of her.

Two children. Little boys, no more than ten years old.

They looked up at her in embarrassment, wondering why she hadn't shouted at them, wondering why she looked more frightened than they were.

'We weren't trying to steal anything,' the older of the two said. 'We would have gone out of a window or something if you'd locked up.'

The other boy nodded vigorously and Kim could almost

feel the relief pouring through her as she looked at them, heads bowed, as if they were about to receive punishment from a teacher. It was all Kim could do to stop herself laughing.

'Come on,' she said. 'I'll make sure you get out. And you can use the doors, not the windows. All right?'

The boys nodded again and ran on ahead of her to the stairs. Kim walked after them, her heart gradually slowing down. She felt both stupid and relieved. It *was* time she went home, she decided; her imagination was beginning to run away with her. She wiped the beads of perspiration from her forehead and actually managed a thin smile as she saw the two boys standing by the exit doors waiting to be allowed out.

'They're open,' she told them.

They hesitated for a moment.

'Go on. Let me lock up,' she called. 'I want to get home.'

They both dashed through the exit and disappeared across the car park. Kim chuckled as she watched them, then she turned the key in the lock, pocketed it and headed back to the staff room to collect her coat and notebook. She'd had enough for one day. All she wanted was to get home, relax in a warm bath and talk to her daughter. Forget everything for the time being. Even the mysterious stone tablets.

As she stepped inside the staff room the figure loomed in front of her.

This time she screamed.

Twenty-Five

'Jesus Christ,' Kim gasped. 'I didn't hear you come in.'

Charles Cooper seemed unconcerned at the fright he'd given her. He merely stood looking around the staff room as if searching for something.

'Where are the tablets?' he asked.

Kim, who was gradually recovering her breath after the shock, held one hand to her chest and felt her heart thumping hard.

'They're in there,' she said, motioning towards the adjoining room.

Without waiting for her, Cooper turned and walked through.

'You frightened the life out of me, Charles,' Kim told him.

'What have you found out about them?' he asked, ignoring what she had said. He picked up her notes and scanned what she'd written. 'Are these accurate?'

'As accurate as possible,' she told him, resenting the harshness of his tone and the implied lack of confidence in her.

Cooper flipped through the pages, his face impassive. 'I was just about to go home,' Kim said, pulling on her jacket.

'But what about the deciphering?' Cooper wanted to know.

'I'll continue in the morning, Charles,' she told him. 'I'm not staying here any longer. My daughter will wonder what's happened to me.'

He exhaled wearily and handed her the notebook.

'How are things going at the dig?' she asked.

Cooper shrugged, as if he didn't know.

'There's still lots of work to be done,' he said vaguely. 'Particularly in the skull chamber.'

'There was writing on the walls inside there,' Kim remembered. 'Have you managed to make any sense out of that yet?'

'No,' he said sharply, turning away from her, his eyes straying back to the stone tablets laid out on the nearby worktop. Then, as if anxious to shift the emphasis of the conversation, he nodded towards her notebook. 'That man claims to be the Great Grandson of Aedd Mawr, the one who actually set up the Druid order.'

'Is that possible?'

'Why should we doubt it?'

'I can't work out who he keeps referring to, such as here,' Kim replied, pointing to her words in the notebook: ' "They know of his day", and "Many will die by his hand". I don't know who *He* is.'

Cooper did not answer.

'Could it be a religious text? Could the writer be talking about one of the Celtic deities?'

'Which one? There were over 370,' Cooper said.

Kim closed the notebook.

'I'll keep at it tomorrow,' she told him.

'How long will it take to decipher all twelve tablets?' Cooper demanded.

'That's impossible to say, Charles. You know . . .'

'How long?' he snapped, interrupting her.

Kim looked at him angrily for a moment.

'I'm not sure,' she said, slowly. 'A week or two. It's difficult to say.'

'Let me know as soon as you have anything important.'

'I'll be coming out to the site in a day or two anyway,' she said.

'Why?' said Cooper, eyeing her suspiciously.

'I need to pick up some of those skulls for carbon dating,' she explained.

'The tablets are the first consideration.'

'I realize that.'

'The skulls can wait,' he said. 'We might not have that much time.'

'What do you mean?'

'Cutler threatened to close the site. We must try to do as much work as possible before he decides to go through with his plan. He doesn't realize what he'll destroy if he builds over that site.'

'Is there nothing we can do about it?' Kim asked, quietly.

Cooper didn't answer. He merely turned and headed for the door.

'Let me know what you find,' he said as he left the room.

She heard the front door as it closed behind him, then, outside, his car revving up. A moment later he was gone.

Kim shook her head, looking across at the tablets. Gathering up her handbag, she flicked out the light above the worktop and prepared to leave, deciding to glance at the animal cages again as she went out.

Every one of the creatures was dead.

Kim's mouth dropped open in shocked surprise. She quickly inspected the cages, gaping at the bodies inside.

The mice were huddled together in one corner of their cage, their small bodies stiff and unmoving. The rats, including the pregnant female, were also stiff with rigor mortis. Kim noted with renewed revulsion that the skin of the female's belly had split, spilling the unborn rats into the bottom of the cage. Their tiny bodies were shrunken and hard, looking more like faeces. The rabbits too were dead. But it wasn't only the fact that the creatures had died so suddenly which caused Kim to shudder. It was also the appearance of their bodies.

All of them were shrunken and shrivelled, their fur patchy and discoloured. The bodies looked only half their normal size. Every one was thin, as if they'd been starved to death.

As if the life itself had been sucked from them.

Twenty-Six

Stuart Lawrence slipped the bookmark into the paperback and laid it on the coffee table. He sat back in his chair, massaging the bridge of his nose between his thumb and forefinger, listening to the wind which whistled around the house. He reached for the glass of white wine on the table and finished what was left, then went into the kitchen and rinsed the glass beneath the tap. Outside the kitchen window the lilac bushes which grew so lushly in summer were now little more than shrunken stumps buffeted by the wind.

Lawrence wasn't one for gardening, but the bushes had been there when he'd moved into the house and he'd decided to leave them. The rest of his considerable garden was laid to lawn so that all he had to do was mow it every now and then. Any garden job beyond that constituted hard work to him, and as far as the young surveyor was concerned, work should be reserved for the office.

He switched off the kitchen light and padded back into the sitting room, checking first that he'd left the porch light on. Ruth would return sometime later, and he didn't fancy having to clamber out of bed in the dead of night to let her in because she couldn't see the lock in the dark. She had been gone since seven that evening, visiting friends in the nearby town of Mossford. No doubt comparing notes on babies, Lawrence thought scornfully. His sister was six months pregnant and staying with him until her husband returned from his three-month stint on one of Shell's North Sea oil rigs. Lawrence didn't object to his sister staying temporarily. It meant that he ate a good breakfast and dinner, and she was company for him, especially in the evenings. Not that being alone bothered him that much; he rarely arrived home before eight. It made a break for Ruth as well, but her little visits would only continue until she had the child. After that, Lawrence would have to find some excuse to stop her visiting so frequently. He didn't want any whining, puking kid messing up *his* carpets. He sat down to watch the tail-end of the late news, then switched the set off and made his way upstairs, taking his book with him. He found it difficult to sleep, but he had discovered that reading seemed to do the trick. He usually nodded off after a couple of chapters. His insomnia he put down to an over-active mind. He was forever turning new projects over in his brain, and at present the Cutler development was occupying all of his working time. He and his partners had worked for the land developer before and had always been more than satisfied with the financial rewards. This time was no exception.

Lawrence tossed the paperback onto the bed, then went into the bathroom to clean his teeth. As he finished he paused and stood listening, a sound from outside having caught his attention.

It sounded like fingernails scraping on glass.

He remained motionless until the sound came again.

Lawrence opened the bathroom window to find the branches of a leafless willow scratching the pane. He decided to leave the window open rather than risk being kept awake by the perpetual tapping and scraping.

He undressed quickly and slipped between the sheets, reaching for the book. The slow, rhythmic ticking of his alarm clock was the only thing that broke the silence of the room. He glanced at it and saw that the time was approaching 11:30. Ruth was late, he thought. He hoped she hadn't missed the last bus; he didn't fancy having to get dressed and drive to Mossford to pick her up.

Just then he heard movement outside the front door and nodded to himself, satisfied that she had finally returned.

A minute passed.

Two minutes.

102

Perhaps she had lost her key and couldn't get in. He waited for the knock.

It didn't come.

The noise seemed to fade and Lawrence returned to his book.

For the first time that night he noticed how cold it was in the room. He lowered his book for a moment, watching his breath clouding in front of him. He shuddered and pulled the covers up higher. He hadn't noticed the chill until now. Christ, it was freezing. He put down the book and tucked both hands beneath the covers in an effort to restore some warmth to them. Perhaps he'd left a window open in one of the other rooms. The draught couldn't be coming from the bathroom because he'd shut that door. After a moment or two he climbed out of bed and padded across the landing, heading for one of the spare rooms.

He opened the door and stepped into the darkness.

Switching on the light, Lawrence saw that no windows were open and decided to try Ruth's room next. Her door was open, but as he walked in he saw that the windows were firmly closed. The surveyor stood with his hands on his hips, puzzled by the unexpected drop in temperature. He turned and headed back toward his own room.

From downstairs there was a deafening crash. A sound like glass being shattered.

Lawrence froze, his heart pounding.

Still on the landing, his skin puckering into goose-pimples, he stood waiting.

Silence.

He swallowed hard and took a step forward, peering over the edge of the balustrade down into the gloom below.

Still there was no sound, only the low hissing of the wind as it swirled around the house.

The surveyor moved to the top of the stairs, muttering under his breath as the uppermost step creaked loudly.

He stood still, wondering if there would be more noise from downstairs.

For what seemed an eternity he remained at the head of the staircase. Finally, with infinite care and slowness, he began to descend. The darkness closed around him and now another sound reached him. The rushing of blood to his ears, driven by his wildly pumping heart.

Gripping the bannister with one hand, Lawrence moved closer to the bottom of the stairs.

He was halfway down when the figure loomed up out of the darkest shadows below.

For an interminable moment the surveyor could not move. His entire body was frozen, transfixed by what he saw, but then, as the figure started up the stairs after him, he found the will to turn and run. Gasping in terror, he fled back up the steps, aware that the intruder was closing rapidly. He could hear the footfalls behind him as he stumbled on the top step and went sprawling onto the landing.

If only he could reach the phone . . .

Lawrence dragged himself upright and sprinted across the landing, hurling himself through his bedroom door, slamming it shut only an instant before the figure crashed into it with a force which almost sent the surveyor flying. But he kept his weight against the wood, his eyes closed, his breath coming in terrified gasps. He felt another crashing impact against the door, so powerful that it was all he could do to retain his balance. Then, nothing.

Quivering madly, Lawrence kept both hands on the door handle waiting for the next blow. Sweat was running from his face despite the numbing cold and his legs felt like water. He pressed his ear to the door, listening for any sounds of movement outside the room.

He heard nothing.

If he could just get to the phone . . .

It was on the bedside table. Five or six feet from the door against which he now leant. But dare he try to reach it?

If he released his grip on the door and the intruder charged it again, there would be no hope for him.

If he did manage to dial the police, would they arrive in time?

If . . .

He released his grip on the handle but kept his shoulder

pressed firmly to the wood, trying to control his breathing in case the figure on the other side could hear him. Only by a monumental effort of will did Lawrence manage to open his eyes and look down at the handle, now smeared with his own perspiration.

He looked across at the phone.

Down at the handle.

At the phone again.

He eased away a fraction from the door.

The handle moved down slowly and it was all Lawrence could do to prevent himself from screaming.

His eyes bulged wildly in their sockets as he watched, then the realization seemed to hit him and he threw all his weight back against the door.

The handle now jerked up and down with terrifying rapidity until it threatened to come free.

Lawrence closed his eyes again as he felt a shuddering impact against the wood. He stood with his back against it, arms spread wide, gripping the frame as his body shook under the repeated hail of blows.

He didn't know how much longer the door would hold up to such sustained punishment.

There was a loud crack and part of it splintered. A great hairline splinter which ran half the length of the door.

Lawrence whimpered in terror, praying that someone would come to his aid, but knowing that there *was* no one who could help him.

The pounding stopped and, in the silence which followed he sank to his knees against the door, fear sapping his strength as surely as physical movement.

He looked around him for something to barricade the door with. The bedroom chair could be wedged under the handle, but how long would that hold the intruder back? A mad idea sprang into his mind, one born of desperation. Perhaps he could wedge the door shut just long enough to jump from the bedroom window. Surely the fall wouldn't kill him. He would be landing on grass. Then he could reach the next house, get help.

It wasn't much of a choice but it was the only one he had.

With his back still pressed against the door he snaked out one leg and hooked his toes around the chair leg, pulling it towards him, waiting for the seemingly inevitable assault on the weakened door.

He dragged the chair nearer, closing his hand around it, then scuttled swiftly away from the door and jammed the chair under the handle.

He backed off and ran to the window, clawing wildly at it.

And now the pounding began again, much louder and more intense than before. Massive blows which shook the door and its frame.

Lawrence chanced a look over his shoulder as he struggled with the recalcitrant window catch.

'Please, God!' he whimpered, tugging at it with hands that shook insanely.

Part of the door was staved in by a thunderous blow that sent fragments of wood spraying into the room.

Another few moments and it would all be over.

He managed to free the catch, panting with renewed hope. He looked out into the night, guessing he was fifteen or twenty feet up.

There was no time to worry about the risks. If he stayed in the room he was sure to die.

He began to clamber onto the sill.

The door exploded inwards with an ear-splitting shriek, the sound mingling with Lawrence's scream of pure terror as the figure bounded across the room towards him.

He allowed himself to slip off the window sill.

A hand was thrust out after him and closed around his wrist. He felt an incredible power in that hand as, by sheer physical force, the intruder hauled him back inside, cracking his head on the window frame in the process.

Lawrence could only stare up at his assailant in disbelief, his terror now reaching an even higher pitch. He was close to madness now.

His attacker wasted little time and the surveyor felt vicelike hands close around his throat, lift him to his feet and then, with almost nonchalant ease, hurl him clear across the bed. He slammed into the dressing table, the impact making him feel sick.

The figure was upon him like lightning and now Lawrence roared in agony as he felt fingers tearing at his eyes, pushing into the bulging orbs, burrowing into the sockets themselves until blood burst from them in crimson spurts. Denied even the mercy of unconsciousness, he felt the fingers driving deep into his skull, tearing the eyes free, leaving pieces of optic nerve dangling over his cheek like bloodied tendrils, before oblivion finally came to him.

Blood pumped in thick gouts from the riven eye sockets, splashing down the dying man's cheeks to form a puddle beneath his head. One of the eyes fell into this red pool, but it was quickly retrieved.

Lawrence's body began to spasm uncontrollably but the killer took no notice.

There were other tasks to perform.

Twenty-Seven

The first thing that struck Wallace as he entered the house was the smell.

He could not help recoiling at the pungent odour as he stepped into the sitting room and looked at the shattered patio doors. Pieces of broken glass were scattered everywhere. It looked as if someone had been at the windows with a sledgehammer.

'Subtle, wasn't he?' Wallace muttered to a constable who was standing close to the doors. 'Have you found a tool he could have used to get in?'

'Not yet, sir,' the PC told him.

Wallace took one last look at the doors, then turned his back and headed for the stairs.

As he ascended the stench grew more powerful. The odour reminded him of bad meat.

On the landing he was greeted by Bill Dayton, and Wallace was surprised to see that the sergeant looked a little pale.

'What have we got, Bill?' he said.

'I'm buggered if I know, guv,' murmured Dayton, wiping the corners of his mouth with a handkerchief. 'I've never seen anything like it in my life.' He swallowed hard and apologized for his lack of composure. 'Young Buchanan was the first one in there.' He hooked a thumb in the direction of the room behind him. 'He's still in the toilet throwing up. I bloody nigh joined him.'

'Has the place been dusted?' Wallace wanted to know.

'Yes. Dr Ryan and the photographer are in there now. I didn't leave any of the men inside. I didn't think it was fair to them.'

Wallace nodded slowly and walked past the sergeant into the room.

He paused at the door, nodding a greeting to the elderly man who sat on the edge of the bed looking down at something which, as yet, Wallace could not see.

Rick Piper clicked off another photo, his flash gun momentarily bathing the room in cold white light.

'Morning, Steve,' said the photographer. 'I think you've got problems.'

He nodded towards the object sprawled at his feet.

'Jesus Christ Almighty,' whispered the inspector, struggling to retain his breakfast. His stomach lurched violently as he gazed at the body of Stuart Lawrence.

The surveyor was spreadeagled on the floor of the bedroom, the carpet all around him matted with dried blood. There was a large quantity splashed over the bed and the walls, too. His mouth was open in a soundless scream and Wallace could see the congealed blood clogged inside, as well as in the torn eye sockets. But, if anything, the ravaged face was the least offensive of the catalogue of atrocities inflicted on Lawrence. Stepping closer, Wallace saw with renewed revulsion that the man's stomach had been torn open. A jagged gash fully twelve inches long had been hacked into his belly from sternum to groin. Lumps of torn intestine protruded from the hole like mushy fingers, and pieces of the entrails had also been scattered around the room like so many bloodied streamers. Clots of blood so dark they looked like tar had formed in the shredded ends of the colon, most of which had been pulled from the riven torso and now lay draped over the shrivelled groin.

Wallace shook his head, fumbling for a cigarette, his eyes compulsively returning to the body time and time again, as if to convince himself that he wasn't imagining what was possibly the worst atrocity of all.

Stuart Lawrence had been flayed as completely as a rabbit in a butcher's shop. Nearly every inch of skin had been stripped from the disembowelled body.

The inspector stuck a cigarette in his mouth and reached for his lighter, flicking it in vain, getting only sparks. He had to be content to chew on the unlit Rothmans.

'The killer must have been covered in blood,' said Ryan, scratching his head. 'There would have been massive haemorrhage from a wound like the one in the abdomen.'

'Have you found a weapon?' the inspector wanted to know.

'It's not my job to find them, Inspector,' Ryan said, smiling.

'Sorry, I meant what do you think was used on him?'

'Well, it's impossible to say for certain until the autopsy has been carried out, but from initial examination, especially of the face, I'd say that there *was* no weapon.'

Wallace shot the doctor a disbelieving glance.

'Those injuries,' Ryan continued, 'were inflicted by hand. Someone literally tore his eyes out, and judging from the appearance of the abdominal wound I'd say the same for that.'

'But who's got the strength to tear through a man's stomach with their bare hands?' Wallace said incredulously as if doubting what the physician had told him.

'You're the policeman, not me. I merely gave you a medical opinion. As for the other injuries, particularly the flaying, I can only assume that a knife or some sharp object was used. Although whoever did it was clumsy.' He pointed to a particularly deep gash on Lawrence's right thigh. 'Not only has the skin been removed but a large portion of the muscle has also been torn away.'

'Flayed,' Wallace murmured. He looked at Ryan. 'You know we found the remains of a goat up in that wood near Dexter Grange. *It* had been flayed too.'

'You think the killer's graduated from goats to human beings?' Ryan asked, cryptically, the slightest hint of sarcasm in his voice.

'It wasn't just that. There are other similarities in the mutilations.' The inspector looked down at the body once more, thoughts turning over in his mind. He shook his head slowly and then glanced up at the doctor again.

'What about the intestines?' he said, removing the unlit cigarette from his mouth and pushing it back into the packet.

'They wouldn't have been too difficult to remove once the torso was opened. Merely a case of pulling,' Ryan said, shrugging his shoulders.

'So where are the eyes?' the inspector wanted to know.

'Nobody has found any trace of them,' Piper told him. 'Nor the skin.'

'Oh, shit, that's all we need,' Wallace sighed. He turned as Dayton re-entered the room. 'Is that right, Bill? There's no trace of the eyes or the skin?'

Dayton nodded, trying not to look at the body.

'We searched every inch of the house,' he said. 'The sick bastard must have disposed of them afterwards.'

'Or kept them,' Ryan offered.

Wallace looked at the doctor for a moment, then sighed and chuckled humourlessly.

'You're a great comfort, doctor,' he said.

'He must be a total fucking nutter to do this,' Piper added.

'I couldn't agree more,' Wallace said, reaching for a

cigarette once again. 'Have any of you got a light?' he asked hopefully.

'Don't look at me,' said Ryan, reproachfully.

Piper obliged and the inspector hungrily sucked in the tobacco smoke. He drew a hand across his forehead and exhaled deeply.

'Who found the body?' he asked.

'His sister,' said Dayton. 'She was the one who called us. They took her to hospital suffering from shock.'

'I wonder why?' the inspector said, bitterly. 'Well, get on the blower and tell the ambulance to pick this poor sod up. Once the autopsy's been done maybe we'll have a bit more to go on.'

'Inspector, I'm afraid there's something else you ought to see,' Ryan told him, getting to his feet.

Wallace followed the doctor around to the other side of the bed, where a sheet had been laid on the floor to cover something. Blood was soaking through the material.

As the policeman watched, the doctor carefully pulled the sheet back.

On the blood-soaked carpet was a thick length of intestine, lying there like some bloated greyish-pink worm.

It had been carefully shaped to form the letter M.

Twenty-Eight

Wallace flipped silently through the pile of photographs, pausing for as long as he could over each one. The fact that they were in black and white didn't make them any easier to look at. The subject matter remained the same. An obscene horror that he wished he could simply expunge from his memory.

There were ten photos in all. Of Stuart Lawrence. Of the room where he was killed. Wallace paused on the last of the batch.

He inhaled deeply on his cigarette and ran the tip of his pencil across the monochrome print, tracing the shape of the letter M which had been created using at least two feet of the dead surveyor's colon. The inspector knew that it was the large intestine because he also had the autopsy report on his desk. He looked once more at the photos, then put them aside and picked up the report, scanning through it to find the salient points. He still could not quite fully comprehend some of the things he read on the carefully typed sheets:

. . .EXTENSIVE DAMAGE TO BOTH ZYGOMA DOUBTLESS CAUSED BY REMOVAL OF THE EYES . . .SPHENOID BONES CRUSHED . . .SOME DAMAGE TO BOTH OCCIPIT-AL AND PARIETAL BONES INDICATING THAT CONSIDER-ABLE FORCE WAS USED TO REMOVE THE EYES.

Wallace blew out a long stream of smoke and turned the page, glancing as he did so at the photo of Stuart Lawrence's face. It was a silent affirmation of what was written in the report:

. . .X-RAY TESTS SHOW NO EVIDENCE OF WEAPON USED TO REMOVE EYES . . .

No evidence of weapon, the inspector thought, shaking his head. He looked again at the photos, noting the savage gashes on Lawrence's cheek bones, then he turned his attention to the shots of the eviscerated torso and the report's conclusions about this:

. . .LARGE PORTIONS OF BOTH THE COLON AND THE DUODENUM REMOVED WITH SUBSEQUENT DAMAGE TO THE BLADDER AND ALSO THE STOMACH . . .CAUSE OF DEATH CARDIAC ARREST PROBABLY PRECIPITATED BY LOSS OF BLOOD BUT EXTERNAL CAUSE CANNOT BE RULED OUT.

And once more:

NO EVIDENCE OF WEAPON.

Wallace looked at his own hands. They, he knew, were not powerful enough to tear open a man's stomach and rip out his entrails. What kind of man, then, was he looking for?

'A right bloody head case,' he muttered aloud, answering his own question. He picked up each of the photos of Stuart Lawrence again, studying them one at a time, his attention drawn particularly to the last one.

That obscenely fashioned letter M

An initial? If so was it the first or last name?

M.

For Maniac?

Wallace almost smiled.

He turned and looked out of his office window at the grey sky with its swollen clouds that promised rain. Somewhere out there he would find the killer but right now he just wished he knew where to start.

He was still gazing out into the gloomy afternoon when the phone rang.

Twenty-Nine

The skull was heavy, despite its small size.

Charles Cooper took the small brush from his belt and flicked some fragments of dirt from the eye sockets, studying the skull a moment longer before putting it into the small wooden crate with the others he had removed. There was still a large pile of them left, however, built in a pyramid shape which rose as high as the archaeologist's waist. He felt as if they were watching him with their sightless eyes, angry that he was disturbing their final resting place.

He had been in the chamber for the last four hours, working alone, resentful of any intrusion by his colleagues. A number of them were working in the tunnels close by, but they had come to realize that Cooper was best left alone while he worked amongst the pile of skulls. And, unlike the others, he seemed not to feel the constant chill which permeated the chamber and tunnels.

It was not only the skulls which interested him.

The carvings on the walls of the chamber were beginning to show up with greater clarity as he removed more dirt. As yet, Cooper was still unable to make much sense of the drawings and the chiselled script. He wondered if it had been done by the same people or person who had been responsible for the stone tablets which had been removed to the museum. He decided to determine this as soon as possible.

The lights inside the chamber glowed with a feeble yellow tinge that belied their hundred-watt strength. They periodically flickered or went dim, but Cooper seemed unconcerned. Now they went out completely, but he merely stood silently in the darkness waiting for the restoration of power.

After a few minutes the lights came back on with a brilliant flash and he saw George Perry standing at the entrance to the chamber.

'Bloody generator must be on the blink again,' Perry said and Cooper noticed that he was shivering, his breath clouding in the dank air.

'What do you want?' Cooper asked, taking a step towards the chamber entrance.

'They've found some more relics in the other tunnels. Gold statuettes and ornaments. I thought you might like to see them.'

'I've got too much to do here,' Cooper told him.

'Charles, you've been down here for four hours,' Perry said, wearily. 'Ever since we found this chamber you've

114

spent most of your time in here. Isn't the rest of the dig important to you any longer? We know that the skulls belonged to those bodies we found. What more can you discover by hiding yourself away in here every day?'

'I don't have to justify myself to you. This chamber could be the key to the whole site, and there's still a great deal of work to be done here. I intend to find out what these carvings on the walls mean.'

'Then let me help you,' said Perry, taking a step forward.

Cooper moved towards him, blocking the entrance to the chamber, his steely eyes boring into his companion.

'I don't need any help,' he snapped.

'What have you found?'

'Look, just leave me to get on with my work, will you?'

The two men eyed each other for long moments, then Perry shrugged and walked away. Cooper watched him disappear along the subterranean passage, making sure he was well out of sight before stepping back inside the cell-like chamber. The silence enveloped him as he returned his attention to the strange series of symbols on the wall before him. There were a number of drawings, each one hacked into the stone, he guessed, with a piece of flint. Beneath each one were letters, some of which formed recognizable words. Others he could make no sense of. As he scraped away more dirt from the stone he saw that the words were beginning to form a sentence. Cooper used a tracer to remove the last vestiges of debris and give himself a clear view of the writing. He read the sentence, mouthing the words silently to himself, his speech slowing as he reached the end.

'My God,' he whispered, his eyes riveted to what he'd read. He scanned it again. And again. More of the Celtic script was carved into other parts of the chamber and he knew that it must all be uncovered, but his eyes kept on returning to the single complete sentence he had so far revealed.

He tried to swallow but his throat felt as if it were full of chalk.

As he stepped back he found that his hands were shaking.

Thirty

'Not bloody cheese again!' groaned Mike Spencer, pulling back one edge of his sandwich and examining the contents. He bit into the bread and chewed quickly.

'Why don't you ask your wife to put something else in them?' Colin Mackay asked.

'I make them myself,' Spencer told him, grinning. 'Cheese was all we had in the fridge, except salami, and I didn't fancy any of that stuff. I'd have ended up smelling like a bloody Italian.'

The other men inside the Portakabin laughed. There were half a dozen of them, all on their lunch break. Outside, on the building site itself, earth-moving machines rumbled back and forth and the roar of powerful engines was a constant background to the men's conversation. Close by, a bulldozer was flattening some ground, the excess earth being scooped up by a JCB. The clanking of caterpillar tracks reminded Spencer of a war film he'd seen the night before. The lorry which he drove back and forth to remove the excess earth was parked on a small incline about thirty feet from the Portakabin. Usually he'd had his lunch at a cafe in Longfield, but that was proving to be expensive so he'd decided to start bringing sandwiches. He'd just come in, having retrieved them from the parcel shelf of the ten-ton Scania.

'You know, I bet the leisure centre is a wreck within six months,' Keith Riley said, gazing out of the window towards the building beyond. 'Once the bloody vandals get at those walls with their spray cans and what have you.'

'I saw a good bit of grafitti in town the other night,'

Spencer announced. 'It was sprayed on the bottom of a poster for abortion, and it said "*You rape 'em, we scrape 'em.*"' He laughed throatily, almost choking on his sandwich.

'I know what Keith means, though,' Mark Little added, pouring himself a cup of tea from his thermos flask. 'I mean, we spent weeks painting that place and it's going to be ruined.'

'You don't have much faith in kids do you?' said Frank King. 'Wait until you've got a couple of your own.'

'Sod off, I'm not having kids,' Little told him. 'They tie you down.'

'Only for the first twenty-five years,' chuckled King.

'So what happens if your old lady gets pregnant, then?' Spencer asked his companion. 'You haven't got the money to pay for an abortion.'

'You can get it done on the National Health, you berk,' Little said. 'Anyway, she'd better not get pregnant. She's been on the pill long enough.'

'My wife's got the coil,' Spencer informed his colleagues. 'On a good day she can pick up Radio One on it.' He burst out laughing again. 'She was going to use the Dutch cap but we couldn't find one to fit her head.'

'How much longer are we supposed to be working on this site, Frank?' Colin Mackay asked the foreman.

'That depends on what Cutler decides to build next,' he said. 'Your guess is as good as mine.'

'I don't care how long we're here,' Spencer said. 'At least the money's good.'

'Come on, fellas,' King said, looking at his watch. 'If *Mr* Cutler decides to pay us a visit I don't think he'll be too happy to find us all lounging about in here.'

Amidst a chorus of complaints and mutterings, the men filed out of the hut. All except Spencer.

'Come on, Mike,' King said.

'Can I just finish my coffee, Frank?' he asked.

'Don't be too long about it,' the foreman said and closed the door behind him leaving Spencer alone.

Inside the Portakabin, Mike Spencer fumbled in his

jacket pocket for his cigarettes, cursing when he realized he must have left them in the lorry. Sod it, he'd wait a few more minutes. He took a sip of his coffee.

If he had been asked to swear on a stack of Bibles, Mike Spencer would have said that he had left the Scania's handbrake on when he parked it on the incline near the Portakabin.

And Frank King naturally would have expected the driver to have done so.

That perhaps was why the foreman was so taken by surprise when he saw the juggernaut move slightly, then begin to roll towards the hut, picking up speed as it did.

For a moment he stood frozen, watching the heavy Scania roll inexorably down the slope, bumping violently over the rough ground as its speed increased. By the time he was able to shout a warning, the lorry was moving at an unstoppable speed.

Still lounging in the Portakabin, Spencer took one last mouthful of coffee, then got to his feet and stretched, becoming vaguely aware of the sound of shouting from outside. He crossed to the window, trying to locate the source of the noise. He frowned in puzzlement as he saw Frank King running towards the hut. Spencer could see him mouthing words but he could not make out what they were.

A second later the lorry ploughed into the hut.

Frank King shouted one last hopeless warning, then he could only stand helplessly and watch as the Scania hit the Portakabin.

The entire structure buckled as the huge bulk of the lorry flattened it.

Others nearby turned to see what was happening, their attention caught by the noise, especially the high-pitched scream which rose from the wreckage.

The foreman started running again, joined by Keith Riley and John Kirkland, and the trio dashed stumbling

118

and swearing across the uneven ground towards the remains of the hut.

Mike Spencer had been caught completely unawares by the collision. The truck had caved in the side wall and the roof of the small building, pinning him beneath the debris, unable to move before the massive rear wheels ran over his legs and thighs. The bones were crushed into pulp by the weight of the huge lorry. Both femurs snapped like matchwood, one jagged edge tearing into his femoral artery before bursting through the skin and muscle of his pulverized thigh. Most of his pelvis was also crushed by the giant wheels. Mercifully, he blacked out as a huge fountain of blood sprayed from the torn artery, rising in a great crimson parabola to splatter the rear end of the truck.

Seated high in the driving seat of the bulldozer, Bob Richardson saw the lorry flatten the hut and immediately jammed the great machine into neutral and switched off the engine. Using one of the caterpillar tracks as a ladder, he began climbing down to join the other men who were running towards the scene of disaster.

He actually had one foot on the ground when the bulldozer's engine roared into life.

Bob looked up in dismay and surprise as the machine rolled forward, instantly trapping his left hand between two of the tread links.

He had one brief second of terrifying realization, then the searing agony began.

As the machine rolled forward he felt an unbearable pressure on his wrist and arm as the 'dozer dragged him a few feet. It was moving slowly but not slowly enough for him to extricate his arm. He shrieked in pain as the tread crushed his wrist and hand, the snapping of bones clearly audible above the clatter of the tracks. He tried to pull himself free, to stop the unbearable wrenching at his shoulder. The entire limb was going numb, the material of his coat tearing under the prolonged tugging.

With one final despairing roar of pain, Bob felt his hand come off.

He sprawled in the mud, the bloodied stump spouting crimson while he screamed for help. His severed hand rolled free of the track as if it had been spat out and he noticed, even through his pain, that the fingers were still twitching.

The bulldozer rolled a few more yards, then stopped.

Bob Richardson continued to scream.

Frank King turned and saw the bulldozer driver sprawled on the ground, his shattered arm spewing blood, the severed hand lying close by. The foreman spun round in time to see Riley and Kirkland, who had reached the smashed hut ahead of him, trying to pull the motionless form of Mike Spencer from beneath the Scania. Apparently they were unaware that too much pressure could rip his body in two. Whether either of the injured men could survive, King didn't know. He stood, hands pressed to his temples, listening to the shouts of alarm from other men running to help, and the next voice he heard was his own, yelling frantically.

'For God's sake get an ambulance!'

Thirty-One

George Perry lifted the crate into the back of the Land Rover, grunting under the weight. He set it down as gently as he could, then stepped back, wiping the dust from his hands.

'There are twelve skulls in there,' he told her. 'That should give you plenty to work with.'

Kim smiled and raised her eyebrows.

'Have you been able to decipher anything from the tablets yet?' Perry asked.

'A little, but I'm still working on them,' she said, looking closely at her colleague, who seemed somehow distracted. 'Is anything wrong, George?' she finally asked.

Perry sighed.

'As a matter of fact there is,' he told her. 'It's Cooper. There's something wrong with him. I don't mean he's ill. It's . . . I don't know, his personality. His entire character seems to have changed in the last day or two. Ever since we discovered the chamber of skulls. He spends all his time in there. He doesn't like anyone else going near it.' The archaeologist sounded indignant. 'He's got no right to do that. I intend having a look myself, whether he likes it or not.'

'Has he found anything else?' Kim wanted to know.

'If he has, he hasn't mentioned it. He seems . . .' Perry struggled to find the right word, 'I don't know . . . obsessed with what he's doing. But it's not only that Cooper's become more aggressive. I think he's frightened as well.'

'What of?'

'I wish I knew. He's found *something* in there and whatever it is, it's scared the hell out of him.'

The two archaeologists looked at one another for a moment, as if both were lost for words.

'Let me know if anything happens,' Kim said finally, climbing behind the wheel of the Land Rover.

Perry nodded, watching as she started the engine and drove off across the field.

He felt a sudden chill sweep through him and it felt uncomfortably familiar. He turned and looked towards the gaping mouth of the shaft.

It took Kim over five hours to carbon-date the first four skulls and put a reasonably accurate fix on their age. Like the rest of the relics recovered from the site, they were at least 2,000 years old. A fluorine test, together with the petrological microscopy, confirmed that fact.

121

As she worked with the skulls, Kim glanced almost unconsciously at the stone tablets still laid out on the worktop. She intended to continue with them as soon as she'd finished with the skulls.

The museum was closed and she worked alone in the silence, having decided that the building was best left shut while she toiled over the finds.

As she worked, though, she was aware of the ever-present chill which filled the air like invisible freezing fog. She got up to check the radiators, deciding that if it got much colder she could not continue working in the museum.

She returned her attention to the skull before her. She had removed the lower jaw and part of one side, leaving the yawning cranial cavity gaping at her. She had used a small portion of the jaw to grind up for a nitrogen test, but it was the cheek bones and eyes which drew her attention. She studied the same features on all the skulls more closely and saw that each of the skulls bore deep, irregular striation marks. Particularly around the eyes, both above and below. As if some sharp object had been used on them at some time. A knife perhaps.

The thought sent a shudder of revulsion through her body.

It looked as if, all those centuries ago, the eyes had been gouged from their sockets.

Thirty-Two

There were twelve of them.

All naked.

The youngest barely sixteen. The eldest yet to reach twenty.

As they moved back and forth in the clearing the dead leaves rustled beneath their feet and the branches of the trees shook spidery fingers at them. The gloom of the starless night was like a black shroud which had closed over the wood as if to hide what was going on.

Henry Dexter stood slightly to one side of the crudely fashioned cross, his face impassive, his grey hair ruffled by the breeze which swept through the wood.

The cross consisted of two large pieces of wood, nailed together at the apex. They were merely particularly large tree branches which had been broken off and joined by three large masonry nails. A youth stood in front of the cross, a lad of sixteen with a smattering of acne on both his face and shoulders. He faced three girls, all of the same age. One was tall and slender, the other two a little overweight, their bellies and thighs slightly too large.

At a signal from Dexter, Gary Webb and another youth stepped forward and pulled the acne-spotted lad towards the cross, tying his arms securely to the cross-beam so that he was spreadeagled. He shuffled uncomfortably, feeling the ropes cutting into one wrist where they had been fastened a little over-zealously. He put up with the discomfort without complaint, however, because he knew what was to follow.

Led by the tallest, the trio of naked girls knelt before the boy, whose penis was already beginning to harden. As the first girl reached out and drew one finger tip along the shaft, his organ rapidly attained its full stiffness.

The second girl leant forward, took his penis into her mouth and sucked gently on it for a minute or two before the next girl did likewise, tasting her companion's saliva as well as the salty taste of the lad's erection. He strained against the ropes as the feeling of pleasure began to grow more intense.

The tall girl took her turn, this time massaging his swollen testicles while the other two ran their hands up and down his thighs.

'The Cross,' said Dexter. 'Symbol of Christ. Monument to that filthy Jew they called the Son of God.' He spat on the ground in front of the cross. 'He who sent his only bastard offspring into the world via the whore Mary. He who watched his own son die on the Cross. He who denies pleasure.'

The youth tied to the cross was moaning more loudly now as the girls began to work more vigorously on his penis, sucking and rubbing until the lad tensed and prepared for release.

The movements stopped and he gasped, looking down first at his saliva-soaked erection and then at Dexter.

Gary Webb stepped forward and handed the older man a large chalice of gold, watching as he moved closer to the helpless boy. Dexter gripped the boy's penis in his powerful hand, beckoning the tallest of the three girls forward once more. His hand was replaced by hers and Dexter watched her pump it rhythmically up and down on the boy's stiff shaft until he pushed his hips forward and moaned loudly.

A thick stream of semen splattered into the chalice, followed by several more spurts until the white fluid covered the bottom of the receptacle. The boy gradually relaxed as the girl slowed her movements.

From the deep shadows around the clearing, Laura Price stepped into view. She crossed to Dexter and looked at him for a moment before dropping to the ground on all fours, her legs spread, her bottom lifted high in the air.

Dexter knelt swiftly before her and offered the chalice to her lips, watching as the liquid trickled towards her open mouth. She swallowed some of it.

'The body of Christ,' Dexter said, smiling. He got to his feet.

It was as he stepped back that Laura caught sight of the dog.

It was a short-haired collie, a sleek-bodied animal restrained by a length of rope around its throat. As she watched, it was led towards her by Gary Webb, who paused, then handed the make-shift leash to Dexter. The dog barked once but Dexter tugged hard on the rope and the animal was silent except for low panting sounds.

The older man nodded and Gary dropped to his knees behind Laura, his penis now swollen and hard.

Another of the young men stepped forward and took up a position beside Dexter.

He carried a long, double-edged knife.

Dexter began winding the rope around his hand, pulling tighter on the dog's leash, causing the animal to yelp in pain as pressure was increased on its throat. It turned and tried to bite Dexter but he merely twisted the rope tighter, listening as the animal's panting subsided into hollow gasps. Then he yanked it hard, lifting the collie off the ground until it dangled by the rope, its legs thrashing wildly. It required a surprising amount of strength to hold the dog up with one hand but the athletic Dexter found it no effort. The dog was now bucking uncontrollably, its eyes bulging wide as the rope throttled it.

The young man with the knife stepped closer, and with lightning speed drew the blade across the dog's throat.

A great fountain of blood erupted from the wound, spraying all those close by with sticky crimson fluid. Dexter kept his hold on the rope, watching as the dog's struggles gradually became less frantic. Blood continued to spurt from its gashed throat and he watched the red gouts for a moment before lifting the chalice to the wound. The blood spilled in, mixing with the semen to form a thick, coagulated mess.

Dexter dropped the dog and held the chalice above his head with both hands.

'The host,' he said, smiling.

He leant forward and tilted the receptacle so that some of the fluid dripped onto Laura's arched back. She felt the warmth of the blood and squirmed. Dexter spilled more onto her buttocks, watching intently as Gary gathered some on his fingers, rubbing it around her vagina.

Laura groaned slightly. Then she felt Gary force his penis into her vagina. He steadied himself, then began thrusting back and forth, both of them grunting like animals.

Dexter dropped the chalice and took the knife from the other boy, who looked on with the rest as Dexter gripped the dying collie by the hair at the back of its neck, yanking its head back.

Gary Webb speeded up his thrusts as he felt his orgasm beginning to build.

Dexter rolled the dog onto its back and drove the knife into its chest, tearing downwards to expose its insides. Then, using both hands, he pulled the reeking tangle of intestines from the gaping cavity, ignoring the vile stench which rose from the slippery coils. Like springs, the entrails seemed to suddenly expand and Dexter continued pulling until the animal was completely gutted, the steaming vital organs lying in a bloody pile beside him.

Laura, meeting Gary's vigorous thrusts with her own, began to shudder as the pleasure grew more intense. She saw that other couples had also begun copulating. The entire clearing was a mass of pale undulating bodies.

Even the youth tied to the cross was not forgotten. The tall willowy girl took his penis into her mouth and began sucking it while another boy drove his shaft into her from behind.

Dexter, his naked form drenched in blood, began skinning the dead dog, tearing off hunks of skin and hair with his vicious cuts. Finally, he managed to rip the complete coat free.

This he draped over Laura's back, and as she felt the warm blood from the hide covering her skin she began to climax.

Her cries of pleasure mingled with those of others in the clearing.

Dexter stood smiling amidst the wild depravity, his grin broadening as he saw the two girls approaching him. They were young, slim and small-breasted. Their nipples stuck out proudly in the chill wind. The first of them, a girl with short red hair, ran her soft hands over Dexter's body and caressed his swollen testicles while her companion kissed the head of his throbbing organ.

Both bore numerous scabs on the insides of their arms, the flesh purple where it had been bruised and punctured so often. Scar tissue had turned into a vivid crust, purple in places where it had been picked away only to grow again in a more purulent form.

Dexter smiled down at them and stroked their breasts, enjoying the mixture of pleasure and anticipation on their faces.

More eyes turned towards him now. Expectantly.

He knew what they wanted and he raised the bag of heroin into the air, displaying it like some obscene trophy.

A chorus of giggles, cheers and cries of delight rippled around the clearing. The two girls standing beside the older man clung more tightly to him, their eyes riveted to the package of white powder as if it possessed some kind of hypnotic power.

Dexter laughed aloud, the sound carried on the breeze to be lost in the dense trees all around the clearing.

'It's time,' he said, quietly.

Thirty-Three

Who the hell did Cooper think he was?

Not allowing anyone else into the chamber of skulls. Ridiculous!

George Perry was muttering to himself as he clambered down the rope ladder, descending deeper into the shaft.

During the day the hole was black enough, but now, in the darkness of the night, it was impossible to see a hand in front of him as he climbed down, bracing himself carefully on each rung, making his way slowly and cautiously into the abyss.

As he reached the bottom he pulled the powerful torch from his belt and flicked it on. The beam pushed a small funnel of light through the gloom. He moved swiftly through the opening which led on into the maze of tunnels beyond. Once inside the main tunnel, though, Perry slowed his pace, careful not to slip or twist his ankle on the dozens of hazards which littered the tunnel floor. Relics, bones and pieces of fallen rock all combined to create an uneven and treacherous surface and, more than once, the archaeologist had to steady himself against the moist walls.

He sucked in a deep breath, surprised at how taxing the walk along the stone corridor was proving to be. His body felt heavy, as if weights had been attached to his legs, slowing him to a snail's pace, preventing him reaching his goal.

His torch beam dimmed momentarily but he banged the light and it glowed more brightly again.

Perry pressed on, knowing that he must be close to the chamber of skulls. Up ahead, dimly illuminated in the light of the torch, he saw the entrance. He immediately quickened his step although the feeling of heaviness was growing almost intolerably strong now. He gritted his teeth and forged ahead, the icy chill seeping into his flesh, into the bones themselves.

George Perry was a fit man, but by the time he reached the chamber entrance he was puffing and panting as if he'd just run a marathon. He sagged against the stone portal, sucking in lungfuls of the stagnant air, waiting for his strength to return. After what seemed hours but was only minutes, he stepped inside and pulled his notebook from the pocket of his jacket. His torch beam played back and forth over the Celtic script which covered the walls of the chamber. He looked all around the small area but could see nothing that Cooper should want to protect. There didn't seem to be any secrets worth hiding.

Then he saw the words.

A large portion of one wall had been cleaned by Cooper, exposing the ancient letters and symbols carved into the stone. Perry now moved closer, a frown already beginning to crease his forehead. He read the words to himself, faltering in places, but the gist of them came through. He went back to the beginning and started again, the full impact hitting him this time.

'Jesus!' he exclaimed, his voice amplified by the

subterranean tomb. It echoed off the walls and died away slowly to a low whisper.

He spun round, listening to the soft, sibilant hiss, realizing after a second or two that it was his own voice he was hearing. Bouncing off the cold stone and reverberating around him.

Jamming the torch into the crook of one arm, Perry began to scribble down what he saw on the walls before him. He wrote quickly, anxious to be out and away from this place. Simultaneously, he was frightened to go back through the tunnel, but he finished writing and pocketed his notepad. He read the words from the wall again, mouthing them silently this time, his skin prickling.

He had wondered what Cooper had found in this underground tomb but nothing could have prepared him for this.

Perry read the words once more, as if to reassure himself that he had got the sense of them right, then turned and hurried, almost fled, from the chamber. The notebook nestled safely in his pocket.

He would re-read the words when he got home.

Then he would decide what to do.

Thirty-Four

At first she thought she was dreaming.

Kim heard the low whispering but merely sighed, rolled over and settled herself again, her eyelids growing heavier. Yes, that was it, she told herself, she was dreaming. She wasn't really hearing the soft, but insistent, whispering. The sound continued and she finally sat upright, realizing that the noises she heard were not the product of her imagination. She could hear them clearly now, beyond the door of her own room, drifting through the darkness.

The sound stopped for a few moments. Kim thought about sliding back beneath the covers, but then it began once more, slightly louder if anything. She swung herself out of bed, pulling on her dressing gown, now drawn irresistibly towards the low whispering.

She paused at her bedroom door, listening, trying to detect the source of the sound. There didn't seem to be any movement, only the noise. Low and conspiratorial, occasionally rising in volume, then dying away completely for a moment or two.

Kim eased her door open, cursing as it creaked on its hinges.

The whispering stopped.

She took a step onto the landing, wishing that the light switch was beside her room instead of being on the far side of the landing. It was dark and she squinted hard in an effort to distinguish shapes in the gloom. She reached out with one hand and touched the balustrade, which felt icy cold. Kim took two more tentative steps forward, hoping that the floorboards wouldn't creak beneath her, wondering why she felt so uneasy.

She heard the hissing once more.

Close to her.

Her heart thudded harder against her ribs as she turned, realizing that the low whispering was coming from her daughter's room.

Kim crossed to the door and put one hand on the cold handle.

'Clare,' she called softly. 'Are you awake?'

No answer.

The whispering stopped again.

Kim hesitated a moment longer, then pushed the door open and stepped into the darkened room, her hand hovering over the light switch.

She heard the sound once more and a slight frown creased her forehead as she realized that it was indeed Clare who was making it. Even in the gloom she could see

130

her daughter's lips moving as she mouthed the words. Whatever they were. The girl was obviously dreaming. She'd thrown her blankets off and lay completely uncovered. Kim stepped to the bed and pulled the blankets up around her once more, afraid that she might catch a chill.

As she bent low over her daughter she heard the words which escaped her fluttering lips and she froze.

They came only sporadically but a few of them were recognizable.

Kim crouched beside the bed, looking at Clare's face and listening.

'Help me,' the girl whispered. 'Time is coming . . . *He* is coming . . . Sa . . .'

Kim listened more closely.

'He knows . . . can't stop . . . too late now . . . He's coming . . .'

The words trailed off as Clare rolled onto her side.

For what seemed an age Kim remained crouched beside her daughter's bed, waiting to see if the girl continued whispering, but she did not. After ten minutes, Kim got to her feet and padded towards her own room, taking one last look at her daughter before closing the door behind her.

She climbed into bed, aware of how cold it had become inside the house.

Her daughter had only been dreaming, she told herself. It was nothing to be alarmed about.

But, for some reason, Kim found it difficult to drift off to sleep again. The hands of the alarm clock showed three a.m. by the time she fell into welcome oblivion.

She was still asleep an hour later when Clare pushed open the bedroom door and looked in.

The girl stood gazing almost mesmerized at her mother for a full five minutes, her eyes wide and staring. Then she turned and walked slowly back to her own room.

However, she did not sleep again that night.

Thirty-Five

Dew lay over the ground like a gossamer sheet and dripped from the roadside bushes like liquid crystal. Spiders' webs looked as if they'd been constructed from spun glass as they glistened in the first rays of dawn light.

Mick Ferguson lit up a cigarette and sucked hard on it, coughing throatily before propelling a lump of mucus into the field behind him. He dug his hands into the pockets of his jacket and leant against the wooden fence behind him, his eyes darting up and down the road which led into Longfield, although he doubted there would be much traffic about at such an unholy hour of the morning. He glanced at his watch and saw that it was not yet six-thirty a.m. He'd already been waiting for fifteen minutes, freezing his balls off. Another five minutes and he was bloody well going.

Now he saw the figure striding purposefully towards him, apparently oblivious to the early morning chill.

Ferguson waited until the newcomer was within three or four yards of him, then hawked loudly and spat into the roadside grass.

'About fucking time,' he rasped. 'I've been standing here like a right prick for the last twenty minutes.'

'It's not my fault you got here early,' Henry Dexter told him, regarding the other man with ill-disguised contempt.

'Have you got the money?'

'If you've got the stuff.'

'Yeah, I've got it. You must have used quite a bit at your little *party* last night,' Ferguson said, sarcastically. 'You'll have to invite me sometime.'

Dexter didn't answer. He followed the other man over to

132

the van which was parked by a clump of leafless trees. Ferguson unlocked it and reached inside, pulling out two small bags. He held the heroin before Dexter.

'Two hundred a bag,' he announced.

'That's fifty more than last time,' Dexter protested.

'Where else are you going to get it?' Ferguson snapped. 'Now either pay up or piss off. I'm the one who runs the fucking risks. I'm the one who takes the chances. I have to pay the dealers I get it from. When they put their prices up, so do I.' He chuckled. 'Just put it down to inflation.'

Dexter hesitated a moment then dug his hand into his pocket and pulled out a thick wad of notes. He counted out four hundred pounds in twenty-pound notes and pocketed the remainder, taking the heroin from Ferguson.

'How pure is it?' he asked, brandishing one of the bags before him.

Ferguson shrugged.

'I got it from a different dealer this time. I don't know.' He smiled. 'You'll just have to take a chance.'

Dexter slipped the bags into his pocket.

'What do you care, anyway?' Ferguson asked. 'You don't use it yourself, do you? You only give it to the kids.'

'That's my business, Ferguson, I've told you before.'

'I know that. It makes no difference to me what you do with it. But when the builders get around to flattening that wood where you hold your little parties, what are you going to do then? It looks like you might have to find something else to occupy your time.' He chuckled.

'I don't know why you think it's so funny. If I stop holding the ceremonies then those who attend will go elsewhere. You'll lose business as well. It's in both our interests to see that the wood stays untouched.'

The two men locked stares for a moment, then Dexter turned and walked away.

Ferguson stood by the van for a moment longer, watching him disappear around a bend in the road, before he started the engine, jammed the vehicle into gear and drove back into Longfield.

Thirty-Six

The light burning in the sitting room was a welcoming sight to John Kirkland as he swung his Metro into the short drive alongside his house. He clambered out of the vehicle and opened the garage door, making a mental note to oil the hinges as he heard them squealing. Then he walked back to the car, got in and drove into the dark garage.

The dashboard clock showed 8:22 p.m.

Kirkland switched off the engine and sat in the gloomy silence, stretching in his seat, feeling the stiffness in the muscles.

Christ, what a day he'd had. Checking every single piece of machinery at the building site to ensure that there were no more accidents like those of the previous day. He and Frank King had been over every one of the vehicles with a fine-tooth comb but had found nothing out of the ordinary. No electrical or mechanical faults of any kind. Just as they had found nothing wrong with the bulldozer the day before to account for it starting up and tearing Bob Richardson's hand off.

They had found no apparent fault with the handbrake of the Scania, either, but it had still managed to roll down that incline and crush Mike Spencer to death.

Kirkland rubbed the bridge of his nose between his thumb and forefinger and exhaled wearily. He was thankful that he hadn't been the one chosen to tell Spencer's wife what had happened. The constable who'd turned up at the scene of the accident had taken it upon himself to perform the task. All part of the job, thought Kirkland, clambering out of the car. He locked it and made his way to the door which led into the kitchen.

His stomach rumbled loudly as the smell of food reached him.

He winced for a moment as he stepped into the well-lit kitchen, the fluorescents presenting a glaring contrast to the darkness of the garage. As his eyes became accustomed to the brightness he noticed a couple of saucepans simmering on the stove. Steam was rising in a white cloud from the bubbling pans, creating a film of condensation on the windows and walls.

On the worktop close by there was a half-finished glass of orange juice.

Kirkland frowned and turned down the heat under the saucepans.

'Jaqui,' he called, wondering if his wife was on the phone in the hall. Yes, he decided that must be the answer. Why else would she leave the kitchen unattended so long while the meal was cooking?

He wandered through to the sitting room, glancing at the television set. The sound was turned right down, but as he approached the hall he could hear no voices. No phone conversation.

'Jaqui,' he called again.

No answer.

Only the low murmurings from the television set.

A thought struck him. One which should have been so obvious.

One which sent him bounding up the stairs two at a time.

He found her in the bedroom.

She was lying on her back, one arm resting across her forehead, her skin as white as milk.

Kirkland crossed to her, taking one of her hands in his, feeling the clamminess of her skin.

'Jaqui,' he whispered, watching as her eyes flickered open. 'Are you all right, love?'

She managed a smile, then nodded almost imperceptibly.

'I felt faint,' she said, answering his unasked question.

She reached for the packet of Dextrosol tablets on the bedside table and popped one into her mouth. In moments Kirkland saw some of the colour coming back into her cheeks. She sat up and kissed him lightly on the lips.

Jaqui Kirkland had been diabetic every since she was nine, and in the twenty years since that discovery she had been forced to inject herself with insulin twice every day. The problem had been well under control until she became pregnant. Now, six months after discovering that she was carrying a child, she had undergone a series of hypoglycaemic attacks due to the fluctuation of her blood sugar level. The doctors had warned her that the level would rise because of the pregnancy but none had told her of the discomfort she would experience when the level dropped. However, the Dextrosol seemed to work for her and so far she had only been admitted to hospital once in those six months. Only occasionally did she succumb to the full fury of an attack.

'I left the saucepans on,' she said apologetically.

Kirkland brushed a strand of dark hair from her face.

'It's OK,' he said. 'We've got our own Turkish bath in the kitchen but there's no harm done.

They both giggled.

'I'm all right now, John,' she assured him, trying to swing her legs off the bed, but he restrained her.

'Stay here,' Kirkland instructed. 'You rest for a while. I'll see to the dinner.'

'I'm all right, honestly.'

'Don't argue with me, woman,' he said with mock sternness. 'Don't you dare move off this bed until I get back. I've got to go and shut the garage door anyway.'

She nodded and squeezed his hand as he got to his feet, turning towards the bedroom door. He made his way down the stairs, through the sitting room and into the kitchen. The steam had not yet dissipated, so Kirkland opened two of the kitchen windows, watching for a moment as the condensation was sucked out into the dark night.

He fumbled in his trouser pocket for the key which would

136

lock the garage door, then stepped into the gloom, closing the kitchen door behind him.

There was a light switch close to his left hand and he flicked it on.

Nothing happened.

The garage remained in darkness.

He muttered something about having to change the bulb, then walked cautiously towards the door which was still letting in some faint light from the streetlamps outside. He cracked his shin on the frame of a baby's pushchair, an early present from Jaqui's parents. Cursing the object, he rubbed his leg and hobbled the remaining few feet to the garage door. Once there he reached up and pulled it down, plunging the garage into impenetrable blackness. There was another light switch nearby and he tried that one too.

For a split second the bulb flickered.

In that instant of twilight Kirkland saw a dark shape close by his car.

He stood still, his heart suddenly beating faster.

The light flickered once more, then went out.

Kirkland snapped the switch up and down frantically, and again the bulb burst into brief life.

The dark shape was gone.

He let out a long sigh and made his way back across the garage, careful to avoid the pushchair this time. He found himself putting out a hand to prevent himself tumbling over any other obstacle that might be blocking his path.

Close by him, something moved.

Kirkland spun round, trying to see in the gloom, screwing his eyes up in an effort to penetrate the darkness that surrounded him.

He heard a metallic scraping sound, then a loud crash, the sound amplified by the silence inside the garage.

For a moment he leant back against the car, his heart pounding. He fumbled in his pocket for his lighter and flicked it on, holding it high above him.

He breathed an audible sigh of relief when he saw the rake lying a few feet away. It had been that which he'd dislodged, and its handle had struck some other garden tools which leaned against one wall and had toppled them like over-sized skittles.

Kirkland closed the lighter, plunging himself back into the gloom. He was now almost to the door which led through to the kitchen.

Strong hands closed suddenly round his throat, jerking upward so powerfully that he was momentarily lifted off his feet.

Eyes bulging in their sockets, blind in the blackness, he could only flail his arms uselessly against his invisible attacker.

Kirkland grunted helplessly as the incredibly powerful hands lifted him fully off the ground before hurling him towards the car.

He hit the vehicle with a sickening thud which jarred him from head to foot and made stars dance before his eyes. He opened his mouth to shout for help, but the pressure on his windpipe had been so great that he could produce only a strangled wheeze.

Head spinning, he tried to rise, clawing his way up the side of the car.

He was upright when he heard the arc of the rake.

The prongs caught him in the side of the face, splintering his cheekbone with the force of their impact. Two of the sharp points pierced his left eye and now he found voice for a scream of agony as blood spilled down his cheek, mingling with the spurts of vitreous fluid from his torn eye.

He crashed to the floor, already beginning to lose consciousness, but before merciful oblivion could claim him he felt fingers tearing at his other eye.

Sharp nails digging into the socket, gouging beneath the sensitive orb, shredding skin and muscle in the process.

Kirkland raised a hand and pushed against the garage door. A thin shaft of light suddenly illuminated his attacker.

Jaqui Kirkland heard the scream.

She hauled herself upright, her heart pounding wildly, a

138

sudden uncontrollable fear spreading through her.

She swung herself off the bed and scuttled towards the stairs, slowing her pace slightly as she reached them for fear of falling.

As she made her way down she spoke her husband's name over and over again. Reaching the hall, she ran through the sitting room with its television that still whispered and into the kitchen.

From the garage there was an almighty crash.

Jaqui hesitated for what seemed an eternity at the door which led to the garage. Finally, with one last surge of courage, she threw the door back, hearing it crash against the garage wall.

Light from the kitchen spilled into the blackness beyond, illuminating the scene before her.

For long seconds she stood upright, her eyes riveted to the ragged bundle which lay by the car. Then, with a moan, she sagged against the door frame, her stomach churning, her lips fluttering soundlessly.

John Kirkland lay like some bloodied, broken mannequin in the centre of a spreading pool of blood. Some of the crimson liquid had sprayed up the side of the car. Great thick smears of it covered the walls. He lay on his side, his stomach gaping open to reveal the slippery lengths of intestine which had been pulled from his belly.

His head, one side of which had been pulverized by the blow from the rake, was twisted around at an impossible angle, the empty eye sockets fixing Jaqui in a sightless stare. Clogged with congealing gore, they reminded her of ink wells filled with bright crimson.

There were deep cuts around his neck and chest, and several reaching from his throat to his pelvis.

Most of the flesh of his torso, arms and legs had been stripped away to expose the bleeding network of muscles beneath.

Jaqui retched, feeling the nausea sweeping over her. She stared, mesmerized, at her dead husband. When she finally tore her horrified gaze from his ruined corpse, her eyes only alighted on something equally vile.

On the windscreen of the car, lying there like some monstrous parasite, still pulsing in places, was a thick length of intestine.

It had been quickly but unmistakably shaped to form the letter S.

Thirty-Seven

'The injuries are identical to those of the first victim,' Doctor Bernard Ryan said, pulling at the end of his nose.

Wallace nodded and glanced at the photos spread out before him on the desk.

'So I see,' he murmured wearily.

In the relative silence of the office, the ticking of the wall clock sounded thunderous. The hands were just moving past twelve noon.

More than fifteen hours had passed since the first policeman had been called to the home of John Kirkland. The screams of the dead man's wife had alerted neighbours who had not been slow in summoning help. Wallace himself had arrived at the house at the same time as the ambulance, less than fifteen minutes after the corpse had been discovered.

The garage and its contents had been dusted thoroughly for fingerprints. Particularly the rake which had been used to fell Kirkland in the first place. But now Wallace looked down at the report and shook his head.

There had been indentations on the rake handle, such was the strength of the hands which had held it.

But it bore not one single print of any description.

The killer had obviously been wearing gloves, Wallace

140

reasoned, but why had Ryan found no trace of fibres from them on or around Kirkland's mutilated body?

Surgical gloves, the inspector speculated.

They would have left no trace.

And yet . . .

He sucked in a weary breath and flipped through the report once more as the doctor sat by silently.

It showed that the eyes had been removed by hand and that the evisceration also had been completed without the aid of any tool or weapon.

No fingerprints, and yet there were scratch marks on the dead builder's face. How could this be if the killer had worn gloves?

Wallace ran a hand through his hair and sat back in his seat, eyes glued to the set of prints before him. The ten monochrome photos only served to compound his obvious bewilderment. They lay there like silent accusations. Constant reminders of his inability to find the leads he so desperately sought.

'The killer has a grouse against the builders on Cutler's site,' he said finally, breaking the long silence. 'You don't have to be Sherlock Holmes to work that out.' He sat forward, glancing up at Ryan as he tapped the photos with the end of his pencil. 'But why go to so much bother mutilating the bodies?'

'Is that a rhetorical question?' said the doctor, 'Or are you asking my opinion?'

'Have you got one?' Wallace asked.

'The fact that the killer steals the eyes and the flayed skin could point to some motive deeper than revenge against the builders.

Wallace looked vague.

'There's something almost ritualistic about these murders,' Ryan continued.

'So you think the eyes and the skin have been taken for a reason?'

'It's a possibility. At this stage I don't think you can afford to ignore *any* angle.'

'Unfortunately it doesn't bring us any closer to

understanding what kind of person actually carried out the killings.' The policeman stroked his chin thoughtfully. He picked up the photo which showed the letter S so crudely yet effectively fashioned from a length of Kirkland's intestine.

What the hell was this bastard playing at? First an M. Now this. Wallace knew of psychopaths who felt compelled to leave evidence of their involvement in bizarre crimes, evidence which would eventually lead to their own arrest. Had he just such a psychopath on his hands now? Was this all part of a monstrous game?

He got to his feet and walked to the large picture window behind his desk. It looked out over the car park of the police station. Down below, Constable Denton, sleeves rolled up, was busy washing down one of the police cars parked on the tarmac.

'You say that the eyes and the intestines were removed by hand,' Wallace said, his back to the doctor, 'but the actual flaying was done using some kind of cutting edge?'

'A piece of broken glass was used on Lawrence,' Ryan confirmed. 'I found a trowel close to Kirkland's body. Both implements were used to remove the skin, although as I said, whoever did it was clumsy. Especially in Kirkland's case. Most of the musculature of the chest had been hacked away too.'

'How much do you know about ritual murder?' Ryan wanted to know.

Wallace shrugged.

'Not enough. I mean, it's not the sort of thing you spend your time studying, is it?'

'It seems as if someone out there disagrees with you,' the doctor said, cryptically.

Wallace picked up the autopsy report on John Kirkland, flipping through it until he found the entry he sought.

His eyes skimmed back and forth over the short sentences as if by constantly re-reading them he would make some sense of them. Perhaps they would at least lose some of their impact.

There was no such effect.

The most disturbing aspect of both murders still remained before him. Something which sent a shudder through the inspector each time he glanced at the neatly typed reports.

Besides the appalling injuries inflicted upon them, both Stuart Lawrence and John Kirkland had suffered massive cardiac arrests.

As if, prior to death, each had witnessed something so dreadful it had simply caused their hearts to burst.

As if they had been frightened to death.

Thirty-Eight

Banks of grey cloud were gathering in the late afternoon sky, signalling the approach of rain. They cast a dull, threatening shadow over the land.

Kim reached for the tracer and cleaned some fragments from the stone tablet she was working on, then blew the dust off and began carefully transcribing the Celtic script onto a fresh sheet of A4 paper. The job was a tortuous one, but already that day she had filled five of the sheets with her neat handwriting.

Yet even though she had now deciphered three of the stone slabs she was no closer to understanding them.

The tablets retained their secrets for the time being.

Kim reached for the mug of tea close by and took a sip, gazing down at what she'd written:

THEY COME FOR THEIR FEASTS AND THEIR DAYS OF PRAISE AND THEY SEE ME PRESENT. THEY WISH ME THERE FOR THEY KNOW I COMMAND HIM WHO THEY FEAR . . .

She tapped the paper with her pen, cradling the mug of tea in her free hand, and read on:

BUT THERE ARE OTHERS TOO WHOM THEY FEAR AND WITH GOOD REASON FOR THERE IS MUCH POWER IN THIS WORLD BEYOND THAT I ALONE AM ABLE TO TREAD.

Kim shuddered slightly, feeling tickling fingers playing icily across the back of her neck as she read:

I AM BOTH MASTER AND SLAVE. FEARED YET FEARFUL.

She sat unmoving on her stool, listening to the silence which seemed to close around her like a living entity.

She felt almost in a trancelike state when the car pulling up outside broke the solitude.

Kim waited a moment, feeling annoyed at the intruding noise, then got to her feet, heading out of the laboratory to the entrance hall of the museum. Her heels echoed noisily in the empty silence. The sign on the outside door said clearly enough that the museum was closed until further notice. She waited in the hall for the new arrival to see it and depart.

There was a loud knock.

'We're closed,' she called. 'There's a notice . . .'

'Police,' the voice replied. 'I'd like to come in.'

She hesitated a moment, then stepped forward, slid the bolt and opened the door.

She recognized Wallace immediately.

'Sorry to disturb you,' he said, smiling.

'Inspector Wallace!' she exclaimed, returning his smile. 'To what do I owe this pleasure?' She ushered him into the hall.

As Wallace stepped inside he drew a breath which felt as though it would freeze his lungs.

It was numbingly cold in the building and he felt as if millions of icy pins were pricking his face and hands.

'I need your expert help,' he said, raising his eyebrows. 'I've just come from the library in Longfield. They didn't have what I wanted so they suggested I try this place. They said you had a considerable collection of books in the building.'

'That depends on what you're looking for,' said Kim, leading him to the right, towards the archway that led into the library.

Wallace scanned the room, which seemed full to bursting with row upon row of volumes in all shapes and sizes, new and old.

'I'm looking for information on ritual murder,' he said flatly, and Kim frowned in concentration as he eyed the shelves.

'That's not my field of expertise, Inspector,' she told him, leading him toward the closest shelf, 'but I think we have a few books here that might be helpful.'

He pulled a packet of cigarettes from his pocket and stuck one in his mouth.

'Is it OK if I smoke?' he asked, fumbling for his lighter.

She nodded, watching as he flicked at the recalcitrant object, unable to raise more than a few sparks.

'You wouldn't happen to have a light, would you?' he asked, almost apologetically.

Kim smiled and turned away, heading for the exit.

'I'll see what I can do. Would you like a cup of coffee a little later?'

He winked at her.

'You're a mind reader.'

Wallace set to work.

4:56 p.m.

Wallace closed the great leather-bound tome and pushed it away from him. He stretched, hearing his joints crack. His back ached and there was a dull pain settling into the base of his skull. He was no closer to discovering the exact nature of the rituals carried out on Stuart Lawrence and John Kirkland, and that irritated him. There was one single word written on his notepad, underlined several times:

WITCHCRAFT.

He closed the pad.

'Did you find what you were looking for?'

The voice startled him momentarily and he spun round to see Kim standing in the doorway holding two mugs of coffee.

'I'm not even sure what I was looking for to begin with,' he confessed wearily, thanking her as she set down his coffee, then pulled up a chair opposite him. Wallace warmed his hands around the mug for a moment before taking a sip. He found his gaze drawn to hers and for brief, but telling, seconds they exchanged glances.

'Do you mind if I ask you some questions, Mrs Nichols?' he said finally.

'My name's Kim,' she told him. 'Unless it's *that* serious.'

Wallace smiled.

'You're aware of the fact that two men working on the building project just out of town have been murdered recently?' he asked.

'There was something in the paper, yes, but no details.'

'Did you know either of them personally? Either Stuart Lawrence or John Kirkland?' He went on to describe them.

'I'd seen Lawrence a couple of times. He came out to the dig a week or so ago with Cutler, the land developer. I didn't know the other man.'

'How did Charles Cooper get on with Lawrence?'

'He hardly knew him.'

'He can't have been too happy about the builders closing down your dig. You told me yourself that he thought it was one of the most important ever.'

'I don't understand what you're getting at, Inspector. You're not implying that Charles had something to do with those men being murdered, are you?'

'Just thinking aloud,' he told her.

'That site *is* very important. I think Charles has a right to be angry at the prospect of it being closed down. Some of the finds are priceless, both in an archaeological and a financial sense.'

'Worth killing for?' asked Wallace.

Kim eyed him irritably for a moment, then took a sip of her coffee.

'Sorry,' he said. 'But I'm only doing my job. I had to ask.'
She nodded.
'I understand,' she told him.
There was a heavy silence, broken by Wallace.
'How's your daughter?'
'She's fine. She'll be wondering where I am, though a neighbour looks after her until I get home.' Kim looked at her watch. 'I'm going to have to throw you out, Inspector,' she said, smiling.
'Steve,' he told her. 'My name is Steve.'
She coloured slightly but returned his smile.
'I need some more information,' he told her. 'I was wondering if you could give it to me. I need to know something about the Celts. I understand you're quite an authority. Only if you're closing up now, perhaps you'd like to discuss it over dinner tonight?'
Kim smiled.
'I don't know,' she said, reluctantly. 'It's not always easy to find someone to babysit for Clare, especially not at such short notice. I'm sorry.'
He felt momentarily deflated and did his best to hide it.
'It would be much easier if you came over to my house,' she suggested. 'I'll cook a meal for us. Then I don't have to worry about Clare. If that's all right with you?'
He laughed, watching as she pulled his notepad towards her and wrote down her address.
'Just in case you'd forgotten,' she said. 'About eight o'clock?'
'That's fine. Thanks, Kim.' He was already getting up. She handed him the notepad and showed him out, ensuring that the door was locked behind him.
Wallace stood in the car park grinning broadly for a moment, then he headed towards his car. However, halfway there he turned and looked back in bewilderment at the museum.
Despite the cool breeze which was blowing, it felt considerably warmer out in the car park than inside the building.

Thirty-Nine

The floor was drenched with blood.

The entire cellar reeked of the sticky crimson fluid.

Mick Ferguson spread sawdust thickly over the gore but it merely soaked through, filling his nostrils with an odour that reminded him of an abattoir. The comparison was particularly appropriate.

The remains of two cats lay scattered over the red-flecked floor. Torn lengths of intestine and lumps of bloodied flesh were strewn over most of the underground room. Ferguson kicked at the severed head of one of the dead animals and watched it roll across the floor, blood still draining from the shredded veins and arteries of its neck.

He turned and looked at the two dogs in the cages behind him, both of them smeared with blood. Rob Hardy sat on the bottom step of the stone staircase smoking a roll-up, his eyes also fixed on the dogs. Particularly the albino terrier. He was pleased that the bloody thing was locked away safely in its cage once more. It frightened the shit out of him. Even Ferguson had no real control over the demented beast. Only the thick chain it always wore prevented it from savaging the two men once it was released from its prison. But now, to Hardy's relief, the bastard was penned up again. He gazed at it, finding his stare returned by those vile pink eyes.

'Do you think he's ready for the pit?' Hardy asked, motioning towards the dog.

Ferguson nodded.

'I heard that some big shot's flying in from Belfast to see the fight,' he said. 'They go a bundle on dog-fighting over there, you know. If he's interested I might sell the dog. For the right price of course.'

Hardy sucked hard on his cigarette, watching his companion scoop up the cat's head and drop it into a plastic bag as he began clearing up the bloody debris.

'You know, I'd bet my life on that dog tearing the shit out of anything sent against it,' Ferguson said, nodding in the direction of the albino. 'But there's one test I'd like to give it before it fights.'

Hardy looked vague.

'I'd like it to have a go at something that could put up a real fight.'

Inside the cage, the dog eyed both men and began barking.

Forty

The footpath stretched away before him, snaking between trees whose skeletal branches bent low as if threatening to reach down and scoop up anyone who came within reach.

Thick bushes also lined the dirt track, which even at its widest point was no more than five feet across.

Jonathan Ashton knew that he shouldn't have taken this route home. He knew because his mother had told him on numerous occasions not to walk the footpath alone. And now, as he hurried along it, he knew that there were other reasons too.

The light of early evening still filled the sky, but beneath the canopy of leafless trees it was already preternaturally dull. Crane flies, some of the last to survive the summer, skimmed through the air and occasionally bumped into

Jonathan as he walked, hands thrust deep into the pockets of his jeans.

Wraith-like swarms of gnats assaulted him every now and then and he quickened his pace, wanting to run but knowing that the extra effort was wasted.

He was over an hour late for tea as it was. His mother would be furious.

If she knew he'd used the footpath to get home she'd be even more angry. He'd be confined to the house for a fortnight, perhaps longer. Jonathan took one hand from his pocket and brushed the fine blond hair from his eyes, glancing around him as he did so. As is the nature of six-year-olds, his imagination was working overtime. He knew that he shouldn't have come this way, shouldn't have strayed from the main streets even though it cut his journey in half. His mother would rather he was even later than have him wandering along the dusk-shrouded footpath alone.

But it was too late now. He was half-way along the dark track. There was no point turning back.

As he walked he kicked with trainer-clad feet at the fallen leaves, humming to himself, noticing how even that soft sound seemed to echo in the stillness.

Only the occasional twittering of birds broke the solitude which bore down on him from all sides.

The bushes ahead of him moved, and Jonathan slowed his pace, wondering if he should turn after all and run back the way he'd come.

He kept walking.

The bushes moved again and this time he felt his heart quicken.

He was only feet away when the blackbird rose from the tangled mass of twigs and soared into the air, a dark arrow-head against the mass of gathering cloud.

Jonathan kept on walking, approaching a curve in the path which would put him on the final three hundred yards. It ended at a broken-down stile and he saw it as the winning post in some kind of race. Once he'd reached it he'd be fine. Up and over the stile then a short run home. He'd get told off by his parents but at least they wouldn't find out he'd used the footpath. If they did, his dad would fetch the wooden spoon for sure. Jonathan didn't fancy three cracks across the backside with that this evening. Again he wished he hadn't decided to take the path home.

The dark trees seemed to glower down at him, but Jonathan tried to keep his gaze fixed on the path ahead.

He rounded the corner.

Another crane fly buzzed him and he knocked it aside angrily, stamping on the insect as it fell to the ground.

It was as he stood watching its last twitchings that he heard the sound.

Further up the footpath, behind him and out of sight, he heard footsteps.

Heavy rhythmic footfalls which grew steadily louder.

And closer.

Jonathan looked around frantically for somewhere to hide.

Should he try to climb a tree?

Hide behind a bush?

He decided to run instead.

Fear gripped him like a metal vice, squeezing tighter as each second passed.

He glanced behind him but could see nothing.

Whoever was behind him had yet to round the corner. But he could hear the footfalls drawing nearer.

Louder.

Jonathan ran as fast as he could, almost stumbling on the uneven surface.

Closer.

He looked round again and almost screamed.

The figure was just rounding the corner, bearing down on him.

Clad completely in black, the figure pounded along the footpath towards Jonathan, drawing closer with each stride. Until finally the figure reached him.

Jonathan stopped running as the jogger in the black track suit went puffing past him, arms flailing wearily, breath coming in short gasps.

151

The youngster watched as the jogger reached the stile about a hundred yards further on. The black-clad man hauled himself over it with what looked like a monumental effort. Then he was gone.

Jonathan was alone once more.

He felt his heart thudding madly against his ribs but he still managed to chuckle to himself, amused at his own fear, glad that he had almost reached the end of the path.

He was still laughing when two strong hands shot out from the bushes and dragged him out of sight.

Forty-One

Wallace sat back in his chair and patted his stomach approvingly.

'That was a beautiful meal,' he said, smiling.

Kim made a theatrical curtsey before carrying the plates into the kitchen. She returned a moment later with two plates of gateaux.

'I hope you've got room for it,' she said. 'It's home-made.'

'I'll make room,' Wallace said and picked up his fork.

They had spoken easily and with unexpected warmth whilst eating dinner, and both had become certain of a strong mutual attraction between them. They felt at ease in each other's company; Kim had found no difficulty explaining how her marriage had broken up, and similarly, Wallace had talked freely about his days as a constable in London and his move to Longfield as an inspector. What had surprised him most was that he had actually felt the need to tell her of his feelings when he was three and his mother had died of cancer, and when his father, years later, had married a much younger woman. His respect and even his love for the man had been eroded and finally destoyed. Now his father too was dead, victim of a massive heart attack only three years earlier. He had no close family left.

With formalities over and confessions exchanged, sipping wine and eating the cake that Kim had made, both of them felt unusually relaxed.

'So, tell me about the Celts,' Wallace said. 'What kind of people were they?'

'They were strange in many ways,' Kim said. 'Great artists and builders, intelligent men, but also barbaric, violent people. But I can't see how this will help your investigation, Steve.'

'Just humour me, Kim,' he asked, pushing a forkful of cake into his mouth. 'I was reading today about the Druids and their practices. Is it right that they burned people alive and watched them die so that they could foretell the future?'

Kim nodded.

'It was a kind of divination, a way of foretelling events to come. That was only done to prisoners of war or lunatics, though. The most popular method of foretelling the future was by studying the entrails of sacrificial victims.'

Wallace looked up, chewing more slowly now, listening to every word as if frightened he'd miss something.

'The victim, or offering, was cut open and the Druid would pull out the intestines and spread them on the ground. The victim's death throes were studied first, then the entrails themselves. Patterns were made with them.'

'Like letters?' Wallace asked, his mind suddenly filled with grisly visions of what he'd seen in Lawrence's bedroom and Kirkland's garage.

'Sometimes,' Kim said.

Wallace exhaled deeply.

'What about flaying the victims, or removing the eyes?' he wanted to know.

'There were so many practices it's difficult to say which ones were most common,' Kim told him. 'Each tribe worshipped a different god or goddess, and the details of sacrificial rituals depended on which deity was involved. At least 394 have been counted.'

'But what about this business with the intestines? Was that widespread?'

'It was one of the few things that was practised by nearly all the tribes.'

Kim looked puzzled as the inspector sat back, brushing a strand of hair from his forehead.

'I don't see how this can help you,' she said.

'When we found Stuart Lawrence and John Kirkland,' he began, ' − and for God's sake keep this information to yourself − both of them had been mutilated. They'd had their eyes torn out, they'd been flayed, and also their stomachs had been torn open. The intestines had been removed and formed into letters.'

Kim swallowed hard and put down her wine glass.

'Now you see why I had to ask you about Cooper,' Wallace said. 'It looks as if the killer has some knowledge of this type of ritual murder.'

'I noticed on your notepad, earlier, you'd written 'Witchcraft'. Are you considering that too?'

He told her about the animals in the wood near Dexter Grange.

'I also read something about the Druids cutting off the heads of their enemies and eating the brains,' he said. 'Why did they do that?'

'Well, the Druids believed that different parts of the body were capable of carrying different powers. If they killed an enemy in battle they'd cut off his head and eat the brains. They felt that the head was the source of all power and knowledge so, by eating it, they'd inherit the strength and courage of the enemy they'd killed. They also thought that by doing that they would stop the soul of their victim from attacking them. They believed in the transmigration of souls. The ability of a dead person's soul to invade the body of another, someone still alive.'

'You mean like demonic possession?' Wallace said.

Kim nodded.

'By destroying the body in a physical form they felt they were destroying the soul too. That way it couldn't take them over. Possess them.'

Wallace laid his fork gently down on the plate.

'Why were Lawrence and Kirkland killed?' Kim wanted to know.

'I wish I could tell you,' Wallace said. 'Obviously someone doesn't want that building project finished.' He shrugged and reached for his wine glass, draining the last drops.

In the sitting room the phone rang.

Kim got up and walked through to answer it, leaving Wallace alone for a moment, gazing at his empty plate. He heard her speaking, then:

'Steve, it's for you.' There was a note of surprise in her voice.

Wallace joined her in the sitting room.

'Sorry about that,' he said. 'I'm on twenty-four hour call, so I had to leave this number with the station.' He took the receiver from her and she retreated into the dining room as he spoke. She knew from the few words he uttered that it was bad news. A moment later she heard the phone being replaced.

'Kim, I've got to go,' he said, heading for the hall, pulling on his jacket. 'There's trouble. A child has been kidnapped.'

He paused for a moment, looking at her, their eyes locked. Then both of them moved forward and embraced gently but firmly, their lips pressed together.

'I'm sorry,' he said, breaking the kiss and turning for the door.

'There'll be other times,' she said, smiling, watching as he hurried out to his car and started the engine. In a second he was gone.

Outside, the wind began to howl.

Like some kind of wailing lament.

PART TWO

'All spirits are enslaved that serve things evil.'

P. B. Shelley

Forty-Two

She had seen the scientific proof, carried out the tests herself.

She had written it down in her notes. It was there before her.

Yet still she could not believe it.

Of the three skulls which Kim had carbon-dated, two were, as expected, of Iron Age origin. Around 1,000 B.C. or earlier, she guessed.

It was the third which had caused her consternation.

She'd checked and double-checked but there was no mistake.

It was less than 500 years old.

She'd written down the approximate date as 1490.

How could it be possible?

Could she somehow have made a mistake with the dating process, she wondered? But the more she thought about it, the more she re-ran the events in her mind, the more her certainty grew. There had been no mistake. More puzzles, she thought, rubbing her eyes, noticing how heavy the lids felt. But those puzzles would have to wait until the next day. It was late and Kim could feel the stiffness in her joints. She stretched, groaning as she felt a dull ache in her back.

She glanced at her watch, muttering irritably when she saw that it had stopped at 5:15 p.m. She looked across to the wall clock.

The hands were frozen at 5:15.

Kim got to her feet and wandered out into the large hallway of the museum, heading towards the clock there.

It too showed 5:15.

She swallowed hard, aware, as ever, of the chill in the air. But it had intensified now to the point where her breath clouded before her as she exhaled.

The silence was pierced by the strident ringing of the phone.

She hesitated a moment, then lifted the receiver.

'Kim?'

She recognized Charles Cooper's voice immediately. 'Have you made any progress with the tablets?' he asked.

'Some,' she told him. 'I've been working on the skulls too, and there's something peculiar about one of them. It's much more recent.' She told him about it.

'It could be a miscalculation on your part,' he countered.

'I've checked and double-checked. The skull is less than 500 years old. I want to examine more of them, see if there are any more anomalies. There could be others from more recent periods.'

'Don't come out to the dig,' Cooper said quickly, and Kim was puzzled by the tone of his voice. 'I'll get someone to bring the skulls to you.'

She paused a moment, bewildered by his attitude.

'How are things going with the dig?' she wanted to know.

'We haven't made any more progress,' he said, a little too sharply. 'Look, I'll send the skulls to you, but I need to know what those stone tablets say.'

Before she could speak again, he replaced the receiver and all she heard was the single tone purr of a dead line. Kim put the phone down and got to her feet, moving quickly about the staff room and laboratory, closing doors and windows, flicking off lights. She didn't bother to check upstairs because no one had been up there. She finally stepped outside, pulling the museum's doors shut behind her, fumbling for the key which would lock them.

'Kim.'

The voice was close to her and its suddenness almost caused her to scream. She spun round to see George Perry standing there, his face impassive.

'You frightened the life out of me,' she said, panting, but Perry seemed unimpressed.

'I need to look at those tablets,' he said.

'Not now, George,' she said, pocketing the key, attempting to step around him.

Perry shot out an arm and grabbed her by the wrist.

She pulled away indignantly.

'What the hell are you doing?' she snapped. 'Look, George, I'm very tired and I want to get home, all right? If you want to talk to me then do it tomorrow, please.' She began to walk past him once more and this time he did not move. He merely turned slowly and watched her as she walked to the car.

In her rear-view mirror, Kim could still see him as she drove away.

Standing.

Watching.

Forty-Three

The water gurgled noisily as it swirled away down the sink, carrying grease and suds with it. Sarah Potter dried her hands on a towel and made her way through to the sitting room, examining her long fingernails, muttering to herself when she saw that another one was chipped. She'd already broken one earlier in the day while typing a letter but that, she told herself, was an occupational hazard. Sarah had been James Cutler's private secretary for the last four years, having secured the job a day before her twenty-sixth birthday. Now she was an integral part of the company, trusted and respected by Cutler himself and also the longest-serving employee on the payroll.

'The washing up's done,' she said, brushing a hand through her tousled brown hair. 'I'm going to have a shower when I've finished this.' She reached for the glass of white wine which was sitting on the dining table. 'Do you want a refill?'

Penny Allen looked up from the pile of exercise books before her and shook her head.

'Later,' she said, smiling. She sat back in her chair and allowed her head to loll back, her fine black hair cascading down her back. Sarah got to her feet and stood behind the other girl, resting both hands on her shoulders. Then, gently, she began to massage the taut flesh, easing away the tension. Penny sighed contentedly and moved her head forward, letting her chin rest on her chest. She wriggled slightly, feeling the stiffness leave her neck, as Sarah kept up her expert manipulation.

At twenty-nine, Penny was only a year younger than Sarah and her round face and the fact that she wore almost no make-up would have allowed anyone who didn't know her to take her for five or six years younger. She was the opposite in almost every way to her companion. Sarah was tall and slender, while Penny, although slim, was more rounded and scarcely five feet tall. She had been a teacher at one of Longfield's largest schools for the past five years.

Two years longer than she and Sarah had been lovers.

It had seemed so natural. They had always been close. They'd attended the same schools, belonged to the same small circle of friends and as time had passed, their friendship had blossomed almost inevitably into love of a kind neither had ever felt with a man.

There was a tenderness about their relationship which Penny had never been able to attain with her husband.

The marriage had lasted only ten months. He'd walked out on her after arriving home early one afternoon to discover Penny and Sarah locked in each other's arms. Neither of the women had attempted an explanation. It was hardly necessary. He'd packed his bags there and then, leaving Penny the house and everything in it. She hadn't heard from him since that day.

There had been no attempt on the part of either woman to hide the nature of their relationship. They still had to put

162

up with the occasional snide remark or sly look when they were out together, but as Sarah had said on numerous occasions, small towns breed small minds and Longfield was no exception.

Penny had been asked to leave her last job, supervising a play-group, as a result of the rumours and innuendo, but other than that, they had encountered little trouble and she had settled easily into her post as teacher.

She leant her head against one of Sarah's soothing hands, allowing her silky hair to flow over it, enjoying the sensations which were beginning to course through her body. Sarah moved closer, pressing herself up against the back of the chair, a familiar warmth beginning to manifest itself within her lower body. She moved to the side of the chair, sighing with anticipation as she felt Penny's left hand brush against her exposed thighs. The short house-coat she wore barely covered her buttocks and she tensed as she felt her lover's gentle fingers gliding over her flesh. Sarah kept up the massage, gradually slipping one hand around to caress Penny's throat and begin removing the blouse from her shoulders.

'Take a shower with me,' she said, softly.

Penny smiled and nodded.

The figure moved quickly but sure-footedly through the darkness, towards the house.

It had seen the silhouettes of the two women against the curtains and now it darted furtively but purposefully towards the window at the side of the building. It was masked from the house next door by a high privet hedge and the night closed around it like a welcoming ally.

It stood before the French windows.

Waiting.

Water splattered noisily from the bulbous head of the shower-spray and Sarah reached forward to adjust the temperature. The room was filled with steam which billowed like thick white mist, covering the mirror and tiles with a thin film of condensation.

Both women stood beneath the spray, enjoying the feel of the warm jet of water on their skin, laughing as they soaped each other lovingly, paying particular attention to each other's breasts.

Inside the glass cubicle they embraced, hearing only each other's voices and the constant noise of running water which masked all other sounds.

Even the noise of breaking glass from downstairs.

The figure drove its hand through the glass of the French windows and strode inside, overturning chairs in its path. It stood in the centre of the room, becoming annoyed by the bright light from the lamp on the table before it.

One powerful swipe sent the lamp hurtling against the wall, where it shattered.

The figure turned towards the door which led into the hall and wrenched it open. The sound of splashing water reached its ears.

It paused for a moment, then began to climb the stairs.

Sarah Potter closed her eyes and allowed the water to spurt over her face, forming rivulets which coursed down her neck and ran between her breasts. She felt Penny's soft touch on the back of her neck and sighed contentedly, turning to face her lover.

She opened her eyes to look at Penny, and it was then that she saw the dark figure outside the shower cubicle.

Through the frosted glass it looked hideously distorted, but Sarah was able to make out the semblance of a shape, like some kind of grotesquely hewn statue.

She opened her mouth to scream.

One side of the cubicle exploded inwards, huge jagged shards of glass erupting into the shower itself.

Penny shrieked as a particularly long shard sliced open her forearm. Blood spurted from the wound, spilling onto the white tiles of the shower, while other fragments cut her feet as she tried to move away from the terrifying intrusion.

Sarah pressed herself into a corner, her eyes bulging wide in horror, and screamed again as she felt a vice-like grip fasten around her left wrist. Bones crumbled under the powerful clamp and she felt searing pain lance up her arm. A second later she was flung effortlessly from the cubicle, as easily as if she had been a rag doll. She skidded helplessly across the slippery floor, knowing in that brief instant that she could not stop herself hitting the mirror on the opposite wall.

She struck it with devastating force, her head snapping forward, powering into the glass, splintering it.

The impact sent her reeling back and she went down in an untidy heap, blood pouring from a vicious gash just below her hair-line. Fragments of the broken mirror rained down on her, slicing her naked body, lacerating her face, arms and chest. She lay unconscious, oblivious now to the screams of her lover.

Penny tried to run, nursing her cut arm, but the figure merely gripped her by the throat, lifting her off her feet for several seconds before slamming her back against the cubicle wall. As she slumped forward again the figure took a firm hold on her hair and forced her face towards the shower-spray.

Penny felt the hot water spattering her skin and it was only that which kept her conscious. She struggled but her assailant was far too powerful to be thwarted.

As she opened her mouth to scream, the attacker pushed her head forward.

Penny's mouth closed over the bulbous head of the shower-spray. Her body bucked madly, but her head was held firm by the vice-like hand. She felt the water gushing down her throat; felt her stomach contract as it filled up. Her body twisted insanely. She gagged violently as the spray touched the back of her throat and the vomit rose, only to be swept back down by the torrent of water.

Penny felt herself blacking out but not before she saw her assailant's hand grasp the temperature control of the shower and turn it to hot.

Blistering, scalding water filled her mouth and throat and she was enveloped in unbelievable agony as the searing cascade gushed through her.

Her lips and tongue were transformed into little more than massive blisters which finally burst in a welter of pus and blood that ran down her chin to mingle with the crimson stains already splattering the shower tiles.

For interminable seconds Penny suffered this excruciating pain, and then her attacker, still using just one hand, slammed her viciously forward.

Such was the force of the movement that the shower-spray itself first gouged through the back of her throat, then burst from the base of her skull. Large fragments of bone broke away and torrents of blood gushed from the hole, washing over her shoulders and back.

She sagged against the wall, arms dangling limply at her sides, held upright by the water conduit which protruded a good six inches from the back of her head.

The figure turned away from her for a moment and moved towards Sarah.

The bathroom was transformed into a dripping slaughterhouse and steam swirled around the room, closing about the figure and its victims like a white shroud.

Forty-Four

Wallace sucked heavily on his cigarette, before stubbing it out in the ashtray. From his office window he could see a good deal of Longfield. If only, he thought, he could see an answer to the questions which now tormented him. He took a deep breath of the cool fresh air in an effort to clear his head.

Who had murdered Stuart Lawrence, John Kirkland and now Sarah Potter and the woman they knew to be her lover?

Was it the same person who had kidnapped little Jonathan Ashton?

What *kind* of person was it who had impaled Penny Allen's head on a shower spray? Who had ripped Sarah Potter's eyes from their sockets? Who had flayed almost every inch of flesh from both bodies using a piece of broken mirror?

Who had gutted them both completely, pulling their intestines from the riven torsos, and then used the slippery, steaming lengths to fashion a crude letter A on the bathroom floor. And, in the bath itself, a bloodied N?

Wallace exhaled deeply and reached for another cigarette. How come nobody ever saw or heard anything? In every case, the killer had forced entry to the homes of his victims, and the extent of the mutilations seemed to indicate that he spent at least thirty minutes, if not longer, on each corpse. Wallace knew from previous experience that people avoided getting involved in police affairs wherever possible, but even so, someone at some time must have seen events taking place before or after the killings which looked odd. This time a neighbour *had* heard something but had assumed that it was kids messing about, throwing stones at the windows of the house where the two women were. By the time he got around to phoning the police it was too late.

The inspector blew out a long stream of blue smoke and watched it disperse in the air.

Four murders and a kidnapping.

'The quiet little town of Longfield,' he murmured humourlessly, but his thoughts were cut short as he heard raised voices in the corridor outside his office.

He spun round as the door crashed open.

James Cutler strode into the room, his eyes fixed on the inspector. Wallace caught a glimpse of Sergeant Dayton trying to pull the land developer back.

'You're supposed to knock first,' said Wallace, unimpressed by the anger which contorted the older man's face into a twisted mask.

'I tried to stop him, guv,' Dayton said. 'I warned him.'

'You incompetent bastard, Wallace!' rasped Cutler, pulling away from the sergeant.

'Right, that's it,' snarled Dayton, gripping the land developer by the arm and twisting.

Cutler hissed in pain but Wallace shook his head.

'Leave him, Bill. Otherwise we'll have Mr Cutler crying police brutality.' The inspector motioned for Dayton to leave the room. Looking a little perplexed, the sergeant did so, closing the door behind him.

Cutler brushed the sleeve of his jacket and glared at Wallace.

'You know why I'm here,' he snapped.

'Telepathy isn't one of my talents,' Wallace told him.

'Another of my employees was butchered last night. When the hell are you going to find the murderer?'

'It isn't as simple as you seem to think, Cutler,' the inspector said, trying to keep his temper. 'There aren't many leads.'

'Then find some,' Cutler hissed. 'God knows who'll be next. It could be me. I initiated this building project. If the killer has a grudge against me and my workers then it's only a matter of time before he comes after *me*.'

'That had occurred to me, too. I know you're a likely target. So is everyone who works for you, but I simply haven't got the manpower to give all of you protection if that's what you're driving at.'

'Then call in some help, for Christ's sake,' the land developer shouted, anger and fear colouring his tone. 'Do your superiors know how you're handling this case? Perhaps it's time they did.'

'What's that supposed to mean?' Wallace said, his own anger now boiling up.

Cutler didn't answer; he merely glared at the policeman.

'If the building project is the cause of these killings then call it off, at least temporarily,' Wallace suggested.

'No. My men are working to schedules,' the older man said. 'To call a halt would mean losing hundreds of thousands of pounds.'

'Well, it's up to you, Cutler. You'll have to decide what

168

price you put on your own life. If there's any way you could stop the project . . .'

'Not a chance!' The land developer turned and headed for the office door, then glared back at the detective. 'I'm telling you Wallace, I want results. Fast!'

'Get out, Cutler,' Wallace said, watching wearily as the other man pushed open the door and strode out, almost colliding with Dayton in the process.

The sergeant hesitated for a moment, then walked in.

Wallace sat down and ground out his cigarette in the ashtray on his desk.

'What is it, Bill?' he said, massaging the bridge of his nose between thumb and forefinger.

Dayton approached the desk slowly, clutching a piece of paper in his hand.

'I just took this message, guv,' he said, quietly. 'Her name's Julie Craig. She's five years old.'

'I'm not with you,' Wallace said, frowning.

Dayton sighed and handed over the piece of paper.

'Another kid's been taken.'

Forty-Five

As Frank King watched, thick white wisps of steam rose from the tar trailer, a cylindrical tank about six feet long which carried the molten fluid. The tarmac-laying crew were careful to keep a safe distance from the blistering black mess as it spilled over the ground, covering an area which would eventually form part of a car park servicing the leisure centre.

The smells of tar and diesel fumes were strong in the air but the foreman seemed oblivious to the odours as he surveyed the building site like some kind of nineteenth-century general inspecting a battlefield.

He shuddered involuntarily as a powerful gust of wind swept past him. He'd be pleased when this bloody project was over and done with. King turned and headed towards the Portakabin, glancing up at the rain-heavy clouds above.

In the cab of the JCB, David Holmes was also watching the sky, but his attention was drawn to his watch as the alarm went off, telling him that it was one o'clock. Lunchtime, he thought with relief. It was freezing in the cab of the JCB. He couldn't wait to reach the relative warmth of the Portakabin. Holmes worked the controls of the machine expertly, guiding the great metal arm around, swinging it in a wide arc before it thudded down into the earth, ploughing deep, scooping up a mound of the dark soil. The arm rose again and Holmes manoeuvred it around so that the load could be dropped into the back of the lorry which stood alongside, its engine idling. He watched as the dirt cascaded from the bucket.

The machine's giant arm swung back into position and Holmes locked it there, twisting the key in the machine's ignition to cut off the power. The JCB stood silent and motionless in the chill wind which was sweeping over the building site.

Holmes checked once more that the vehicle was securely locked up. Then, using one of the caterpillar tracks as a step, he lowered himself to the ground.

There seemed to be fewer men working on the site today, he thought, pausing to extract a cigarette packet and matches from his pockets. He knew that because of the accidents of a few days ago and now the news filtering through of Cutler's employees being murdered, a number of men had simply refused to work on the project anymore. But Holmes was not one to be frightened easily. Besides, he needed the money. The blokes who'd chucked it in must be mad or well off, he hadn't figured out which yet.

A gust of wind blew out the match as he tried to light his cigarette. He struck another match but the wind blew it out, too.

The gusts seemed to increase suddenly in ferocity, drowning out the creak of the JCB's metal arm.

As Holmes struggled with a third match the great machine seemed to move an inch or two, its massive bulk like some lumbering metallic dinosaur.

The metal arm came free.

Even above the roar of the wind, Holmes finally heard the rush of air as the heavy bucket came hurtling towards him as if to scoop him up.

He did not hear it in time.

The metal edge hit him just above the waist, shearing through muscle and bone effortlessly. Slicing his body in two.

Blood and intestines erupted from the severed torso which was sent pinwheeling across the ground, spraying crimson in all directions. Fragments of pulverized spinal column mingled with a trail of viscera. Like a decapitated farmyard chicken, Holmes' lower half staggered a few yards, as if searching for the other half, then buckled and fell to the ground, blood still fountaining madly from the torn arteries. The torso, blood now running from the dead man's nose and mouth, finally came to a halt on its torn base. As the blood poured out in a wide pool around it, the body looked as if it had been buried up to the waist in a thick gore.

The bucket of the JCB swung slowly back and forth, gobbets of flesh and streamers of crimson dripping from it.

The cigarette which Holmes had been trying to light was still stuck firmly between his cold lips. Blood had soaked into the filter like ink into blotting paper.

Forty-Six

The classroom was large, holding somewhere in the region of thirty children. From that considerable group, a steady babble of excited chatter rose.

Clare Nichols seemed oblivious to any extraneous sound as she carefully considered the set of coloured crayons before her. So many colours to choose from. Where should she begin her drawing? Beside her, Amanda Fraser, Clare's best friend (at least for the past week she had been), was already busy on her own drawing. As were most of the children in the room.

Clare tapped her bottom lip with the blue crayon and decided to start with the sky, so she scribbled a blue border along the top of her paper, glancing up as Miss Tickle moved from desk to desk inspecting the work of the others.

Clare giggled. She always did when she thought of Miss Tickle. Not just her name, but those funny red tights which she always wore. It looked as if someone had painted her legs the colour of a letter box, Clare thought, reaching for the yellow crayon. She gripped it firmly, and just beneath the rim of blue she drew a large yellow sun, remembering to add spoke-like rays around it. It was going to be a nice sunny day in her drawing, she'd decided. Not like it was outside.

Rain was coursing down the window panes in torrents and Clare hoped that it would have stopped by the time she had to go home. Still, perhaps her mother would pick her up in the car. Or, if not, she could always get a lift from Amanda's mother.

Clare liked Mrs Fraser. The large wart with its three ever-present hairs growing beneath her chin never failed to mesmerize the small girl. She glanced out of the window once more, watching the rain as it ran down the glass and she felt a chill run through her.

Clare swallowed hard and looked down at the paper, wondering why her hand seemed to freeze as she reached for the green crayon which she needed to draw the grass. Her hand hovered over the wax stick for a moment longer, then she picked up the black one, and with swift strokes began to draw.

Her breath was coming in low sighs and her eyelids had partially closed, yet still her hand worked over the paper, moving in unfailing curves and lines, fashioning an image which she herself could see only in her mind's eye.

Amanda spoke and looked over at Clare and her drawing, but the girl seemed not to hear.

Her eyes were now almost completely closed and her lips fluttered rapidly as she mouthed soundless words, the crayon moving back and forth across the paper with dizzying speed.

The black crayon, then the red one, then the black again.

Clare heard a loud noise from beside her and the sound seemed to rouse her.

She looked up, like a dreamer awaking from a deep sleep, her eyes focussing on Amanda, who was backing away from her, eyes riveted to the drawing before her. Miss Tickle was making her way towards the desk, her face knitted into that familiar look of concern.

She saw how pale Clare looked. How the colour seemed to have drained from her cheeks. The child looked like death.

Miss Tickle approached her slowly, seeing that Clare was about to faint. She was swaying from side to side on her chair, one crayon still gripped in her hand, gliding across the paper.

'Clare,' the teacher said, softly. 'Clare, are you all right, dear?'

It was patently obvious that the child was not.

Miss Tickle turned to a boy near her and told him to run and fetch the nurse. All other eyes in the classroom turned towards Clare, who had now turned the colour of rancid butter.

She was still swaying back and forth, and now Miss Tickle rushed towards her, seeing the child's eyes roll up in their sockets.

From somewhere deep inside her Clare heard a sound like rolling thunder. A deafening roar which seemed to hammer at her eardrums. So loud that it hurt.

She screamed and fell forward onto the desk.

Miss Tickle reached the girl and cradled her in her arms, lifting her away from the desk. As she did so she looked down at the drawing, and she, too, felt an unearthly chill run through her.

'Oh God,' she murmured, softly.

Kim knelt beside the bed and brushed a strand of hair from her daughter's forehead, feeling the soft skin with the back of her hand.

'There's no sign of a temperature,' the school nurse told her. The woman was young, Kim's age, but painfully thin, the dark uniform she wore accentuating this feature. 'She woke up as soon as we got her in here,' the nurse continued, making a sweeping gesture with her hand to encompass the school sick room. It was small, clean and smelt of disinfectant. There were pictures of animals and toys on the walls, competing for space with cabinets and shelves.

'How do you feel, sweetheart?' Kim asked her daughter.

'I'm all right, Mummy,' Clare assured her, the colour having returned to her cheeks. She sat up quite happily and sipped the plastic beaker full of orange squash which the nurse had given her.

'I think it might be best if you took her home, Mrs Nichols,' said the thin woman and Kim agreed, fumbling in her jacket pocket for her keys. 'It's a good job we were able to reach you at the museum,' the nurse added.

Miss Tickle, who had been standing by the doorway throughout the conversation, now stepped forward and beckoned to Kim.

'Might I have a word?' she asked, almost apologetically.

Kim smiled, noticing as she approached the woman that she held a piece of paper. The two of them moved out into the corridor, while inside the room, the nurse helped Clare into her shoes and coat.

'Your daughter was drawing when she . . . passed out,' the teacher said. 'This is what she'd done.'

Kim took the paper from the other woman and looked at it, her brow furrowing.

'I didn't know what to make of it,' the teacher confessed. Kim noticed that goose-pimples had risen on the woman's flesh.

Drawn in thick black crayon, sketched with remarkable dexterity for a child so young, was a large figure. The features were smudged apart from the red eyes. At its feet Kim saw several hastily drawn small stick figures, each one surrounded by a smear of red. There were more of the small figures in the black shape's hands, too, with red dripping from them. But it was the lettering over the top of the shape which Kim found the most disturbing. In letters two inches high were scrawled four words:

HIS TIME IS COME

Forty-Seven

The loud knocking seemed to echo throughout the wood-panelled interior of Dexter Grange, bouncing off the walls and high ceilings until it faded away to a low hum. After a moment or two of silence the banging came again, louder and more insistent.

Laura Price hurried down the wide staircase and crossed the hall to the door, anxious to silence the knocking and also curious as to who could be calling at the house with evening approaching. The grandfather clock nearby struck six as she pulled open the door.

The figure barged past her, arms pinwheeling in an effort to remain upright.

Laura, taken by surprise, screamed and turned to look at the intruder, who was standing unsteadily in the centre of the hallway, clothes soaked by the rain which was still falling outside.

The youth was in his early twenties. His face was twisted with pain and a thick growth of stubble covered his cheeks and chin. He wore a T-shirt which had at one time probably been white, and a pair of faded jeans tucked into scuffed ankle boots.

She recognized him as Tony Evans. As he stood dripping wet before her she could see the suppurating sores on his arms, grouped around the insides of his elbows.

'Where's Dexter?' he barked, his throat sounding tight.

'What do you want?' Laura demanded.

'I want some stuff,' he snapped. 'I've got to see Dexter.' His breath was coming in gasps. 'I'm fucking strung out.'

Laura looked past him towards the two figures approaching from the corridor behind Evans. He noticed the movement of her eyes and turned, almost overbalancing.

Henry Dexter approached him slowly, running appraising eyes over the wretched youth.

'Dexter, I need some stuff,' he moaned. 'I need a fix. Now!'

'Why did you come to the house?' Dexter said. 'You were told never to come here. Any of you.'

'I fucking need it,' Evans rasped, taking a faltering step towards the older man.

Gary Webb stepped ahead of Dexter, his imposing frame stopping Evans' advance.

'You could have been followed,' Dexter said, angrily. 'Anyone could have seen you.'

Evans dug his hand deep into his jeans pocket and pulled out a handful of crumpled five pound notes.

'I've got money,' he said. 'Just give me the stuff.'

'Where did you get that?' Dexter demanded. 'Did you steal it?'

The youth was already clutching his stomach, wincing as he felt another powerful contraction.

'Please,' he whimpered, doubled up in pain. 'Take the money. I promise I'll never come here again. Just let me fix.' The money fell from his quivering hand.

'Get him out of here,' Dexter said, looking at Gary.

'You bastard,' roared Evans and ran at the older man. His reactions, however, were dulled and Gary merely stepped between them, driving one powerful fist into the other youth's face. There was a loud crack as Evans' nose broke. He toppled forward, but Gary caught him by the front of his T-shirt, held him up and drove another pile-driver blow into his face, shattering two of his front teeth, driving one of them through his upper lip. Blood ran down Evans' chin and he burbled incoherently as Gary threw him to the floor and drove a kick into the base of his spine.

'If you speak to anyone about this,' Dexter said, looking down at the injured youth, 'I'll kill you. If one policeman turns up here, I'll kill you. Do you understand?'

Grabbing Evans by the hair, Gary lifted his head a foot or two off the ground then slammed it down, hard enough to open a gash below his hairline.

'Understand?' he said.

'Yes,' Evans whimpered as he was hauled to his feet.

Laura opened the front door and Dexter watched as Gary hurled the other youth out onto the driveway. He rolled over twice and lay still, the rain lashing his exposed body. He lay on his back, one arm twitching slightly, mumbling to himself through his split lips and broken teeth, groaning every now and then as a fresh contraction knotted his stomach muscles.

The three of them stood watching, waiting for him to drag himself to his feet which, moments later, he did. He looked back once, then stumbled off down the long driveway, falling once.

Dexter closed the door.

'Do you think he will go to the police?' Laura asked, apprehensively. 'Not just about the drugs, I mean . . .' She paused, aware of Dexter's unfaltering gaze upon her. 'I . . . You know, about what we've been doing?'

'The police won't find out,' he replied, striding back down the corridor.

The two youngsters followed Dexter into the library, where he crossed to the wall safe, fiddled with the combination and opened it. He placed the notes Evans had dropped inside with the money that was stacked there beside bags of heroin, glancing at the store of cash and drugs indifferently. Gary looked at Laura then at the heroin. He took a step forward, as if the drug were some kind of magnet, drawing him. Laura, too, felt a tingle run through her. She nudged him and a knowing look passed between them, unseen by Dexter.

'If one of us was ever strung out,' Laura said, 'you wouldn't treat us like you treated Evans, would you?'

Dexter smiled and closed the safe, shaking his head almost imperceptibly.

'If anything happened to you, how would we get hold of the stuff in the safe?' Gary asked.

Dexter smiled again.

'But nothing *is* going to happen to me,' he said, brushing past them as he left the room.

Gary looked at the older man, then at the wall safe with its precious contents.

But it was on the ornamental dagger over the fireplace that his gaze finally came to rest.

Forty-Eight

The rain which had been falling all day finally disappeared soon after the onset of night. It was replaced by a chill wind which swirled and eddied around the houses of Longfield, occasionally rattling window frames like a mischievous child.

Frank King looked up from his newspaper as a particularly powerful gust howled around the house. He was the only one in the room who seemed to notice it. All around him his family were engaged in pursuits of their own.

His wife Linda was sitting on the floor studying the large jigsaw puzzle laid out on the coffee table. He saw her smile triumphantly as she slotted a piece into the maze of shapes and colours.

Behind him his youngest son, Ian, was busy trying to destroy the next Imperial walker as it lumbered across the snow. He manoeuvred his X-wing fighter expertly, pumping shot after shot into the evil agent of the Empire. The scores lit the multi-coloured screen of the TV set as he punched buttons on the computer, teeth gritted in concentration.

'Dad,' he said, not taking his eyes from the screen. 'When will you be able to finish that desk you're making for me?'

'Your father's trying to rest, Ian,' Linda reminded the lad.

'I only asked,' he muttered, narrowly avoiding a laser blast from a marauding Imperial craft.

'I was going to do some work on it tonight,' said King.

'Oh Frank, for heaven's sake,' Linda protested, fitting another piece into the jigsaw. 'It's freezing out in that workroom.'

'I don't notice it when I'm working. Besides, there's not much left to do now. I've nearly finished,' King told her.

'I don't know why you couldn't have built the shed closer to the house instead of putting it right at the bottom of the garden.'

'That, my dear,' he said, getting to his feet, 'is so I don't disturb you with hammering and banging when you're busy with your puzzles.' He picked up a piece of the jigsaw and slotted it smugly into place.

'I'll be making a cup of tea in a little while,' she told him.

'What's Simon doing?' asked King, wondering where his other son had disappeared to.

A moment later the floor above seemed to shake as the older boy switched on his record player. King stood listening to the rhythmic thud of the bass for a moment and then, smiling, he shook his head and headed for the back door. He heard Linda yelling to the boy to turn the record player down as he stepped out of the kitchen.

The darkness closed around him and he shivered as the wind jabbed icy fingers into his flesh.

Ahead of him, barely visible in the gloom, was his workshop. King had built it himself two years earlier, shortly after the family had moved into the house. Since then he'd worked in it most nights, turning his mechanical and practical skills to useful ends. He'd built them a dining room table and the six chairs which went with it, all finished in dark wood and carefully varnished.

He hurried down the path towards the workshop, fumbling in his trouser pocket for the key.

The trees which overhung the structure bowed and shook as the wind blew with renewed ferocity. King let himself in and clicked on the light.

The dark figure saw the light flash on inside the hut.

It saw Frank King illuminated in the window.

Keeping close to the trees and bushes at the bottom of the garden, the figure moved closer.

Linda was right, thought King, shivering. It was freezing inside the workshop. He rubbed his arms briskly for a moment, trying to restore some circulation before he moved over to the workbench and picked up a piece of sandpaper. He set to work on the legs of the desk.

It had taken him barely a week to complete his latest project. Copying the design of some that he'd seen in a stationer's the previous weekend, he had worked quickly but methodically to construct the article, and he was pleased with his handiwork. Ian had been going on for months about wanting a desk on which to put his computer.

The lad was fascinated by the bloody gadget, but King couldn't make head nor tail of how it worked. When he'd been eleven, no one had even heard of calculators, let alone computers, and the thought that his kids would be using them in school one day would have been beyond the bounds of imagination.

King's other son was a year older, but electronic wizardry held no such appeal for him. He was much more at home with his records and tapes. Despite the diversity of their interests, King was pleased to find that the two of them got along well together. There was little of the rivalry, even open hostility, which was usually associated with brothers. Especially two so close together in age.

Frank King was more than happy with the way his children and his marriage had turned out. Life had been kind to him, and for that he was grateful.

The wind howled mournfully around the workshop, the sound reminding King of a dog in pain.

He heard a harsh scraping sound on the roof of the hut.

Like bony fingers being drawn across the canopy.

King looked up briefly, listening to the disembodied sound. It promptly ceased and he continued with his task.

Something smacked against one of the windows and he spun round, squinting to see what it was.

He straightened up and walked over to the window, cupping one hand over his eyes so that he could see out into the wind-blown night.

Nothing moved except the trees.

As he stood there a sudden movement immediately in front of him caused him to step back in surprise.

A low branch from one of the trees had swung down and scraped against the glass. Clattering against the pane as if trying to gain access.

King shook his head, annoyed at his own jumpiness. Perhaps the thoughts of what had happened to Stuart Lawrence, John Kirkland and those two women were causing his mind to play tricks, he told himself. He returned to his job, trying to blot out the night sounds.

He finished sandpapering the desk and blew the wood dust away, reaching for the tin of varnish on the worktop. He stirred it thoroughly, enjoying the smell of the fluid.

The door of the workshop rattled in its frame and King looked up, watching it for long seconds, listening to the wind and the creaking wood.

He shivered slightly and frowned. His imagination *must* be playing tricks now.

It seemed to be getting colder inside the hut.

King continued stirring the varnish, his eyes still on the door.

The handle turned a fraction.

He almost dropped the tin.

The handle moved again, twisting full circle this time, and at last King put down the varnish. He stepped quickly across to the door.

He stood by it for interminable seconds, watching the handle twisting back and forth, but there seemed to be no attempt to push the door open.

Outside, the wind howled with ever-increasing force.

The rattling of the handle stopped and the puzzled man was left staring at it, as if expecting more movement at any moment.

He reached for the key in his pocket, wondering whether or not he should lock it.

But why? he asked himself. What was he locking out?

Then again, could the wind move door handles?

The key hovered close to the lock.

The handle moved again, more slowly this time.

Could it be one of the kids winding him up, he wondered?

If it was, he'd teach the little bugger a lesson.

King moved closer to the door, his hand reaching towards the knob.

'Come on,' he whispered. 'Try it again.'

He waited for the handle to move.

The wind screamed, banshee-like, shaking the small structure to its foundations.

The door shook in its frame.

Quick as a flash, King gripped the handle and wrenched open the door, taking one step out into the night.

'Right, you little sod . . .' he began, but let the sentence trail off.

There was no one out there.

From where he stood he could see the light in the kitchen of the house, nearly a hundred feet up the garden.

He could see a figure silhouetted against the lowered blinds, but apart from that, he saw nothing.

Just the darkness.

He stepped back inside the hut and closed the door.

Linda King lit the gas under the kettle, then dropped a tea bag into her husband's mug.

'Ian, take your Dad his tea when it's ready,' she called and received a belligerent affirmative from her son, who had just been hit twice by Imperial tie-fighters.

She flicked off the light and returned to the sitting room.

The scratching on the roof of the hut continued, and Frank King made a mental note to cut away the bare branches of the overhanging trees when he got a moment. The noise was irritating him.

He looked up sharply when he heard the door being rattled once more in its frame.

This time he stepped back because the movement was not caused by the wind. The powerful gusts had ceased for the time being, yet still the door of the hut rattled and shook as if it were going to explode from its hinges.

King felt ever more penetrating cold wrapping itself around him and he backed off, eyes fixed on the door, fear now gripping him tightly. It was as if all rationality and reason had left him, only his fear remained.

He stood with his back to the window, waiting for the door to open.

Waiting.

He snatched up a hammer from the workbench and hefted it before him.

If there was someone out there then the bastard would not catch him unawares.

The wind shrieked loudly. A cry of the damned which pounded shrilly in his ears.

He gripped the hammer more tightly and watched the door, which rattled furiously again.

He waited.

The window behind him exploded inwards with an earsplitting crash.

Glass sprayed into the hut, cutting the back of his neck and grazing his scalp. Before he could turn, hands had closed around his throat and were pulling him backwards.

He struck at them with the hammer but to no avail. The vice-like grip only tightened and King grunted as he was slammed back against the wall with bone-numbing force. He dropped the hammer and clutched feebly at the hands which were throttling him. His eyes bulged in their sockets and he gasped for air as the clawed fingers dug deep into the flesh of his throat.

White-hot agony lanced through him as he felt his larynx splinter under the pressure. It finally collapsed and he heaved as blood filled his mouth and ran down his throat.

His attacker now released one hand and grabbed King by the hair, spinning him round, tugging his head down towards the jagged glass which poked up in uneven peaks from the window frame.

Stars danced before his eyes and he fought in vain to prevent what was about to happen.

The powerful hands were forcing his neck onto the glass.

King tried to scream but his shattered larynx would

produce only a liquid croak which caused fresh blood to spill over his lips.

With his last reserves of strength fading rapidly, he still fought to free himself, but it was useless.

Six inches away from the glass, and he could feel incredibly cold air rushing through the broken window, bringing with it a nauseating stench which reminded him of rotting meat.

Five inches.

His attacker was exerting even more pressure in an attempt to force King down.

Four inches.

The desperate man felt his knees going weak, realized that he was losing the strength to resist.

Three inches.

As he tried to scream again an agonizing pain filled his head and neck and he tasted blood, warm and coppery in his throat.

Two inches.

The longest points of glass were actually brushing the bruised flesh of his neck.

One inch.

Frank King knew he was finished.

The hands of his attacker thrust his head down, dragging it back and forth across the jagged glass, allowing the short lethal splinters to act as a rasp. The razor-sharp slivers sliced easily through the flesh and muscle of King's neck, severing veins and arteries, carving a path through the flesh as the sawing action was speeded up.

Blood erupted from the torn neck in great jets which splattered the floor and walls of the hut, spraying from the sliced blood vessels like water from a fountain.

King's body began to spasm uncontrollably as his assailant continued to rake his throat back and forth over the glass until it seemed his head would be severed. Then, suddenly, the hands hurled King back, blood sprayed out in a wide arc as he fell, his body crashing onto the desk he had made with so much care.

He hit the floor with a thud, the massive gash in his throat opening and closing like the gills of a fish, blood still spurting from it.

King was unconscious, close to death, as his attacker entered the workshop.

The figure hauled itself in through the broken window and dropped to the floor, standing over King's prostrate form for long seconds, oblivious to the stench inside the small structure and the thick slicks of crimson which were splattered everywhere.

It knelt beside the corpse and began its work.

As she heard the shrill whistle of the kettle, Linda King got to her feet, peering for a moment longer at the jigsaw before her, then at the piece she held in her hand. As the kettle continued to squeal she muttered something to herself and put the piece back on the table.

She patted Ian on the head as she passed and he grunted. The momentary disturbance caused him to sustain slight damage to his X-wing fighter as a neutron blast from one of the walkers caught him unawares.

Linda switched off the kettle and poured boiling water onto the tea bag in Frank's mug, stirring it around briefly.

'Ian,' she called, peering through the blinds towards the hut at the bottom of the garden. 'Take this tea down to your Dad, will you, please?'

No answer.

'Ian. Did you hear me?' she repeated, puzzled by what she saw from her vantage point in the kitchen.

The light in the workshop went out and then came back on again, twice in rapid succession. She wondered if the wind was affecting the power lines. But if that was the case, why were the lights in the house all right?

She watched as the light went on and off once more, then finally came back on and stayed that way.

'Ian,' she called again. This time the boy appeared in the doorway.

'Why can't Simon take it?' he asked irritably. 'I was on my highest score ever.'

She seemed unimpressed and handed the boy the steaming mug of tea.

'I asked *you*,' she said. 'And tell your Dad to hurry up or I'll lock him out for the night.' She chuckled and opened the back door for her son.

The boy braced himself against a particularly strong gust of wind, then set off down the path towards the hut where his father was working. As he drew closer, Ian felt the flesh on his arms rising into goose-pimples. He slowed his pace somewhat, looking around him in the gloom.

'Dad,' he called, but his voice was snatched away by the wind.

He reached the door and knocked twice, calling to his father again.

No answer.

Ian pushed on the door, surprised when it wouldn't open. His dad never usually locked it. He put more force behind it, almost spilling the tea in the process.

It moved slightly, and as it did, a noxious stench filled his nostrils, drifting from inside the hut.

The boy recoiled momentarily, then began pushing again, harder this time, now ignoring the cold wind which whistled around him.

'Dad,' he called, his voice catching slightly. 'Open the door.'

The wooden partition suddenly gave, as if a weight on the other side had been removed, and Ian found himself stumbling inside, enveloped by the obscene smell which he'd first noticed outside.

He stood transfixed, his body shaking uncontrollably, as he took in the scene of carnage before him. And saw what had once been his father.

He dropped the tea, the brown liquid mingling with the thick red fluid which seemed to be everywhere inside the hut. On the walls, on the floor, even on the ceiling.

Ian gulped down huge lungfuls of the foul air, his eyes darting back and forth, to his dead father, then to the broken window, then to the blood.

He turned and tried to run, but felt as if someone had injected his legs with lead.

It was like standing in a slaughterhouse. His head was swimming, his stomach contracting violently, threatening to empty its contents onto the floor with the spilled tea and the congealing blood. Finally he found the strength to run, a strength born of horror.

Horror made absolute by the sight of what lay on his father's workbench.

Forty-Nine

The wind had, to some small extent, helped to dispel the vile stench of blood and excrement from the workshop. Even so, the odour still hung like an invisible pall, causing Wallace to cough every time he inhaled too deeply.

The inspector reached for his cigarettes and stuck one in his mouth. He patted his pockets, looking for a light. One of the ambulancemen standing close by came to his rescue and lit the cigarette for him. The inspector nodded his appreciation and sucked in the smoke gratefully, his eyes scanning the scene of slaughter before him.

Frank King lay on his side, his head twisted back savagely, the muscles severed as far as the spinal column. The killer could hardly have been more thorough if a chainsaw had been used. The head was practically severed.

The face, rent by numerous deep gashes from the broken glass, was lacerated particularly badly around the nose and cheeks.

The eyes had been ripped from their sockets.

King's shirt was open to reveal the horrendous injuries inflicted on his torso. A massive wound running from neck to navel had been opened up, and the torn edges of the stomach wrenched back to allow the killer access to the intestines. Several thick lengths lay scattered around the hut, now stiffened and covered in caked gore.

Most of the flesh had been flayed from the body with a blood-stained chisel which lay close to the corpse. But the thing which drew Wallace's closest attention was the object lying on the dead man's workbench.

Two thick lengths of entrail had been used to fashion a reeking letter A.

'I hope this bastard isn't working his way through the alphabet,' said Sergeant Dayton, who held a handkerchief to his face to prevent the worst of the smell from penetrating.

'If he is, then he's dyslexic,' Wallace said sardonically. 'He started with M.'

'Can we move the body now, Doctor?' the ambulance-man asked, looking down at Dr Ryan, who was still hunched over the dead man.

He nodded and got to his feet, careful not to step in any of the puddles of sticky crimson gore which were splattered all around.

'Did you speak to the boy?' he asked.

'The poor little bastard can't say a word,' said Wallace. 'All he does is grunt.'

'Traumatic shock syndrome,' Ryan informed the police-man.

'Your brilliant insight does surprise me, Doctor,' Wallace said, his voice heavy with sarcasm. He caught the anger in Ryan's eyes and apologized. 'Could you let me have the autopsy report as soon as possible? I know it hardly seems worth it but . . . this other business . . . about the hearts.'

'You mean you want to know if King was frightened to death, too?' said Ryan. 'I doubt it. I think he died from massive loss of blood from the wounds in the throat, but I'll check.'

'Died of fright?' said Dayton, looking puzzled. 'You mean that's what happened to the others?'

Wallace nodded.

'But not a word to anyone else, Bill. If that reaches the papers then we'll all be cleaning shit off the walls because it's going to hit the fan faster than any of us can imagine.' He took a long drag on his Rothmans.

'*Frightened* to death,' the sergeant repeated. 'What the hell happened to them? What did they see before they were cut up?'

Wallace shook his head.

'You tell me,' he said, cryptically. 'But if it was that bad, I'm not so sure I *want* to know who killed them.'

Clare Nichols swung herself out of bed, perspiration soaking through her nightdress. She padded slowly to the bedroom window and peered out into the night, the image of the dream still strong in her mind. She gazed out at the street lamp on the other side of the road, its sodium glare casting cold light around it.

She stood there for a long time, peering into the gloom as if searching for something which she knew was there but which she could not see.

Not yet.

But it was coming.

Coming soon.

Fifty

It was nine o'clock the next morning when Wallace swung the Sierra into the street which led to Longfield police station. He braked, allowing a couple of children to cross the road. The sight of them sparked thoughts of the two children who were missing. As far as he knew there had been no further word on either, despite the efforts of his men to find them. Both killer and kidnapper — if they were not one individual — were managing to keep an annoyingly low profile for a town the size of Longfield, Wallace thought.

He brought the Sierra to a halt in the police station car park, then clambered out and strode across the tarmac towards the main building.

As he walked in, Sergeant Bill Dayton looked up and nodded feebly. Wallace frowned.

'You've got a visitor, guv,' he said.

'Who is it?' Wallace wanted to know. 'Oh Christ, not Cutler again . . .'

'The Chief Inspector,' Dayton told him. 'He's in your office.'

Wallace nodded and walked on, his forehead wrinkled in surprise, and also irritation. What the hell did his superior want, dropping in like this? As he reached the door of his office he paused, wondering whether to knock or not. He hesitated a moment longer, then knocked once and walked in without waiting for an invitation.

Chief Inspector Gordon Macready looked up at the sudden intrusion, his cold grey eyes fixing Wallace in an unflinching stare. The inspector thought that his superior's features appeared to have been modelled from wax. His expression did not change as he looked up at Wallace.

Macready was in his early fifties, balding and over-weight. The buttons of his waistcoat strained to meet across his stomach and Wallace expected them to explode open at any moment. Despite the bald patch on top of his head, the older man sported thick sideburns and a bushy mane of hair at the back. Speckles of dandruff dotted the shoulders of his jacket.

Wallace noted with slight annoyance that his superior had made himself at home in the inspector's own chair. He rocked gently to and fro on the back legs, eyeing the younger man up and down.

The two of them exchanged greetings and Macready motioned to Wallace to sit down.

'I've read the files on the murders,' the older man said. 'And the kidnappings.' He folded his arms across his chest. 'You're not making any progress, Wallace. You're no closer.'

'If you've read the files then you'll realize what we're up against, sir,' Wallace said, his eyes never leaving the other man. 'The killer's a clever bastard. We've got virtually nothing to go on. He leaves no clues. Nothing.'

'What about the kidnappings? Any motive for those?'

'Not that I can find.'

'Do you think the killer and kidnapper are one and the same?'

'I'd have thought it was a pretty safe bet, yes.'

Macready made a clucking sound with his tongue and looked first at the files before him, then at Wallace.

'As from now, Inspector, I will be taking over this investigation,' he said. 'I think it's fair to say that the incidents which have occurred are somewhat beyond your capabilities.'

'You mean you're relieving me?'

'That's exactly what I mean. This case needs, shall we say, an older head.' He smiled condescendingly. 'Wouldn't you agree?'

Wallace clenched his teeth, the knot of muscles at the side of his jaw pulsing angrily.

'Yes, sir,' he muttered.

'I've already asked for more men to help with the search,' Macready told him. 'We might even need to cordon off the town eventually.'

'I'd requested extra men, sir,' the inspector said, trying to mask his annoyance.

'I'm aware of that, Wallace,' Macready said.

'Whose decision was it to replace me, sir?'

'That isn't important.'

'It's important to me,' rasped Wallace, a little too vehemently.

Macready regarded him reproachfully for a moment.

'I said it isn't important,' he muttered, keeping his voice low. 'You haven't been suspended. You're still on the case, but from now on you will report directly to me and you'll take your instructions from me. Clear?'

'Yes, sir,' Wallace said through clenched teeth.

There was a heavy silence, finally broken by the younger man.

'May I go now, sir?' he asked.

Macready nodded, watching as Wallace headed for the door. As he closed it behind him he let out an angry breath.

Inside the office the phone rang.

From the police station Wallace drove to the museum, a little puzzled to find the car park empty when he arrived. There was no sign of Kim's Land Rover. He drove up to the main doors, got out and knocked three times. He waited several minutes for an answer, but only silence greeted his arrival. He knocked once more, then walked around the building to the window which looked into the laboratory.

The blinds were down. As he stood listening, he heard no sounds of movement from inside.

Wallace strode back to his car, clambered in and drove off.

He reached Kim's house in less than fifteen minutes.

The Land Rover was parked outside, so Wallace drew up behind it. He climbed out and walked up to the front door, brushing a hand through his hair as he knocked. The door opened a moment later.

Kim smiled happily as she saw him.

'Steve! Come in,' she said, touching his hand as he entered. She felt him squeeze hers softly. They looked into each other's eyes for a moment and felt that tingle they'd experienced the other night.

'When I couldn't get hold of you at the museum I thought something might be wrong,' he told her, wandering through into the sitting room.

Clare was sitting on the floor in front of the television, one eye on 'Sesame Street', the other on the dolls which lay before her. When Wallace entered the room, she turned and looked at him. A smile which spread from her lips to her eyes lit up her whole face.

'Clare, this is Inspector Wallace,' Kim told her. 'He's a policeman.'

'Hello, gorgeous,' Wallace said, smiling at the child, struck by her radiant beauty. She looked strikingly like her mother, he thought.

'Are you friends with Mummy?' Clare asked.

Wallace grinned and looked fleetingly at Kim.

'You could say that,' he answered.

'Are you her best friend?'

It was Kim's turn to smile.

She ushered Wallace through to the kitchen where he sat down at the table, watching while she switched on the kettle.

'A very astute young lady,' the inspector said, waving to Clare through the partially-open door. She waved back. 'And very beautiful, like her mum.'

Kim coloured slightly.

'You didn't come round here just to pay me compliments,' she said. 'What's happened?'

'Another man's been killed, another of Cutler's employees. The method was exactly the same. It happened last night.'

'Oh, Christ,' she murmured as she dropped tea bags into the mugs on the draining board.

He also told her about the arrival of Macready.

'So you're really no closer to finding the killer?' she asked.

'Or the kidnapper,' he added. 'Kim, it's like looking for a bloody ghost.' He sighed, then seemed to push the questions aside momentarily. 'Why aren't *you* working? I thought you still had things to do at the museum.'

Kim crossed to the door and pushed it shut, then spoke in a lowered voice.

'It's Clare,' she said. 'She's been having nightmares for the past week or so, and she hasn't been sleeping too well. I thought it best to keep her out of school for a while.' She paused for a moment, then told him about the incident at school the previous day. From a cupboard above the sink, where it lay rolled up and held by an elastic band, Kim pulled out the drawing and unfurled it in front of Wallace.

He studied it, puzzled by the grotesque image and the scrawled words.

'Clare says she doesn't remember drawing it,' Kim told him, switching off the kettle as it began to boil. 'Or writing those words.'

Wallace picked up the drawing and held it before him as if that simple act would reveal its secrets.

'Is she ill?' he wanted to know.

'In perfect physical condition, the doctor said. I took her to see him earlier today. She's just tired. Like I said, she hasn't been sleeping very well. She says she has bad dreams but she can never remember them the following day. At least not what they were about.' Kim handed the policeman his tea, wandering round to stand beside him. They both looked down at the drawing.

'Perhaps this figure is what she's been seeing in her dreams,' Wallace offered.

'It's possible,' Kim sighed. 'Do you believe in premonitions? Second sight?'

Wallace shrugged.

Kim picked up a notepad from the worktop nearby and handed it to him. It contained more of the transcribed words from the Celtic tablets she was working on.

'I finished the transcription yesterday teatime,' Kim told him, her eyes following the words across the page:

ONCE IN EACH YEAR THE TIME COMES. TIME OF FEAR FOR THEM. TIME OF FEAST. OF TARBFEIS AND OF THE OFFERINGS. THEN I AM NO LONGER A WANDERER. THE KING IS SELECTED BY THE OFFERING OF A MARE. A WHITE MARE IS SLAUGHTERED AND IN THE HOT LIQUID THE KING DRINKS AND BATHES UNTIL HE HAS ABSORBED THE SPIRIT OF THE DEAD ANIMAL. FOR THOUGH DEATH COMES IT BRINGS LIFE TO OTHERS. DEATH THROUGH LIFE. THE DEATH OF ONE MAN MEANS POWER TO ANOTHER. AND THE DEATH OF MANY MEANS POWER TO HIM.

Wallace looked at the drawing done by Clare and then at the final phrase which Kim had written down. It was underlined three times.

'His time is come,' he read aloud.

Kim nodded.

'Clare did that drawing and wrote those words yesterday lunchtime,' she said. 'Three hours *before* I'd deciphered the writing on the tablet.'

'I'll call you later,' Wallace said as he slid behind the wheel of the Sierra. He looked up at Kim and smiled. She bent forward and kissed him on the lips, surprising him with the suddenness of her movement, but he responded, still more surprised by the passion which he felt. He felt her tongue probing against his lips, pushing past his teeth to find the warm moistness of his tongue. He gently touched her cheek as he returned the kiss with equal fervour. When they finally parted it was very reluctantly.

'Take care,' she said as he drove off.

He could see her in one wing mirror as he drove away, but his thoughts were interrupted by the harsh crackle of the two-way. He immediately snatched it up.

'Wallace.'

'It's Dayton, guv. The C.I. wants you back here straight-away.'

Wallace didn't ask why. He merely acknowledged and put his foot down.

He reached the police station in a little under ten minutes, parked his car and walked across the tarmac towards the entrance, wondering what Macready wanted.

As he entered the station he heard unfamiliar sounds.

A woman crying.

Puzzled, he glanced around, trying to find the source of the anguished sounds.

The frosted glass partition was down and locked, separating the entry-way of the police station from what lay behind it. There was no one in sight and the only sound was of the woman crying.

196

Wallace climbed the stairs to his office, knocked once and then walked in.

Macready was standing with his back to the door, gazing out of the window. He turned as the younger man entered the room and Wallace saw the worried expression on his superior's face.

The chief inspector said nothing. He reached for something on his desk and handed it to Wallace.

It was a photograph. A wallet-sized snap of a young boy, no more than six years old, the inspector guessed. Short brown hair, one front tooth missing, the gap revealed by a wide and cheeky grin.

Wallace felt an uncomfortably familiar chill creeping up his spine as he looked at the picture.

'Carl Taylor,' Macready said. 'He's not quite six years old.'

Wallace suddenly understood why the woman downstairs was crying.

Macready sighed and continued:

'He disappeared from outside his home an hour ago . . .'

Fifty-One

The huge Scania lorry rolled inexorably up the slope towards the site, the first of a massive convoy of steel vehicles. Belching diesel fumes in great bluish-grey clouds, the trucks and other metallic juggernauts made their way over the uneven ground as easily as a tank rolling over a shell-ravaged battlefield.

Alongside the lorry, looking curiously incongruous, was James Cutler's Jensen. The car bumped and bounced over the ruts in the earth, but its suspension prevented the land developer from feeling the worst of the uneven ride.

Charles Cooper stood close to the entrance of the ancient shaft, watching the vehicles drawing closer, feeling the anger boiling up inside him. So, this was it. The end. The most valuable archaeological find of its type for years was to be wiped out by bulldozers and earth-movers. All in the name of profit.

'What's going on?' asked George Perry, appearing beside him, his gaze also drawn to the convoy of lorries heading towards them. Other members of the dig, alerted by the roar of engines, were also watching apprehensively.

'Cutler,' said Cooper, angrily. 'It looks as if he's finally getting around to doing what he threatened.'

The Jensen sped on ahead of the heavier vehicles and came to a halt at the top of the slope. Cutler got out, muttering to himself as he saw that the mud was sticking to his shoes. He walked towards Cooper, a thin smile on his face.

'My men won't be starting work until tomorrow,' he said. 'You and your people will have plenty of time to move your things out.'

Cooper clenched his fists, his anger preventing him from speaking.

'Come on, Cooper, you knew it would happen eventually,' Cutler said. 'You've already had longer on this dig than you originally envisaged.'

'But our work isn't finished,' Perry said.

'I'm afraid it is,' Cutler told him. 'I'm very sorry but we made an agreement when the site was first discovered. I'm sure I don't need to remind you.'

'How can you do this?' Cooper hissed. 'Still, asking you to appreciate *true* value is like asking a dog to shit in a toilet.'

Cutler waved a finger reproachfully.

'I didn't come here for a slanging match, or to be insulted. I came to tell you to move off *my* land. I hoped that it could be done amicably but I see that it can't.' The land developer's tone had hardened. 'Now I'm telling you,

Cooper, I want you and all your people away from here by tonight. Otherwise I'll call the police in and press trespass charges. Understood?'

Cooper suddenly lunged forward, hands outstretched in an effort to reach Cutler. The other man stepped back, avoiding the frantic attack. The archaeologist slipped and sprawled in the mud but he dragged himself upright immediately and went for Cutler a second time. This time he was stopped by two of his colleagues.

'Do you want assault charges added to those for trespass?' Cutler asked scornfully. 'Now, get out of here. I won't tell you again.' He walked back to his car and climbed in. 'I'll be back first thing in the morning, and I don't expect to see you here,' he said and started the engine. The wheels spun in the mud for a moment, then the Jensen roared away. Only then did Cooper's companions release him.

'You bastard,' he bellowed after the car, hurling a handful of mud in its direction.

George Perry looked on in silence.

Cooper stood for a moment longer, then turned and stalked away towards his tent.

Fifty-Two

The chink of ice against crystal sounded almost unnaturally loud in the peacefulness of the room.

James Cutler dug his hand into the ice bucket and dropped more of the frozen squares into the whiskey tumbler before pouring a generous measure of Johnny Walker.

He drank deeply, allowing the amber fluid to burn its way to his stomach. The land developer had drunk three or

199

four scotches at the restaurant an hour or so earlier, and he wondered how he had managed to remain so stone-cold sober. He didn't even feel a hint of light-headedness. He poured himself another drink, wondering how long it would take him to get smashed.

Even though the liquor inside him was warm and the central heating was on full-blast he still felt cold. As if icy fingers were tickling the back of his neck. He took his drink and sat down facing the television set. He didn't bother to turn the set on but merely gazed at the blank screen, sipping his drink a little too hastily.

Beside him his dog, Rebel, a red setter, lay with its head raised as if listening to something in the distance.

Cutler reached down with one hand and stroked the animal's head, surprised when it growled.

'What's the matter with you?' he said, withdrawing his hand an inch or two.

The dog's ears had pricked up and it was now looking round, its head jerking from side to side. Finally it contented itself with glaring at the sitting room door.

Cutler looked at the dog a moment longer, sipping more of his drink.

'You're a temperamental so-and-so tonight,' he said, patting the dog again, more cautiously this time.

Again the animal growled, low in its throat. It got to its feet, padded across to the door, and stood facing it, its growls gradually building into barks.

Cutler frowned and rose from his chair.

'What the hell is the matter, Rebel?' he asked as if he actually expected the dog to tell him.

Once more he felt those icy fingers at the back of his neck but with more cause now. His dog wouldn't behave this way unless it had a reason.

The animal was now barking, growling and whimpering by turns. It stood unmoving by the door as Cutler approached. He pulled the door open, expecting the setter to run out, but it remained where it was, looking out into the darkened hall and the front door beyond.

He himself looked at the wood-panelled door, then back

at the large bay window with its curtains still undrawn. Cutler suddenly felt very vulnerable.

And frightened.

Couldn't dogs sense the presence of others? he thought.

They could tell when there was an intruder about.

An intruder.

Or a murderer perhaps?

The thought struck Cutler like a thunderbolt and he moved away from the door towards the windows, hastily drawing the curtains across, shutting out the darkness of the night.

His house stood on the outskirts of Longfield, surrounded by two acres of grounds. He was, in short, isolated. Cut off. And, with what had been happening recently to those who worked for him, the land developer felt suddenly afraid.

The dog had now moved out into the hall slightly, still growling.

Cutler followed it, moving slowly in the gloom, his ears alert for any sound from outside the house.

He listened intently but heard nothing. Still the setter growled, its lips sliding back over its canine teeth.

Cutler glanced to his right, up the stairs, then to his left, towards the dining room. The dog seemed intent on the front door and now, as he watched, it began to bark frenziedly, the sound echoing in the stillness of the house.

The land developer crossed to the door, one hand resting on the lock.

Should he let the dog out? Let it chase whoever was out there?

But if he did open the door . . .

He swallowed hard, looking down at the setter, which was now barking loudly, its body stiff. The only part of it moving was its head.

Open the door? he asked himself.

He finally slid back the bolt and pulled it open, letting the setter scurry out into the night. He slammed the door quickly behind it and stood with his back to it, shaking. If

201

there was a burglar or prowler out there, then Rebel would soon see them off, he thought, trying to reassure himself.

The barking ceased abruptly and silence descended once again.

Cutler listened, waiting for the noise to continue.

Nothing.

Maybe the dog had been unable to find anyone. Perhaps it was even now trotting back towards the house. Cutler glanced at the phone on the hall table and wondered if he should call the police. If he did, what would he tell them? That his dog had been barking at sounds he himself could not hear? It was scarcely a good enough reason to bring two panda cars screeching to his door. He closed his eyes for a moment, surrounded by the darkness, wondering what to do.

He heard his dog yelp wildly and his blood froze.

The cry died away on the breeze which swirled around the house.

Cutler looked across at the phone once more.

Should he phone?

What if the killer were outside?

He had a right to be protected.

Again he hesitated, peering out of the window beside the door in an effort to see where the dog had got to. The darkness was impenetrable. The light switch which controlled the porch lamp was close to his hand. If he put that on he would be able to see. He flicked the switch.

As the front path was bathed in light, Cutler sucked in a strangled breath.

His dog was lying about ten yards from the house in a spreading pool of blood.

Its head had almost been severed. It hung at an impossible angle, twisted to one side to reveal a jawbone which was shattered into crimson mush. Both eyes had been torn out, leaving only the weeping sockets, and Cutler noticed that one of the dog's long ears had also been ripped away by its killer. The ear lay discarded a couple of feet away. The body was still twitching spasmodically, one rear

202

leg quivering insanely as the last muscular movements racked it.

Cutler turned immediately, snapping off the porch light, and dived for the phone. He snatched it up and dialled three nines.

The line was dead.

Shaking uncontrollably he dialled again, not stopping to think that the lines had most likely been cut.

With a final despairing moan he threw the receiver down and blundered into the sitting room, slamming the door behind him, his breath now coming in short gasps.

He heard scratching outside the front door, the sound gradually building until a series of loud bangs rang through the house.

Cutler looked around desperately for something with which to defend himself.

The bangs became blows of sledgehammer proportions and the land developer heard the strain of cracking wood.

He ran from the sitting room, through the kitchen, and unlocked the back door.

If he could just get to his car . . .

The garage was about thirty feet from the house at the end of a long tarmac drive.

With the sound of the splintering front door still echoing through the night he plunged on towards the garage, slipping once on the grass. He rolled over and sprang to his feet, not daring to look back. The cold air rasped in his throat as he gulped down huge lungfuls. Finally, with a whimper of relief, he reached the garage. Only then did he afford himself a look back over his shoulder.

No one was following him.

He flung open the garage door and scurried around to the driver's side of the Jensen, fumbling in his pockets.

He'd left the keys in the house.

His heart seemed to accelerate to an impossible speed, hammering madly against his ribs.

He tugged on the car door in his anger and fear, knowing that he had no choice but to go back for the keys. Clenching his teeth he turned and sprinted back across the grass towards the open back door, the sound of splintering wood still loud in his ears.

Another few moments and the intruder would be inside.

Cutler crashed into the kitchen table in his haste, bruising his hip. He ignored the pain, intent only on finding his car keys, on escaping with his life.

He looked around frantically for the keys, aware that the front door could not hold out for much longer. Each hammer blow rained upon it brought his would-be killer closer.

'Oh God,' he grunted. Where had he put the bloody keys?

A huge lump of wood was torn from the door, clattering into the hall. Cutler spun round, his eyes darting back and forth.

He saw the keys on the drinks trolley and snatched them up, hurtling back out through the hall and the kitchen.

The front door finally crashed inwards and the intruder blundered into the hallway, catching sight of the fleeing land developer.

He knew without turning round that he was being pursued but that knowledge only spurred him on to greater effort and, seconds later, he was outside again, sprinting towards the garage, praying that this time he didn't slip and fall.

Behind him, his attacker followed.

Cutler reached the garage. Only then did he turn and look back.

The sight he saw nearly caused him to drop his keys.

The would-be killer was within twenty feet of him.

Cutler smelled the noxious odour, saw the blood, felt the searing cold.

He kicked open the side door of the garage, dashed through and slammed it behind him, slipping the bolt, praying that it would keep the intruder at bay long enough for him to get away.

His hands shaking madly, Cutler struggled to push the key into the lock on the car door.

There was a deafening crash as the first powerful blow landed against the garage door. It was followed by many more.

Murmuring to himself, Cutler struggled with the keys again.

They fell from his grasp but he hurriedly snatched them up and rammed the appropriate one into the lock. In an instant he was behind the steering wheel.

As he jammed in the ignition key he heard the side door of the garage beginning to give.

It would only be a matter of seconds now.

He twisted the key savagely, stepping on the accelerator simultaneously. The engine roared into life and he rammed the Jensen into gear, but his foot slipped off the clutch and the car stalled.

On the verge of hysteria now, he started the engine once more, the loud roar drowning out all other sounds.

Cutler didn't even bother opening the main doors. He merely ducked low behind the wheel and put his foot down.

The Jensen shot forward as if fired from a cannon, smashing through the double doors and out into the night, skidding on the tarmac for precious seconds as Cutler struggled to control the vehicle.

He heard and felt a tremendous thud which seemed to rock the entire car and, for a second, he thought with delight that he'd managed to run his attacker down.

It took him a second to realize that the thud had come from above.

There was someone on the roof.

He braked hard, trying to dislodge the attacker, but as he did so, a powerful hand swung down towards the driver's window.

Glass exploded inwards under the impact and Cutler shrieked as he felt the slivers cutting his skin. The scream was silenced a moment later as the hand fastened itself around his throat.

He swerved, running the car onto his front lawn, skidding to a halt, both hands now clutching at his assailant's arm and at the hand which was throttling him.

His attacker slid from the roof of the car without releasing the strangling grip on Cutler's throat.

He felt himself being pulled towards the broken window and, for one bizarre moment, he thought his assailant was going to try to pull him through the tiny opening.

Instead he saw another hand reaching in, clawing at his face, at his eyes. Sharp nails started digging into the soft flesh of his lids, curving inwards to scrape the sensitive orbs themselves.

Pain enveloped him and he struggled even more fiercely, but his frantic movements only seemed to inflame the attacker more.

Cutler felt his head being turned to an impossible angle, felt the muscles and bones creaking and popping.

Then suddenly, he was staring into the face of his attacker.

Horror such as he had never felt before overwhelmed him and he felt sharp pain stabbing at his heart.

He managed one final scream.

Gripping his head like a bottle top, the killer twisted with incredible ferocity.

The bones in Cutler's neck cracked with a strident shriek, the muscles tearing like paper as the killer continued to twist.

Cutler slumped forward, his head turned completely around, facing backwards.

Without a second's hesitation, the assailant tore open the car door and dragged the body from the confines of the vehicle, which already reeked of excrement and blood.

The killer stood over the corpse for a moment, then fell upon it.

There was much still to be done.

PART THREE

'His heart is black,
His blood is cold,
Returning to destroy our World.

Warrior

Fifty-Three

WHEN THE LEAVES DIE ON THE TREES THEN THEY FEAR
HIM. WHEN THE WIND IS COLD THEY FEAR HIM. AND
THEY KNOW THAT ONLY THE DEATHS OF OTHERS CAN
STOP HIM RISING SO THEY KILL. THEY KILL IN HIS NAME
BUT THEY KILL IN FEAR OF HIM AND HIS POWER WHICH
IS SUCH TO SPLIT THE WORLD IN TWO. NONE CAN STAND
AGAINST HIM FOR NONE POSSESS SUCH POWER AS HE.
SAVE ONE. THEY KNOW LITTLE OF THIS OTHER. OF THE
ONE WHO IS ALWAYS WITH HIM. THE ONE WHO SEEKS
LIVING BODIES NOT DEAD ONES. THE ONE WHO LIVES IN
OTHER MEN'S MINDS. I HAVE PLACED THIS KNOWLEDGE
IN MANY PLACES. HIDDEN. FOR I SERVE HIM AND I
CARRY THE SECRETS.
THE LEAVES ARE DYING ON THE TREES. THE YEAR IS AT
AN END. THEY MUST KILL AGAIN.
DAGDA COMES.

Kim sat back from the notebook and exhaled deeply.
Wallace stood beside her, looking down at the words which
she had so painstakingly transcribed from the stone tablets.

'Who the hell is Dagda?' said Wallace, glancing at the
notes once more.

'Each Celtic tribe worshipped its own individual god or
goddess,' Kim told him. 'For instance, Maponus was a
Northern God, but the lord of them all was Dagda. He was
the most powerful, the most feared. Supposedly grotesque
to look at. He's described as an immense figure with
incredible powers.'

'What about the other name?' the inspector said,

pointing to one which was underlined further down the page.

'Morrigan, the Queen of Demons, Dagda's mate in fertility rituals. She was also known as *Nemain* which means panic, or *Badb Catha*, the raven of battle. In some ways, thought to be as powerful as Dagda himself.' She looked down at her own scribblings.

WHEN COMES THE SEASON OF COLD THEN COMES DAGDA UNLESS THEY ARE WILLING TO OFFER TO HIM THE YOUNG OF THEIR TÚATH.

'The Celtic year was divided into two halves,' Kim said. 'The season of warmth and the season of cold, basically summer and winter. They had no concept of spring and autumn, only that there was one time of the year for growing crops and another for storing them.' She sighed. 'But don't ask me how all that ties in with the murders.'

Wallace shrugged, sipping at his coffee, looking down at the photos of the murder victims spread out on the table in front of Kim. The most recent one showed the butchered remains of James Cutler. His body had been flayed, his eyes torn from their sockets, his stomach cavity almost emptied. Beside him lay the final abomination.

Three lengths of intestine used to form a capital letter I.

The clock on the mantelpiece struck one a.m. and Wallace rubbed his face with one hand, simultaneously stifling a yawn. He had driven to Kim's house after leaving the scene of Cutler's murder, returning quickly to the police station to collect the photos. That had been three hours ago. He stretched and looked across at Kim, who was dressed only in a short house-coat, her slender legs drawn up beneath her. He did not drop his gaze when he saw her look back at him.

'You look exhausted, Steve,' she told him, brushing a stray hair from his forehead. As she withdrew her hand she held it and kissed her slender fingers. She responded by moving closer, snaking one hand around the back of his head, pulling him to her as they kissed.

The scream which echoed through the house caused them both to gasp aloud.

It came from upstairs.

From Clare's room.

Fifty-Four

Kim leapt to her feet and dashed for the stairs taking them two at a time in her haste. Wallace was right behind her, the scream still drumming in his ears.

They reached the landing and he followed as she pushed open the door of her daughter's room and hurried in.

'Oh God,' Kim gasped as Wallace joined her and they both stood gazing down at the girl.

Clare was lying spreadeagled on the bed, the covers thrown off in an untidy heap. Her head was moving slowly from side to side, her lips fluttering constantly, expelling a series of low mutterings. Her eyes, though, were closed tightly.

Kim moved forward but Wallace stepped in front of her.

'Don't wake her,' he said, seeing that the girl was obviously still asleep. He picked up the covers and laid them gently back on the bed, moving closer to the sleeping girl. Her entire body was quivering gently, as if a mild electric shock were passing through it. Kim crouched beside the bed, touching her daughter's hand, feeling how cold the skin was despite the thin film of perspiration which covered her face, matting her hair across her forehead and beading into minute crystal droplets on her arms.

The low whispering continued, like some kind of muted litany, the same mumblings repeated over and over again as the girl's head moved from side to side.

'This happened to her once before,' said Kim, anxiety etched on her face. 'It must be another nightmare.' She bent close to her daughter's face, brushing a strand of hair away. As she did so, she realized that it wasn't a string of words which Clare was mouthing. It was one single word. Kim strained her ears to pick it out.

'Can you understand what she's saying?' Wallace asked.

Kim merely raised one hand to silence him, the word now becoming more distinct.

It sounded like steam escaping as Clare mouthed that one word over and over again.

'*Samain. Samain. Samain.*'

Kim frowned, unsure at first if she had heard right, but Clare continued and there was no mistaking the word.

Wallace saw the look of concern on Kim's face.

'What is it?' he asked.

'*Samain. Samain. Samain,*' Clare breathed, more insistently now.

The sound stopped abruptly. In the silence they both heard the girl's breathing return to a semblance of normality. The rigidity in her limbs seemed to disappear and she curled up into a ball beneath the covers. Kim sat on the edge of the bed, one hand resting on her daughter's shoulder, her eyes never leaving the girl.

'I'll sit with her for a while, Steve,' she said softly.

Wallace nodded and walked slowly from the room. Kim heard his footfalls on the stairs as he descended. From the kitchen she heard the sound of the kettle being filled.

Clare continued to sleep peacefully.

Kim found that it was she who was quivering now.

'Is she all right?' Wallace asked as Kim entered the sitting room, closing the door behind her.

She nodded and sat down beside him on the sofa, gratefully accepting the mug of coffee which he handed to her. A heavy silence settled over them, finally broken by Wallace.

'What was she saying, Kim? That word, you seemed to recognize it,' he said.

She nodded slowly, her eyes drawn towards the photos of the murder victims before her. Kim put down her cup, her own breathing now becoming more rapid. She looked at each of the photos that showed the letters which had been formed from lengths of bleeding intestines. She pulled a notebook towards her, one eye on the grisly photos, and said, 'When the letters the killer left behind are placed in the correct order they do make a word.'

Wallace watched as she wrote down in block letters:

SAMAIN

'Samain,' she said quietly. 'It's a Celtic word. It means the end of summer. The Celts held a great festival to mark its ending.'

The inspector swallowed hard.

'Is there any way Clare would know that word?' he asked. 'Could she have seen it written in one of your notebooks?'

'It's possible, I suppose,' Kim said, her brow furrowed. 'That's what the writing on the stone tablets must refer to: "When comes the time. Time of cold. Time of Samain." Whoever carved those tablets was a very powerful Druid. He claims to have had power over Dagda. "When comes the season of cold then comes Dagda," ' she re-read.

'So what happened at Samain?' Wallace asked.

'In order to ensure that their crops would grow in the coming year, the Druids would sacrifice children to Dagda. It was like a kind of fertility rite but also a means of appeasement to prevent Dagda from rising and entering this world. It was done every year.' She pointed to a line of the transcript.

ONCE RISEN HE CANNOT BE STOPPED. ONLY THE OFFERING OF THE YOUNG WILL PREVENT HIS COMING.

'Steve, don't you see? The children's skulls that we found in that underground chamber must have belonged to sacrificial victims killed in the name of Dagda, to prevent him from rising. Every one of those children had been

213

decapitated and the eyes gouged out. It was part of the ritual. Except that the carbon-dating tests I ran on the skulls showed that not all of them came from the same period. They weren't all Celtic sacrifices. One of them belonged to a child who was murdered in 1823. Other people, in the past, have found those tablets and deciphered them. The knowledge has been passed down through the ages, the superstition continued for thousands of years. Right up until 1823 when that last child was murdered.'

Wallace felt a chill envelop him.

'Children must have been sacrificed on that same spot for thousands of years. Since 1,000 B.C. that site had been used for the ritual murder of children,' Kim continued.

'Was it always children?' the inspector asked.

'Young children. They would be killed on the night of Samain. Usually three at a time because three was a mystical number to the Celts. How many children have been kidnapped from Longfield?'

Wallace stiffened.

'Three,' he said quietly. 'When was Samain? The date?'

'October 31st,' she told him.

'Christ, that's tomorrow,' said Wallace. 'October 31st. Halloween.'

'The name changed but the festival has persisted in different forms,' Kim told him. 'The early Christians called it Hallowmas. Then in the Middle Ages, November the 1st was consecrated as All Saint's Day so the night before became All Hallow Even. Over the years it was shortened to Halloween.'

'The kidnapper must have some knowledge of all this,' Wallace said, agitatedly.

'When you were at the museum you were reading up on witchcraft,' she reminded him. 'Halloween is the most important time of the witches' year too.'

Wallace nodded, remembering the butchered animals that had been found in the wood near Dexter Grange. His gaze strayed to the photos of the murder victims, slaughtered in a similar, though even more horrendous fashion. But one question plagued his mind.

'Why would the killer spell out the word?' he mused, looking at the pictures. There was a heavy silence.

'The three kids that have been kidnapped,' he continued, 'obviously whoever's got them is going to use them as sacrifices tomorrow night.' He looked at Kim. 'Charles Cooper would know about this ritual, wouldn't he? *And* he had it in for Cutler and the others that were killed.'

'You could say the same about anyone who was part of the archaeological team on that dig,' she told him. 'They all had a grievance against Cutler.'

'Maybe,' he said, unconvinced. 'But three kids are going to be murdered tomorrow night unless I find out who's got them. I've got to concentrate on the likeliest suspects first.'

'But what if the legends about Dagda are true?'

'Kim, you're not serious?' he snorted.

'A lot of people *have* been serious about this over the past few thousand years. Serious or frightened enough to murder children to prevent unleashing this . . . evil, whatever it is.'

'So you think I should let the kids die?'

She lowered her head.

'I've got to find them.'

Kim gripped his hand.

'Do you have to leave tonight?' she wanted to know. He heard the anxiety in her voice.

He leant forward and kissed her lightly on the lips.

'No,' he said softly, pulling her closer, but as she wrapped her arms around him he glanced at the table once more. At the sentence from the transcript which made him shudder:

WHEN COMES THE SEASON OF COLD THEN COMES DAGDA UNLESS THEY ARE WILLING TO OFFER HIM THE YOUNG . . .

215

Fifty-Five

The policeman slammed the knocker down three times and stepped back, waiting for Charles Cooper to open the door.

There was no response.

Wallace knocked again.

Still no answer.

He pushed open the letter box and peered through. It looked dark inside the hallway. He called the archaeologist's name, then wandered halfway back down the path, glancing up at the bedroom window. The curtains were open.

The inspector spotted a gate which he guessed led around to the back of the house. It was flanked on one side by the house itself, on the other by a high privet hedge, now leafless and bare. Through it, Wallace could see the woman next door peering curiously at him, a yard broom held in her hands.

'You looking for Mr Cooper?' she called.

'Yes,' Wallace replied, tersely, without looking at her. He reached the back of the house, and cupping one hand over his eyes, peered through the kitchen window.

The place certainly looked empty.

'You a friend of his?' the woman asked.

'You could say that,' Wallace told her, knocking on the back door. 'Have you seen him about today?'

'No, but then I don't see him much anyhow.'

'Terrific,' murmured Wallace and made his way back to the waiting Sierra. He picked up the handset and flicked it on.

'This is Wallace. I want a car sent to 12 Elm Street now.'

'Anything wrong, guv?' asked Dayton at the other end.

'I don't know. Yet. Look, when the car arrives I just want the blokes in it to watch the house. But if Charles Cooper shows up I want him pulled, got it?

'What's the charge?' Dayton wanted to know.

Wallace sucked in an impatient breath.

'Indecent exposure,' he snapped. 'I don't give a toss what they use. I just want Cooper brought in for questioning. Over and out.' He replaced his handset before the sergeant had a chance to reply. Wallace sat looking at the house for a moment longer, then started his engine and drove off.

It was 10:56 a.m.

As Wallace guided the Sierra through the gateway which led up to Dexter Grange he peered through the windscreen towards the gaunt edifice as if looking for signs of movement within the house.

The gravel of the driveway crunched loudly beneath the wheels of the car as he swung it around before the imposing structure. He got out of the vehicle and stood looking up at the house for a moment before striding up to the front door. He banged loudly three times.

No answer.

Muttering to himself, Wallace walked back to the car and pressed hard on the hooter, keeping his hand there until even *he* could stand the strident wail no longer. He then hurried back to the front door and banged again.

There was still no reply.

'Shit,' he murmured, wandering past the large windows which led into the library, the study, the lounge. He reached the side of the house and a set of French doors. The inspector hesitated a moment, and then, cupping one hand over his eyes, he peered in through the glass. Nothing moved inside the room. The policeman took off his jacket and wrapped it around his fist and lower arm. With one swift punch, he stove in a panel of glass close to the door handle. The glass shattered loudly, small shards spraying into the room. Wallace snaked a hand through, careful not to cut himself, twisted the handle and let himself in.

There was still no sound or movement inside Dexter Grange. No one had heard, or else they had chosen not to hear, Wallace thought as he made his way across the room to the door which he knew led out into the corridor.

He paused for a moment, then stepped out onto the polished wood floor.

He moved quickly from room to room, pushing open doors, something at the back of his mind asking him what the hell he was going to say should Dexter appear. But the inspector swiftly administered himself a rebuke. He was searching for evidence. More to the point, three missing children. He didn't need a search warrant and if Dexter started mouthing off then *he'd* be hauled down to the station too.

But there didn't seem to be any sign of either the recluse or his young girlfriend. If, Wallace thought, that was the right word.

As he reached the front door he saw that two large bolts had been slipped into position.

Obviously Dexter didn't want any visitors.

Wallace glanced to his right, towards the broad staircase.

The steps seemed to climb precipitously up to a landing which looked strangely dark and forbidding. Wallace told himself that some curtains up there must be drawn, cutting out the daylight, and the sky was grey and overcast in any case.

He began to climb.

The stairs were uncarpeted so he trod as softly as he could.

The sound of his shoes echoed in the stillness and more than one of the steps creaked protestingly under his weight as he drew nearer the top of the flight.

He thought about calling Dexter's name but decided against it.

He reached the landing and stood still, looking around at the closed doors which faced him. The solitude was almost oppressive on this floor and Wallace, for some unaccountable reason, felt strangely apprehensive about approaching the first of the doors.

'Come on,' he whispered to himself, annoyed at his own reticence. He strode towards the door and flung it open.

There wasn't a stick of furniture in it. No carpet either. A thick film of dust covered the floor and Wallace coughed as the choking particles swirled before him, disturbed by his sudden entrance.

It was the same in the next room.

And the next.

He approached the fourth door, his initial apprehension having given way to annoyance.

He threw open the door and walked in.

The sight which met him caused him to freeze momentarily.

He frowned, his eyes drawn to what lay in the centre of the room.

Drawn on the bare boards was a huge pentagram.

At the apex of each of the five points of the star there was a small silver bowl. In the centre lay another, larger than the others.

Wallace moved closer, kneeling beside the carefully drawn shape. He touched the closest line, surprised to find that it was fresh. Chalk smudged his finger tips.

What the hell had Dexter got in mind? Wallace thought. And, more to the point, where was he?

The policeman straightened up. Taking one last look at the pentagram, he walked out of the room and headed down the stairs.

He made his way back through the house and out through the French doors, glancing towards the wood which lay about a mile or so from the building. With the dark clouds gathering above it, the sight made Wallace shudder.

'Witchcraft,' he muttered to himself.

Witchcraft. Ritual murder. Kidnapping.

A thought struck him, at once logical yet absurd.

Could both Cooper and Dexter be involved together in the killings and kidnappings? Both men had motives for wanting Cutler and those who worked for him dead. Both had knowledge of ritual murder.

He slid behind the wheel of the Sierra and started the engine. He threw the car into a screeching turn and drove rapidly away from Dexter Grange.

Fifty-Six

'You were in breach of regulations, Wallace.'

Chief Inspector Gordon Macready sat back in his seat, his fingers clasped across his stomach.

'You had no right to break into Dexter's house. He could prosecute you for trespassing and he'd be perfectly within his rights. You had no search warrant, no authorisation of any kind.'

'I think that reason to suspect he's holding three kidnapped children is authorisation enough, sir,' Wallace snapped, trying to light a cigarette.

'There are certain procedures to be followed in a case like this . . .'

Wallace cut him short. 'My only concern is to find those kids. They could be dead by morning.'

'Your concern should be with carrying out correct police procedure,' Macready told him, his voice taking on a menacing tone. 'You also had no business calling a car and two constables to keep watch on Charles Cooper's house.'

'How the hell else are we supposed to find him?'

Macready sat forward in his seat, his dark eyes fixing the younger man in a piercing stare.

'Look, Wallace, I came to Longfield to replace you because you weren't getting results. I also told you that you were to take your orders direct from me. Now *I* didn't order surveillance on Cooper's house, did I?'

'But you do agree that it's rather strange that the two

prime suspects in this case are . . . unobtainable?' he said, acidly.

'Strange, yes, but I don't attach the importance to it that you do.'

'Maybe it's a pity you don't, sir,' Wallace replied, sucking hard on his cigarette.

Macready studied him for a moment, the knot of muscles at the side of his jaw pulsing angrily.

'You also had no business showing the results of our investigation to that woman,' he said.

'We *had* no results until I showed her,' Wallace gasped. 'She was the one who told me what those bloody letters stood for!'

The older man was unimpressed.

'And you expect me to believe that these murders and kidnappings are being done by someone who practises witchcraft? Just because the letters happen to spell out some mythical name? What do you take me for, Wallace? It's only a coincidence that the letters spelled out a word this woman recognized. We don't know that the word is Celtic. More likely it could be a foreign word and mean something completely different. For God's sake, man, you're a policeman. You're supposed to think rationally, not believe the first piece of mystical hocus-pocus you hear.'

'How do you explain the accidents on the building site, then?'

'That's precisely what they were. Accidents. Nothing more. There's nothing sinister about them.'

'Two men died.'

'That was unfortunate. You have no proof to support any . . . occult links.'

'But the murders have a basis in ritual, you have to agree with that. A ritual which could apply equally to witchcraft or to Celtic sacrifice. And the kidnappings too. Children are or were used in both Celtic ceremonies *and* the Black Mass.'

Macready sucked in a deep breath.

'No, I'm sorry, Wallace,' he said. 'I can't accept that

there's a supernatural element involved here.'

'Well then, if you won't do anything about it, at least let me. I *do* care if those kids are killed.'

'One more word out of you and you're suspended. I mean it.' Macready pointed an angry finger.

Wallace sucked hard on his cigarette, locking stares with the older man for a moment.

'From now on you do everything by the book, got it?' Macready continued. 'You report to me, you don't do anything without my say-so. You step out of line once more and you're finished.'

The inspector took one last drag on his cigarette, then ground it out in the ashtray next to his superior.

'I'm going to drive around, if that's OK, sir,' he said sarcastically. 'Perhaps I can help the men who are looking for the children.'

'Keep away from Cooper and Dexter,' Macready warned him. 'They'll be brought in for questioning when, and if, we find enough real evidence to link them to this case. Understood?'

Wallace nodded, turned and left.

Outside the office he looked at the door, as if glaring through the wood itself at his superior beyond.

'Bastard,' he hissed.

He headed out towards his car.

It was 12:08.

Fifty-Seven

'Come on, come on.'

Mick Ferguson tapped on the wall agitatedly as he waited for the phone to be picked up at the other end. He waited a full minute, finally tiring of the persistent ringing in his ear. He slammed the receiver down, waited a moment, then tried again. This time he only had to wait a few seconds.

'Dexter?' he snapped.

'This is Henry Dexter,' the voice on the other end informed him.

'Where the fuck have you been? I've been ringing for the last half hour,' Ferguson snapped. 'Do you want this stuff I've got or not?'

'Of course I want it, but don't come to the house.'

'Bollocks,' the other man interrupted. 'I've got two kilos here, I want to unload it quick. I'm coming straight out there now.' He paused for a moment. 'And by the way, Dexter, it's going to cost you £3,000 for this little lot. You could say my supply's about to dry up. The bloke I bought it off was collared by the law yesterday.'

'Will they be able to trace his contacts?' Dexter asked, apprehensively.

'Do you think I'd have touched the stuff if I thought they could?' Ferguson added scornfully and put the phone down. He turned to see his wife standing in the sitting room doorway. 'I've got to go out,' he told her.

'More business,' she said. 'I overheard.' The anger in her voice turned to something akin to pleading as she approached Ferguson. 'Mick, just dump the heroin. If the law find you with it they'll lock us both up. What with that and those bloody dogs.'

'Get out of the way,' Ferguson snapped, trying to push past her, but she grabbed his arm.

'No, you bastard. You're not dragging me down with you. I'll ring the law myself, tell them it was you. I'll tell them what's been going on.'

Ferguson eyed her malevolently for a second.

'You wouldn't dare,' he hissed.

'Wouldn't I?'

She took a step towards the phone.

Out of the corner of her eye she saw her husband lunge forward, but before she could avoid his flailing arms, he was upon her.

223

Wallace reached for the packet of Rothmans on the parcel shelf of the car, cursing when he found that it was empty. He tossed the empty pack out of the window, startled when the radio crackled into life, the message coming across in metallic tones:

' . . . Respond . . . We've had a call about a disturbance at number twenty-five Victoria Road . . . check it out, will you . . .'

He listened for a moment longer, then picked up the handset.

'Base, this is Wallace, over.'

The man at the other end sounded somewhat startled to hear his superior's voice.

'Oh, hello, guv, it's Dayton here,' he said.

'I know who it is, Bill. Look, what's this about a disturbance in Victoria Road?'

'Some woman rang up about ten minutes ago, reckons she heard screaming.'

'Who's the occupant of number twenty-five?'

'Mick Ferguson and his wife.'

'I pulled that bastard about six months ago for GBH but he got off. Have you sent a car? Well, I'll cover it too.' He replaced the handset and put his foot down.

He was less than ten minutes from Victoria Road.

Fifty-Eight

The woman was on her knees in front of the house.

As Terry Laidlaw brought the police car to a halt close to her, he could see that the blouse she wore was ripped in several places. One flap hung open to reveal her left breast. She turned briefly, and in that split second Laidlaw saw the blood which covered her face.

'Jesus,' he muttered, clambering out of the car.

Constable Roy Denton followed him toward the woman who they now knew was Carol Ferguson.

She seemed oblivious to their presence as they approached her, her eyes never leaving the house before which she knelt. The blouse she wore was also stained with blood, and as the two policemen drew nearer they could see vicious gashes on her face. One eye was swollen and surrounded by blackened, puffy flesh. It looked as if it had been pumped up. A repulsive, throbbing balloon.

Her nose had been broken; the bone was shattered and the flesh misshapen.

As the two policemen drew level with Carol they heard her muttering to herself, the words forced out through lips which were split and weeping blood.

'Bastard,' she mumbled. 'Bloody bastard.'

Denton knelt beside her, slipping one hand beneath her arm to help her up.

'Come on, love,' he said, quietly.

'Get off me,' she rasped, twisting loose. Then she suddenly seemed to find untapped reserves of strength. She dragged herself upright and bellowed towards the house.

'Some man you are. You're a fucking animal just like those bloody dogs you keep.'

'Let's get her into the car,' Denton said to his companion and they took one arm each and tried to guide her towards the waiting vehicle.

'Come on, now,' Laidlaw said, urging the defiant woman to move.

'Leave me,' she hissed, turning to face him, forcing him to look upon the hideous extent of her injuries.

Her features were little more than a crimson mask. A patchwork of cuts and bruises. The constable also noticed several angry red marks on her throat.

'I'm going to call a doctor for you,' the constable said, using all his strength to guide the injured woman towards the car as she still resisted. Denton asked if he needed help but the other man shook his head.

Both men turned as the Sierra skidded to a halt about ten yards away.

Wallace jumped out and strode over to the waiting men. He took a brief look at the battered face of Carol Ferguson and shook his head.

'Is Ferguson still inside?' he wanted to know.

Before either of the uniformed men could answer, the inspector had set off towards the front door. Denton followed him.

'You cover the back,' he told the constable. 'If Ferguson comes out, flatten him.'

The constable looked surprised.

'Lay him out,' Wallace repeated. 'Because you can be bloody sure he won't hesitate to deck you if he gets the chance. Give me five minutes. If he hasn't come out by then, *you* come in. Right?'

Denton nodded, then disappeared around the side of the house.

Wallace banged three times on the front door and waited.

There was no response.

He didn't try a second time.

Wrapping his handkerchief around one fist he smashed one of the glass panels of the front door, hurriedly fumbling for the key which would unlock it. He twisted the key and hurled the door open, stepping into the long, narrow hallway.

Ahead of him was the staircase, to his left the sitting room, to his right a white door, firmly closed.

In the momentary silence, Wallace heard frenzied barking and it took him only a second to realize that it was coming from below. From the cellar.

He tugged at the white door, surprised when it opened so easily.

The heavy bulk of Mick Ferguson came hurtling through the door, ducked low, catching Wallace in the midriff. Both men crashed into the sitting room, toppling over a coffee table and upending a standard lamp as they struggled.

Wallace, despite being taken by surprise, managed to bring his knee up hard between his attacker's legs and Ferguson groaned in pain, rolling off.

The inspector struggled to his feet, his hand closing around the leg of a small stool.

As Ferguson rose the policeman swung the stool like a club and caught the bigger man across the shoulder with it. It broke apart in his hand and he was left holding the one leg. Hefting it before him like a truncheon he steadied himself for his opponent's next attack. This time, the bigger man ducked beneath the swing and drove a fist into Wallace's stomach, winding him, the impact propelling him back over a chair.

Before he could react, Ferguson was upon him, both ham-hock hands grasping the policeman's throat, the thumbs pressing into the windpipe. He found himself looking up into a face which was distorted into a mask of sheer rage.

Wallace struck out with his left hand, driving two fingers into his attacker's eyes.

As Ferguson screamed in pain, Wallace tore the large hands from his neck and rolled to one side, scrambling to his feet. The bigger man struggled to rise, but the policeman kicked him hard in the side, hearing the sharp crack of breaking ribs. Ferguson went down in a sprawling heap, clutching his injured side, and Wallace saw him spit blood. A second later he was up again, lashing out wildly, catching the inspector across the face with a backhand swipe that split his bottom lip. Blood spilled down his chin, and for precious seconds white stars danced before his eyes.

The lapse was enough to give Ferguson the upper hand.

He launched himself at Wallace, knocking him back into the hall, slamming him up against the wall with a bone-jarring thud. As the policeman slid to the floor Ferguson drove the toe of his boot into his stomach twice in quick succession, then tore open the front door and prepared to flee.

He cursed as he saw Laidlaw running towards him.

Ferguson ducked back into the house, wrenched open the white door and bolted down into the cellar.

Wallace struggled upright, helped by Laidlaw, and both men hurried after their quarry, struck by the foul smell as they entered the cellar.

Now they heard the barking of the dogs, echoing around the subterranean room until it was deafening.

In the gloom, Wallace saw Ferguson over by the two cages, fumbling with the lock which held the black dog firmly behind bars.

Laidlaw ran at the bigger man, apparently unaware of what was about to happen. Wallace's restraining arm wasn't enough to halt him.

The cage door swung open.

Jaws open wide, long streamers of saliva dripping from them, the pit bull terrier bounded forward, snarling madly.

As Laidlaw opened his mouth to scream, the dog launched itself at him.

Fifty-Nine

The cellar had become a madhouse.

Shouts from the men mingled with the frenzied barking and growling of the dogs in a deafening cacophony.

The black dog crashed into Laidlaw, and as he raised both arms to protect his face, it clamped its jaws over his right forearm, shaking its head back and forth frenziedly as if the arm were a rabbit. With horror the policeman felt the material of his tunic tearing, and an instant later the sharp teeth found his flesh.

The skin and muscle were shredded as easily as by a meat grinder and the taste of the blood which jetted from the wounds inflamed the ravenous dog further. It jerked its head away and struck at the policeman's unprotected stomach, tearing through his clothing until it reached his midriff. He screamed in pain and fear as he felt the sharp teeth gnawing at him and grabbed desperately at the beast's head.

Laidlaw succeeded in grasping the beast by the ears and dragging its head up by sheer force, but he knew that he wouldn't be able to hold on forever. The brute twisted and writhed in his grip, its fetid breath strong in his face as it struggled to snap at the hands which held it.

Wallace, after fighting his way past Ferguson, now dashed across and drove a powerful kick into the animal's side, almost grinning as he heard bones splinter under the impact. The dog rolled over, then came hurtling back at Laidlaw, as if sensing which was the weaker of the two men. This time he could not raise his arms in time and its snapping jaws closed over one of his ears like the sprung blades of a man-trap, severing the fleshy appendage with ease.

The dog swallowed the severed ear and came at the policeman once more.

He was moaning in pain, one hand clapped to the place where his ear had been. Now there was just a ragged hole which pumped crimson down the side of his face. Some hair had also come away, torn from the roots to leave a bloodied bald patch above the hole.

The bull terrier skidded on some blood and this time only succeeded in sinking its teeth into Laidlaw's belt.

He gripped it by the ears once again and dragged it off him, trying to hold the snapping, squirming beast at arm's length.

Wallace, meanwhile, spotted Ferguson preparing to free the other dog and made a dash for him, knocking the bigger man backwards over the second cage.

They grappled as the albino dog leapt and barked at the bars, anxious to be free of its prison, to taste blood in its mouth.

Wallace picked up one of the stainless steel trays used to store the dog's meat and swung it in a wide arc at his opponent.

There was a dull clang as it caught Ferguson full in the face, shattering his nose and causing him to stagger back, blood pouring down his face. Wallace struck again, using the side of the tray in a backhand swipe that splintered two of Ferguson's front teeth and opened a hideous gash in his upper lip.

The bigger man dropped to his knees, the barking of the dog loud in his ears. Beside the cage lay a palette knife which Ferguson used to cut up the meat and offal which he fed the beasts. In one swift movement he snatched up the weapon and lashed out at Wallace.

The broad blade caught the inspector on the thigh, slicing effortlessly through the material of his trousers and into the muscle. He winced in pain and drew back, blood running freely from the cut.

'Fucking coppers,' rasped Ferguson, moving towards the front of the cage which held the albino. His free hand fumbled for the lock while he kept the knife lowered towards Wallace.

The inspector knew he had only seconds to act.

Using the metal tray as a shield, he ran at Ferguson and managed to swing the object downwards to deflect the thrust. The knife went spinning across the floor, but Ferguson lashed out with his other hand and Wallace groaned in pain as the backhand swipe connected with his throat. He tumbled backwards, rolling close to where Laidlaw still struggled with the first dog.

The black beast had, by now, all but slipped loose of his desperate hands and it twisted its head to one side, closing its jaws on the policeman's left hand. He shrieked as the razor-sharp teeth penetrated, but fear gave him an added strength and he threw himself on top of the dog, using his free hand to rain blows down on its skull.

Still it would not release his left hand.

Wallace knew that he would never reach Ferguson before he could set the other dog free. All he could do was look around for something to defend himself with.

The bigger man slipped the lock on the albino brute's cage.

Wallace leapt to one side, his hand closing over a stout

length of wood which had been broken off from a fruit box during the struggles in the cellar.

Two long nails protruded menacingly from one end, their points rusted but razor sharp.

Ferguson threw open the door of the cage. The insane barking of the dog reached nerve-shredding heights as it flew forward as if fired from a cannon.

Wallace braced himself for the onslaught.

Ferguson gave a shout of triumph which turned suddenly into a yell of fear as the dog rounded on *him*.

The powerful beast leapt at its owner and, with one well-aimed bite, fastened its steel-trap jaws around his genitals.

Ferguson shrieked in uncontrollable agony as the white brute bit through his jeans, its teeth shearing through his scrotum and most of his penis.

With one powerful twist of its head it tore his testicles away, ripping a thick length of penis with them.

Blood erupted from the massive hole, spraying the floor beneath and also covering the dog, which merely swallowed the fleshy ovoids as if they had been boiled eggs. Blood dripped from its jaws, the smell exciting it as much as the taste.

Wallace was transfixed by the sight, watching helplessly as Ferguson screamed and dropped to his knees, both hands clutching at the torn mess between his legs, his fingers sinking into the gore-filled chasm. He was helpless as the dog attacked again, its frenzied charge knocking him onto his back.

Horrified by what he saw, Wallace reacted in the only way possible. He lashed out at the dog with the slab of wood, the two nails cutting open its right shoulder. But the animal seemed oblivious to the wound, reluctant to let go of its prey.

Its head darted forward and it snapped its jaws together around Ferguson's throat, crunching the larynx to pulp, ripping away most of the skin and muscle beneath his chin.

Huge fountains of blood burst from the severed arteries,

rising a full three feet into the air, some of the red liquid spattering Wallace. He struck out at the dog once more as it began to shake Ferguson, whose head rocked back and forth with such terrifying speed that Wallace feared the beast would rip it from his shoulders.

The animal was drenched with blood, looking as if it had just emerged from an abattoir.

The policeman struck at it again with the spiked wood, and this time the nails punctured the side of its head, almost gouging one of its watery pink eyes from the socket.

Snarling in pain, it turned on him.

Wallace swung the piece of wood again but the dog caught it between its teeth. The inspector gripped both ends, hearing the timber crack as the dog bit through it and, in horror, he hurled the two ends away, throwing himself to the blood-soaked floor in an effort to reach the knife.

As his fingers closed around the handle he felt agonizing pain shooting through his leg.

The dog had fastened its teeth in his calf, practically ham-stringing him with the ferocity of its bite. But he lashed out with his other foot and drove a piledriver kick into its face, forcing it to release its grip for precious seconds. Wallace rolled over as it launched itself at him again, teeth aimed for his throat.

He raised one arm to protect himself, and with the other struck upwards with the knife, using all the force he could muster.

The dog's jaws closed around his wrist, lacerating flesh and almost snapping the bone, but the pain was only momentary.

He drove the knife into its belly and, using all his strength, tore downwards, gutting the beast with one savage cut.

Its stomach opened and Wallace moaned in revulsion as its intestines spilled onto him like thick, reeking spaghetti. An evil smelling flux of bile and viscera splattered him and it was all he could manage to prevent himself from vomiting. The stench was unbelievable. But the grip around his wrist loosened and he managed to push the creature off, rising unsteadily to his feet, his head swimming now, pain gnawing at his arm and leg.

Laidlaw was still struggling with the first animal, still trying to force the beast to release his left hand. It took Wallace a second or two to realize that the creature was actually dead. The blows which the constable had been raining down on its head had finally succeeded in shattering the skull. His hand was coated in a sticky greyish-red porridge which Wallace realized must be the brain.

As he staggered across to the injured constable, Wallace felt his leg starting to go numb. He stumbled, then fell, sprawling alongside the dog, the knife slipping from his hand. He felt sick, his clothes sticking to him, soaked in blood.

'Oh, my God!'

He heard the voice from the top of the cellar steps and looked up to see PC Denton scuttling down, his face draining of colour as he saw the carnage before him.

Wallace exhaled almost painfully, coughing up blood which, for a moment, he thought was his own. With disgust he realized that he must have swallowed some of the albino brute's blood. The thought made him violently and uncontrollably sick and he rolled onto his side, retching until there was nothing left in his stomach.

'The ambulance is on its way,' Denton said, struggling to retain his own self-control.

'Terrific,' murmured Wallace, using his handkerchief to staunch the flow of blood from the bite on his leg.

Laidlaw had blacked out.

Sixty

The light above the worktop flickered once then went out.

Kim looked up and muttered to herself, annoyed at being plunged into darkness for long moments until the power came back on again. Outside, the wind was roaring like an enraged animal and she wondered if it had brought down a powerline somewhere in the vicinity.

The light flickered again, and this time she decided that enough was enough. She'd been at the museum since three that afternoon, having left Clare in the capable hands of Wendy Barratt, a neighbour from across the street. Now, as the hands of the clock reached 9:45, she decided to ring her home and tell Wendy she was on her way.

Kim had spent most of her time at the museum carefully packing and labelling the stone tablets and skulls as well as the scores of other relics which she'd examined over the past couple of weeks. Now they were all secure in wooden boxes. She wondered what would become of them and the other relics found at the dig now that work there had ceased. That decision would be up to Charles Cooper, but her attempts to contact him throughout the evening had proved futile.

She gazed at the box containing the tablets, her eyes narrowing slightly. Although Kim had sealed it herself, one corner looked loose, as if it had been prised open slightly with a chisel. She picked up the hammer which lay nearby and banged each nail twice to ensure that the lid was adequately fixed on, then she returned to the staff room and picked up the phone, dialling her own number. She waited for the receiver to be picked up.

The wind shrieked around the building.

She waited.

Finally she pressed down the cradle, waited a moment, then dialled again.

The ringing tone sounded loudly once more.

Twice. Three times.

No answer.

Kim tapped on the worktop with her index finger, waiting.

Waiting.

The lights suddenly went out and, as they did, there was a tremendous hiss of static from the phone, so loud that she held the receiver away from her ear.

The line was dead.

Kim dropped it back onto the cradle, cursing the storm. She bumped her shin on the stool as she turned, waiting for the lights to come back on.

It was a full minute before brightness once more flooded the room.

She rubbed her eyes as the fluorescents flashed on, illuminating the staff room and the laboratory beyond it. Kim swallowed hard and took a step into the other room, her eyes fixed on the box which held the stone tablets.

There was a pungent odour in the air, like burnt wood, and she waved a hand before her as she moved into the lab, her breath coming in short gasps.

The lid of the box lay on the floor, the nails twisted and bent.

As if the lid had been torn free with great force.

There were dark patches on the lid and sides of the box.

Like burn marks.

Sixty-One

The house was in darkness.

Kim brought the car to a halt, pulling up the collar of her jacket as she climbed out, shivering as the wind swirled around her.

Perhaps some power lines actually had come down. Maybe that was why not one single light burned in her house. She approached the front door glancing to her right and left. The houses on either side were both well lit, and the street lamps too were on.

Why was it only *her* house which remained in darkness?

She fumbled in her pocket and pulled out the key, turning it quickly, walking into the hallway.

The house was as quiet as a grave. The only sound Kim heard was her own muted breathing as she pushed open the sitting room door, reaching for the light switch.

The lights came on instantly.

The television set was on too, but the sound was turned off.

On the nearby coffee table was a mug of tea. Full but cold.

'Wendy,' she called, wondering where the child-minder had got to.

Kim moved through to the kitchen, flicking on that light too. The fluorescent sputtered into life, bathing the room in a cold white glow.

'Wendy,' Kim said again, softly, her voice almost a whisper.

She felt the first twinge of fear then. As if cold hands were being placed on her back and neck.

236

She turned and headed through the sitting room, towards the hall and the stairs. She tried the light at the bottom but it merely flickered once, then went out.

The staircase remained in darkness.

Kim began to climb slowly, her eyes never leaving the black-shrouded landing.

'Clare,' she called, feeling a much stronger fear now.

Was her daughter alone in the house?

There was no answer.

'Clare!'

Still nothing.

She reached the landing and paused before her daughter's room.

There was a dark stain on the white paintwork of the doorframe, visible in the dull sodium glare from the street lights which penetrated the landing window.

Kim froze, her hand shaking as it hovered near the dark smear.

She touched it and almost screamed.

It was blood.

The smell was unmistakable.

From inside her daughter's room there was a thud, followed by a low moan.

Kim gritted her teeth until her jaws ached; then, bracing herself, she flung open the door, her shaking hand reaching for the light switch. She felt more of the sticky fluid on the switch. The light came on, and she saw that there was blood on the walls, too. And on the sheets, which had been ripped away from the bed.

Of her daughter there was no sign, but huddled in one corner of the room was a crumpled shape which she recognized as Wendy Barratt.

Kim rushed to the other woman who, she now saw, was bleeding badly from two savage wounds on her head. One of them, just above the right ear, seemed to be the worst of the two. The other had almost laid open her forehead, though, and blood had poured down her face and into her eyes.

'Wendy, can you hear me?' Kim said, frantically,

squatting beside the injured woman. 'Who did this to you?'

Wendy could only look at her with eyes full of fear and pain and gently shake her head.

'Did you see who it was?'

'No,' she croaked, her eyes widening as she saw the amount of blood she was losing.

'Where's Clare?' Kim demanded.

'Oh God, I'm hurt badly. Get an ambulance.'

'Where's Clare?' Kim rasped.

'I don't know.'

Kim felt her stomach contract.

'Who took her?' she demanded, her concern for the injured woman now secondary to her fear for her daughter. 'Who took her, Wendy? You have to remember, please.' Her voice had risen close to a shout. Unable to help herself, she shook Wendy. 'Who took her?'

'I didn't see who it was.'

With one despairing moan the woman blacked out.

'Oh God,' Kim gasped, scrambling to her feet, blundering down the stairs, almost stumbling at the bottom. She crashed into the sitting room, tears brimming in her eyes. Tears of desperation and fear.

She snatched up the phone, praying that it hadn't been cut off, almost crying out loud when she heard the dial tone.

With shaking hands she dialled Longfield police station.

Sixty-Two

From the time she put the phone down until the time the ambulance screeched to a halt outside her house, each minute seemed an eternity to Kim Nichols.

She'd sat with Wendy, holding the woman's hand as she

burbled incoherently, occasionally drifting off into unconsciousness. Throughout that time, Kim's only thoughts had been for her kidnapped daughter. Fear and foreboding such as she'd never experienced before filled her. When the emergency vehicle and its stricken cargo had finally left she'd begun pacing the floor.

Now, as she heard the squeal of tyres from outside, she dashed to open the front door.

Wallace hauled himself from the Sierra and sprinted up the path towards her, ignoring the pain from his injured leg.

'It's Clare,' she blurted. 'She's been taken.'

'Come on,' the policeman said, unhesitatingly, beckoning her towards the car.

She looked puzzled.

'Kim,' he said, a note of urgency in his voice as he slipped back behind the wheel and re-started the engine.

She clambered into the passenger seat and the car sped off.

As the inspector glanced across at her he could see that her eyes were puffy and red-rimmed from crying. He tried to coax some more details from her, and tears began to course down her face. He squeezed her hand tightly.

'We'll find her,' he said.

'She could already be dead,' Kim said, wiping the tears from her eyes with a sodden handkerchief.

Wallace didn't answer.

The streets of Longfield seemed strangely deserted as Wallace guided the car towards its destination. Here and there street lamps had gone out, adding further darkness to the gloom which already seemed to hang over the town like a blanket.

The lamp outside Charles Cooper's house burned brightly, though, and Kim looked up in surprise as she saw where they were. Wallace was already out of the car and heading towards the front door when Kim scuttled after him.

'Why would Charles take her?' she wanted to know, aghast at the prospect of her colleague being a kidnapper.

'He would have known about Dagda, wouldn't he?'

239

Wallace said. 'About the need for sacrifices.'

Kim swallowed hard and watched as the inspector banged hard on the front door.

There was no answer.

The house remained in darkness, silent and defiant.

Wallace hurried around to the back of the building, Kim following breathlessly. Without waiting he drove one foot hard again the back door, hearing wood splinter under the impact.

'What if you're wrong?' she asked.

'Then I'm wrong,' he rasped, using even more power against the barrier. It swung back on its hinges and crashed against the wall. Wallace stepped inside, moving quickly through the kitchen, flicking on lights as he went.

The smell reached him as he came to the sitting room.

A cloying odour which he thought he recognized.

He slowed his pace, moving more quietly now, listening for any sounds of movement from upstairs. Kim followed, her heart thudding against her ribs as they began to climb the stairs. This time Wallace did not turn the light on. They climbed in darkness, one of the steps creaking in protest, the sound echoing through the silent house.

The smell was getting stronger.

He paused as they reached the landing, peering into the gloom, trying to make out the dark shape ahead.

Kim stifled a gasp.

The inspector fumbled for the light switch at the top of the stairs and the sixty-watt bulb burst into life.

This time Kim screamed.

Dangling by his neck from the attic trapdoor was Charles Cooper.

The step ladder which he had used to climb up lay beneath him, kicked aside before he jumped. Wallace approached the body, reaching out to touch the cold, rigored flesh. He ran appraising eyes over the corpse, trying to ignore the smell as he stood close by.

Cooper's eyes bulged in their sockets, the flesh beneath them blackened, the skin of his cheeks as white as milk. He'd obviously been dead for some time, thought the

240

inspector. The rope was thin and poorly suited for the job. It had cut deeply into the archaeologist's neck, drawing blood which had caked hard over the hemp itself. There was no knot at the back of the neck. Cooper had probably choked to death. Dark stains at the front and back of his trousers had dried stiffly and Wallace saw a puddle of stale urine beneath the body. A swollen tongue protruded from his mouth like a bloated leech.

Wallace exhaled deeply and looked around at Kim, who was standing at the top of the stairs, her gaze lowered slightly.

It took the policeman a second or two to spot the piece of paper sticking out of Cooper's trouser pocket. He pulled it free and unrolled it. Kim looked up as he began to read the note aloud:

'I realize that suicide is the coward's way out, or so they say, but it takes more strength than anyone knows to take your own life. I know I am going to die soon. We all will.'

Wallace frowned, looked at Kim, then continued reading:

'No one would have believed me anyway if I'd told them what I had discovered in the chamber of skulls. I knew how to stop this horror, how to prevent it, but I could not bring myself to take the lives of children. Someone else may have seen the writing on the wall of the chamber. If so, then I pray that he has the strength. I am sorry for the children but there is no other way. If there is a God, let him help us all. The children in the chamber must die but I cannot do it. When the end comes I don't want to see it.'

Wallace folded the note and slipped it into his pocket.

'Jesus,' he murmured. 'Come on.' He gripped Kim's arm and together they hurried down the stairs.

'If Cooper couldn't kill the children then he might have an accomplice,' Kim said as Wallace snatched up the phone from the hall table. He dialled and waited for the receiver to be picked up at the other end.

It was finally answered and he recognized Sergeant Dayton's voice.

'Listen to me, Bill,' he snapped. 'This is Wallace. I want a car sent to Dexter Grange now. If the men can't find Dexter there, then tell them to search that wood nearby.'

'But guv,' the sergeant began.

'Don't argue with me,' Wallace rasped. 'Do it. I also want another car to meet me at the archaeological site in twenty minutes. Got that?'

'I can't do that. The Chief Inspector told me to disregard any orders you gave me,' Dayton protested.

Wallace gripped the receiver so tightly it seemed he would snap it in two.

'Fuck Macready. Just do it. Do what I tell you, Bill, please. *I think I know where those kids are.*'

There was a moment's silence at the other end.

'Did you hear me?' he repeated.

'The cars are on their way, guv.'

Wallace managed a small grin of triumph. He told the sergeant to send an ambulance to 12 Elm Street but didn't say why and, before Dayton could ask, Wallace had replaced the receiver.

He and Kim dashed out to the waiting Sierra.

.

Sixty-Three

'And don't forget, make it convincing,' said Gary Webb. 'Dexter's no fool.'

'What if something goes wrong?' Laura Price wanted to know.

'It won't,' he assured her, raising a hand for silence when he heard footsteps in the corridor outside the room. A second later Henry Dexter entered the room. He looked closely at his two young companions, particularly Laura, who was lying on the leather sofa with both legs drawn up to her chest, her face contorted.

'She's strung out,' Gary said. 'She needs some stuff now.'

Dexter eyed Gary for a moment and the youngster found that he couldn't hold the older man's gaze.

Laura moaned softly and rubbed at the crook of her left arm.

'Please, Henry,' she said, sucking in a sharp breath as she feigned a contraction that made her wince.

Like a doctor, the older man crossed to the sofa and sat down on the edge, looking at Laura impassively, brushing a strand of hair from her face. She squirmed beneath his gaze and closed her eyes in mock pain, waiting until he got up once more and crossed the room towards the wall safe where the heroin was kept. Gary edged closer to the mantelpiece, one eye on the ornamental dagger which hung above it.

'Open it,' he said, swallowing hard as Dexter turned to look at him.

The older man hesitated.

'What would you do with all this heroin?' he asked. 'Sell it? Use it yourselves? And the money? How would you spend that?'

'Just open the safe,' snapped Gary.

Dexter grinned broadly.

'Subtlety was never one of your strong points, was it, Gary?' he said, the grin fading. 'I wondered how long it would take for you to try this.'

Gary snatched the dagger from the wall and moved towards the older man.

'Open that fucking safe now. I don't want to hurt you but I will if I have to,' he rasped.

Laura sat up and looked anxiously at the two men.

'And if you kill me, who's going to open the safe?' Dexter asked, fixing the youth in a cold stare. 'Put that knife down before I use it on *you*.'

Gary took another step forward, the blade glinting wickedly.

Dexter braced his foot against the coffee table nearby and kicked out, sending the object skidding towards Gary. It slammed into his shins, the suddenness of the assault causing him to lose balance. Dexter was on him in an instant, one hand grabbing for the knife.

Laura screamed as the two of them grappled. She leapt up off the sofa, moving towards the fireplace, her hand reaching for the poker which stood beside it.

Gary, despite being at a disadvantage, managed to turn the blade on his attacker and Dexter grunted as he felt the cold steel cut into his forearm. He slammed Gary's hand down hard against the floor and the knife skidded from the youth's grip. Blood from the cut ran down Dexter's arm as he reached for the boy's throat and fastened both hands around it, squeezing hard. Gary first gripped his assailant's wrists and then, unable to relieve the pressure on his throat, struck out at Dexter's face with a punch which sent him sprawling sideways. Gary leapt to his feet, his eye on the knife, but the older man swung his left foot and kicked the youth's legs out from under him.

He fell forward heavily, cracking his head on the floor, stunned by the impact.

Dexter leapt on him, one knee pressed between the lad's shoulder blades while he slipped both hands beneath his chin and tugged his head back. Gary could feel unbelievable pressure on his neck and spine and he actually felt the muscles tearing. Another moment or two and Dexter would break his spine.

Laura, galvanized into action by this sight, lunged forward and brought the poker down with bone-crushing force onto the back of Dexter's head, opening a large gash on his scalp. The loud crack of bone filled the room and the older man sagged forward, collapsing onto Gary, who tried to roll free. Laura helped him shift the motionless form of Dexter and then supported him as he got to his feet. Gary took the poker from her and aimed a blow at the combination lock of the safe. The metal rod sang off it and vibrated in his hand, so he struck again. And again.

It wouldn't budge.

Behind them, his head throbbing from the powerful

blow, Dexter began to crawl towards the momentarily forgotten dagger.

Gary struck the safe again, desperation now aiding his efforts. Laura looked on anxiously, both of them too intent on their task to see that Dexter had reached the knife and was dragging himself upright.

Still the safe door would not give and Gary paused for a moment, his breath coming in gasps, the pain at the back of his neck growing with each movement.

It was Laura who heard the sounds from behind them.

She screamed as she saw Dexter run at Gary, his face a mask of rage.

The warning came too late and Gary turned only to take the knife-thrust in the stomach.

He felt as if he'd been punched, the wind knocked from him. Dexter dragged the blade free and drove it home with even greater ferocity, up under the boy's sternum, feeling it grate against bone as he tugged the bloodied weapon out, ripping open the upper part of Gary's torso in the process. He gripped his victim by the hair, powering more knife strokes home with ferocious strength.

Blood splattered the floor as Gary began to sag to his knees. As he fell, Dexter drove the knife forward once more. The blade tore into his open mouth, slicing through gums and tongue before bursting from the base of his skull.

Laura screamed once more and jumped at Dexter, scratching at his eyes, forcing him to drop the knife. Her desperate fingers found the hilt and, with a blow that owed more to luck than judgement, she brought the knife down with terrifying force, driving it through Dexter's left eye, pressing down on the hilt until she felt the blade puncture the floor beneath.

The dying man screamed in agony and writhed helplessly, held firm by the blade through his eye, blood shooting from the wound like crimson rain.

She collapsed, sobbing, between the two bodies, looking up at the door of the safe.

It had swung open, revealing the money and the heroin inside.

Laura smiled bitterly through her sobs, looking at the

bags of white powder, smelling the stench of death all around her.

Seconds later, she heard the loud knocking on the front door.

Sixty-Four

As Wallace swung the Sierra around the corner of the road he could see the police car already parked across the entrance to the field leading up to the archaeological site.

One of the two uniformed men was caught in the glow of the Sierra's headlamps as he stood urinating into the long grass.

Neither Kim nor Wallace paid him any heed.

The nearest of the two policemen crossed to Wallace's car and looked in at the inspector.

'How long have you been here?' the inspector asked.

'A couple of minutes, sir,' Buchanan told him.

'Right. Follow me up to the site. Get that bloody car out of the way.' He jabbed a finger at the panda car and Buchanan signalled to his colleague, Kendall, to move it. The constable reversed leaving a clear path.

'A message just came through from the other car,' Buchanan said. 'They found Dexter in his house. He'd been killed.'

Wallace chewed his lip contemplatively, listening as Buchanan recounted the details. Then the inspector nodded and pressed down on his accelerator.

'Follow me,' he instructed and the constable sprinted back to the waiting police car.

Both vehicles skidded over the uneven ground, the wheels of the Sierra spinning as they reached the crest of the rise. The headlamps cut through the darkness, illuminating the rope barrier which was around the entrance to the shaft.

Wallace swung himself out of the car, snatching a torch from the glove compartment in the process. Kim joined him along with the two uniformed men.

'Kendall, you stay up top,' Wallace said. 'If we're not back here in thirty minutes you'd better get help.'

Kim took the policeman's torch from him and looked at Wallace.

'I'm going with you,' she said determinedly.

Wallace thought about protesting but finally merely nodded his agreement. He turned towards the rope ladder which dropped away into the black abyss.

'Thirty minutes,' said Kendall, checking his watch.

Wallace nodded.

They began to descend.

It was 11:32.

Sixty-Five

The torch beam was swallowed up by the murky blackness, unable to penetrate the tenebrous depths for more than a few feet.

Wallace finally switched it off, jamming it into his belt, leaving two hands free to grip the rope ladder. He shivered as he climbed down, the icy air searing his throat, filling his chest so that it was difficult to breathe. He moved with agonizing slowness, as if unable to coax any more speed out of his legs. Already he felt as if he'd run twenty miles. His muscles were throbbing with the effort of the climb although, he guessed, they couldn't have been on the ladder more than a couple of minutes.

Above him, moving just as cautiously, Kim and Buchanan clambered downward.

The inspector gritted his teeth. Trying to push through the darkness was like fighting against a solid object. He grunted loudly, the sound bouncing back off the walls of the shaft. He pulled the torch from his belt and shone it down into the depths.

The beam glinted off something metallic and he realized that they had almost reached the bottom.

He tried to move quicker but the effort was beyond him.

The air itself seemed thick and oppressive. Unclean, he thought.

As he reached the bottom a particularly noxious odour reached him for the first time, a dank, cloying stench which seemed to float about like invisible tendrils, filling his nostrils and lungs until he thought he was going to be sick.

Kim jumped down beside him. Then the two of them were joined by Buchanan who also coughed as he drew breath and smelled the rank scent.

'What the hell is that?' he croaked, dragging a handkerchief from his pocket to cover his face. But even the fabric couldn't mask the fetor, such was its intensity.

Wallace shone his torch over the floor of the shaft, the beam picking out many relics left behind by the archaeologists. Spears, swords, torcs, the odd piece of pottery.

But there was something which *didn't* belong.

On the tall pointed stake which formed the centrepiece of the pit was a piece of fabric. Clean and new.

Wallace pulled it free and turned it over in his palm.

It was brushed cotton.

The sort of fabric that might be used to make a child's dressing gown or similar garment.

Kim took the fragment from him, her hand shaking slightly.

She said nothing, merely followed Wallace as he

advanced towards the first tunnel entrance, his torch cutting a path through the blackness.

The smell remained as strong as ever.

They moved quickly, sure-footedly through the tunnel until they came to a fork.

The two tunnels yawned like hungry mouths and Wallace exhaled deeply, his breath forming a white fog in the freezing air.

'We should split up,' said Kim.

'No,' Wallace whispered. 'If the murderer *is* down here we're better off together.'

'But it could take all night to search these tunnels. We haven't got all night,' Kim reminded him, clutching the piece of fabric. 'I know these tunnels. Let me search that one.' She pointed to the stone corridor on the right.

Wallace shook his head.

'Buchanan. *You* search it. If you find anything, shout. If you hear me, then come running. Meet us back here in twenty minutes.'

The young constable swallowed hard, his face, already drained of colour, looked sickly yellow in the reflected beam of the torch. He hesitated a moment, then nodded uncertainly and headed for the opening. Wallace watched as his torch beam slowly disappeared, consumed by the darkness.

'Come on,' he whispered to Kim, and they too pressed on, down the left-hand tunnel.

Wallace had his right hand outstretched, feeling his way along the walls. He suddenly recoiled as his fingers slipped into something wet and slimy. The putrescent moss stuck to the policeman's fingers like noxious porridge. The stench was unbelievable. They moved on, treading carefully now over piles of bones and more relics.

There was another tunnel immediately to the left.

An icy breeze was blowing from it, further lowering the already sub-zero temperatures in the tunnels. Wallace was convinced, anyway, that it must be below freezing. His hands and face felt numb and he only forced himself to continue walking by a supreme effort of will.

He passed the tunnel entrance, the torch flickering as he reached the other side.

'Shit,' he murmured, shaking the light, cursing when the bulb failed completely, plunging them into total blackness.

'Kim,' he whispered. 'Give me your torch.'

No answer.

'Kim.'

The silence was as total as the gloom.

He reached out a hand behind him, trying to touch her.

His fingers clutched only empty air.

The policeman banged his torch on the tunnel wall, and to his surprise it came back on, flooding the narrow stone passageway with light, momentarily driving back the dark. He turned and shone the torch behind him.

Kim had gone.

He was alone in the tunnel.

It was then that he heard the sound ahead of him.

Sixty-Six

For interminable seconds Wallace froze, unsure of what to do.

Should he go back and look for Kim?

The muffled sound from ahead came again, distracting him once more.

He frowned, trying to make out what the sound was. It was muted. A soft, almost asthmatic wheezing punctuated by low moans.

'Kim,' he whispered again, shining the torch into the secondary tunnel. She must have stepped down there.

She'd told him she knew the network of underground walkways. Perhaps she knew a quicker route.

But to where?

The children?

The murderer?

Wallace shuddered and moved on, the sound ahead of him growing louder, then suddenly dying away. Only the silence remained. He paused again, his heart thudding just that little bit faster, then, gripping the heavy torch like a weapon, he moved on.

Constable Mark Buchanan pressed himself close to the wall of the tunnel and advanced slowly, ears and eyes alert for the slightest sound or movement. Despite the numbing cold below ground he could feel a thin film of perspiration forming on his forehead. His breath was coming in short gasps even though he struggled to control it. The smell which had filled the tunnels from the outset seemed to be growing worse, if that was possible. Buchanan slowed his pace even more, also trying to breathe through his mouth to lessen the effect of the noxious air.

He heard movement behind him.

Buchanan turned quickly, shining the torch in the direction of the sound.

The beam quivered from the shaking of his hand as he tried to pick out the source of the noise.

The silence was thunderous, the rushing of blood in his ears like a tidal wave.

He could see nothing.

For what seemed an age he stood there, and then, very slowly, he moved on. Every few paces he would turn and point the torch over his shoulder. Just in case someone was following him. He tried to tell himself that his imagination was playing tricks but the thought did not ease his mind. Fear continued to grip him, steadily squeezing tighter.

There was movement behind him again.

This time he spun round in time to see some small rocks toppling from a ledge in the side of the tunnel. They fell to the ground with a sharp crack and Buchanan breathed a sigh of relief as he realized he must have dislodged them himself.

Or had he?

He still wasn't completely satisfied with his own explanation. It did little to calm his already tattered nerves. However, it was all he had and he clung to it as a drowning man would cling to a piece of driftwood. He *wanted* to believe that the falling stones were all he'd heard if only his mind would let him.

As he moved on he found that the tunnel was beginning to curve to the left.

He stopped and glanced over his shoulder again, then walked on.

He heard another noise.

This one came from ahead of him.

An almost imperceptible mewling sound. A stealthy murmur.

Buchanan frowned.

The sound came again.

He moved on.

Whatever was making the noise, Wallace decided, was closer than he'd first thought. What he couldn't figure out was why it was so muffled.

He shone the torch ahead of him, watching as the beam bounced off the rough stonework. Bones crunched beneath his feet, causing him to wince. If anyone was up ahead, they would hear him coming. He stood still for a moment. Listening.

The noise ahead continued. Low, beckoning.

His flesh was crawling.

The atmosphere inside the tunnel had also changed. Almost impossibly, it had become still more oppressive until he felt as if he were literally pushing against the darkness and the cold as he walked. They sucked the strength from him as surely as invisible parasites. But he fought it, battled the urge to lean back against the wall and rest. He forced himself to continue, the sound ahead acting as a guide.

Or was it bait?

Wallace suddenly had the uncomfortable feeling that he was walking into a trap, but he rapidly shook the thought away, more intent on finding the source of the strange sound.

Beneath him he heard, and felt, a low rumble.

The ground vibrated for long seconds and the policeman shot out a hand to steady himself, only to find that the walls of the tunnel were also shuddering slightly. Several fragments of stone fell from the tunnel roof and Wallace tried to shield his head as they rained down around him.

He struggled to retain his balance as the ground beneath him throbbed menacingly.

The tremor stopped as suddenly as it had started.

Wallace stood motionless, stunned by the unexpected event, waiting to see if there were any more earth movements. The tunnels were stable as far as he knew. There had been no mention of subsidence. But if the whole network should collapse . . .He let the thought trail off, not allowing himself to dwell on the idea of being buried beneath tons of rock and earth.

He wondered where Kim and Buchanan had got to.

They must have felt the tremor too.

Perhaps both had left the labyrinthine tunnels at the threat of collapse.

Perhaps they were waiting at the bottom of the shaft for him to emerge.

Perhaps the killer had found them first.

He swallowed hard and pressed on more cautiously, his torch beam picking out something ahead.

The disembodied moaning sound came again, louder. Wallace realized that he was close to its source. Very close.

He saw the stone slab.

He saw the piles of skulls inside the chamber.

He felt the cold breeze from another secondary tunnel, this time to his right, as he drew nearer the chamber, shining his torch inside, allowing the beam to move over the mounds of skulls.

Wallace took a step inside. It was clear now that the

muffled sound was within the chamber.

He didn't think to look over his shoulder.

Had he done so, he would have seen the figure approaching him.

Sixty-Seven

PC Kendall rubbed his hands together in an effort to restore some warmth to the freezing extremities. He blew on them, but to little effect.

The headlamps of the police car were still aimed at the entrance to the shaft, but he had heard nothing from Wallace and the others since they descended almost twenty minutes earlier. Leaning on the bonnet of the car, he glanced at his watch and shook his head, deciding that it would be warmer inside the car.

As he slid into the driver's seat the two-way crackled.

'Unit three, come in,' the metallic voice rasped and the constable frowned. It wasn't Sergeant Dayton's voice. The harsh tones belonged to Chief Inspector Macready.

'Unit three, come in,' the voice repeated.

Kendall reached for the radio, his hand shaking slightly. He told himself it was because of the cold.

'Unit three. Go ahead.'

'Where the hell are you?' Macready snapped.

'I'm at the archaeological dig, sir . . . '

Macready cut him short.

'Did Wallace order you there?' he demanded, already knowing the answer.

'Yes, sir.'

There was an angry silence, then Macready came on again.

'Let me speak to Wallace. Quickly.'

'He's not with me, sir. He and PC Buchanan and a woman . . .'

'What woman?' the older man demanded.

'She's one of the archaeologists, I think. The three of them climbed down into the tunnels. The inspector said he knew where the missing children were.'

'Jesus Christ!' snarled Macready, angrily. 'Listen to me. Don't move from there. I'll be over as quickly as I can. Wallace has some explaining to do.'

The radio went dead in his hand and Kendall replaced the handset. He groaned as he thought of Macready's reaction. What the hell, thought the constable, he was only doing what he'd been told. If Wallace got his head chewed off that was tough shit. Kendall knew that *he* hadn't done anything to merit a bollocking.

He glanced down at the dashboard clock and checked it off against his own watch.

11:51.

He wondered if they'd found anything yet.

Kendall was still wondering when he felt the ground begin to tremble.

He sat bolt upright in the car, looking out of the windows as the vehicle slid back a foot or so, shaken from its stable position by the minor tremor.

He heard an ominous rumbling which seemed to come from deep within the earth. The vibrations rapidly spread through the car until the whole vehicle seemed to be shuddering. The rumbling continued for no more than ten seconds, then ceased abruptly.

Kendall didn't move at first, Then, cautiously, he stepped out of the car, treading gently on the ground.

There was no more movement.

He sucked in a worried breath.

What the hell was going on?

Sixty-Eight

A rough estimate indicated that there were up to three hundred skulls in the chamber. For long moments, Wallace stood looking at them, their sightless sockets seeming to stare back at him. Then he raised his torch, allowing the beam to trace a pattern over the walls, across the ancient writings which covered the stone.

He never heard a sound from behind him.

He only felt the hand as it closed on his shoulder.

The inspector almost shouted aloud in fear, twisting around, pulling away from the hand, swinging the torch up like a club. He ducked down, ready to face the intruder, the heavy torch poised to strike.

PC Buchanan seemed as startled as his superior.

He stepped back, avoiding the impending swing of the torch, his face pale.

'It's me, guv,' he gasped.

Wallace let out a long breath and glared at the constable.

'Sorry if I startled you,' the constable said, apologetically.

'Startled me?' Wallace gasped. 'I nearly had a fucking heart attack. Why the hell couldn't you have warned me? Jesus.'

'I didn't find anything in that other tunnel,' Buchanan explained. 'But I heard a noise, like . . .well . . .like an animal. Like something trapped.'

'Yeah,' Wallace said. 'It's coming from in here.' He motioned around the chamber, trying to locate the exact point from which the sound was emanating.

'There,' the inspector said, pointing to a place beneath a pile of skulls.

The two men began removing them, throwing them aside in their haste.

The sound grew louder.

The last of the skulls was flung aside and Wallace saw that they had covered an oblong stone set into the ground.

'Help me lift this,' he said, digging his fingers under the rim.

Both of them strained for a moment, then the stone slab began to lift with surprising ease, rising like the lid of a coffin until they pushed it back against the wall and peered down into the hole below.

'My God,' murmured Buchanan.

Lying in the hole, which was roughly six feet long and four feet wide, were four children.

Each one was tightly bound. Gags had been stuffed into their mouths. Wallace studied the faces, their eyes bulging wide in fear.

Jonathan Ashton. Julie Craig. Carl Taylor.

And Clare Nichols.

The missing children.

Wallace and Buchanan lifted the children from their tomb-like prison and laid them on the ground next to the hole. Clare and one of the boys were crying, making a soft, muted mewling sound.

The two policemen untied the children, pulling the gags from their mouths. Immediately, Clare embraced the inspector, who kissed her on the cheek, pulling her close to him.

'It's all right now, sweetheart,' he said. 'All of you, it's going to be all right. We're policemen. We're going to get you out of here.' He felt another minor rumble from beneath them. His breath was now coming in gasps. 'You're going to leave now. I want you to go with the constable. Will you do that for me?'

The children agreed in a pitiful chorus of whines and sobs.

'Take them out now,' Wallace said to the other man. 'I've got to stay and find Kim.'

Buchanan hesitated.

'Go, for Christ's sake,' the inspector urged. 'There isn't much time. This whole place could come down around our ears in a minute.'

Buchanan, carrying Clare, nodded and gathered the other children around him. He felt one of them clutching the leg of his trousers as he tried to walk. He struggled on, out of the chamber.

The constable caught only a glimpse of his attacker as the shape emerged from the blackness.

He heard the air part as something heavy was swung at him, then suddenly he felt a bone-cracking impact against his right temple.

The flat of the sword smacked savagely into his head, splintering his skull and opening a cut which sent blood shooting into the freezing air.

He went down in an untidy heap, his slack arms losing their grip on Clare, who fell with him, her scream drumming in his ears as his blood splattered her.

Wallace pulled the nearest child to him, shielding it against the attacker, gripping his torch in a vain attempt to defend himself. He shone it at the face of the one who wielded the rusted blade.

Illuminated by the powerful beam, George Perry stood before him.

Sixty-Nine

'They have to die, Wallace,' the archaeologist said, flatly. 'I wish there was some other way but there isn't.' He glanced briefly at his watch.

It was 11:52.

'In eight minutes it will be too late,' Perry told him. 'Dagda will rise. Dagda, the Celtic God. The Lord of

Destruction. I read it here.' He gestured about him toward the walls of the chamber with their strange words and symbols. 'This creature, or power, whatever it is, exists. Perhaps it only exists in men's minds or perhaps it has a tangible form but it lies dormant in the earth for years at a time until it's disturbed, the way this dig disturbed it. And then, the only way to stop it is by sacrifice. At midnight on the day of Samain, unless three children are sacrificed on this spot, Dagda will rise.'

Wallace could see that he was shaking.

'We can't begin to understand the extent of the power we're dealing with, Wallace,' Perry told him. 'This thing . . . if it's allowed to rise, is unstoppable. Dagda will destroy us all. These children must die. Cooper knew that too. We spoke about it. He knew what had to be done but he was weak. It's my job now.'

'You'll never get away with this,' Wallace reminded him. 'Even if you kill me too.'

'It doesn't matter. What can they do to me? Lock me up for life. What are the lives of three children compared to so many? A drop in the ocean. It's a small price to pay to prevent such obscene evil entering our world. Entering and destroying.'

'You're insane!' Wallace shouted.

'I'd be insane if I did nothing,' the archaeologist countered.

'Why did you kill James Cutler and the others?' Wallace wanted to know.

Perry smiled crookedly.

'Cutler and the others were killed by Morrigan.'

Wallace frowned. The name rang a bell.

'The Queen of Demons,' Perry told him. 'A being able to take on the form of a human. A creature with incredible strength. She fed on the flesh of her victims. The Celts used to flay sacrificial offerings and lay the skin on the altars of Morrigan.'

'This is bullshit,' rasped Wallace, watching as Perry pulled one of the children to him, the sword poised at its throat.

'You still don't understand, do you?' Perry snarled. 'That was why I took *her* daughter. I had to bring *her* here tonight. I had to make sure *she* would come so that I could destroy her.'

'Who?' Wallace demanded.

'The Queen of Demons, the creature that killed Cutler and all the others. The one possessed by Morrigan.'

Wallace shook his head.

'No,' he murmured.

'She murdered them. Kim Nichols killed them all,' Perry told him. 'Or at least what once was Kim Nichols. Morrigan has found a new host body now. She was safe inside Kim until I discovered the truth in the writing on these walls. Kim is possessed. She has been since we opened this chamber. Only now I know it for sure.'

Wallace shook his head, edging closer to Perry, ready to jump him if the chance arose.

'Let the children go.'

The voice lanced through the blackness and both men turned to see Kim approaching them.

'Stay back,' Perry said, a look of absolute terror crossing his face.

'Let them go,' Kim said again, and Wallace too was shocked as he heard her voice deepen from its normal feminine pitch to a thick deep bass.

'Release them,' she said, the words now almost slurred due to the depth of tone. They boomed around the tunnel and Wallace stood transfixed as Kim moved closer, her body beginning to shudder. She stood still, only feet from him, her head tilted backwards slightly, her arms stiff by her sides. The shudders intensified and suddenly she let out a roar which froze his blood.

Her head snapped forward and Wallace found himself witnessing something plucked straight from a nightmare.

There was a sound like tearing fabric and the skin on her face split in three or four places, peeling back to reveal dark, pitted, rotted flesh beneath. It welled through the rifts like pus-filled growths, expanding and contracting as even greater convulsions racked her body. The flesh beneath Kim's own skin was sickly yellow and Wallace saw a number of liquescent boils pushing through it like fingers through wet pastry. Like a mask, her entire face seemed to peel off, hanging by a thick tendril of skin from her stubby neck.

And now he saw her chest and stomach undulating madly, the clothes she wore stretching over each fresh bulge, ripping in places to reveal the scabrous flesh beneath.

Her eyes rolled white, the pupils disappearing, and the glistening orbs then turned red as blood vessels dilated and swelled. She opened her mouth to reveal an array of sharply pointed teeth, all blackened and stained like her lips, which reminded Wallace of swollen leeches. Only they were dark blue, like two corpulent bruises framing a leering mouth which stretched wide and expelled a blast of air so rank that both men almost vomited.

Her hands and arms twitched madly as more flesh peeled back in great leprous folds, dropping away as if she were some kind of snake undergoing a sloughing process. Thick veins pulsed obscenely beneath the new, odorous skin, throbbing like blackened, animated worms.

Wallace shook his head in horrified disbelief as her fingers seemed to reshape themselves into points, not just the nails but the digits themselves, which contracted until they were like bloated needles.

He suddenly understood why they had found no fingerprints on the bodies of the murder victims. This beast had no pads to leave indentations.

Her hair turned grey, then white. In stark contrast to the colour of her putrescent skin.

The change was complete.

The thing which had once been Kim Nichols threw back its head and uttered a loud ululation which could never have come from anything human.

Wallace felt his bowels loosen, the screams of the children now also drumming in his ears.

With another inhuman roar, Morrigan launched herself at Perry.

The archaeologist screamed and went down in a heap beneath the raving monstrosity, the sword falling from his grip.

Wallace took his chance.

'Run,' he shouted at the terrified children. 'Go on, down the tunnel. Now.'

They set off in the darkness, crying in terror, stumbling over bones and other objects as they went, but they struggled on, Clare sobbing with a particularly despairing tone.

Wallace turned to look back at the writhing forms close to him. He heard Perry scream in agony as one of Morrigan's clawed hands slashed open his cheek, exposing the bone, ripping a large portion of the flesh away.

'Slaughter the children,' the archaeologist wailed. 'Stop Dagda.'

Wallace felt as if he was frozen to the ground, unable to move as he watched the creature lift Perry with one scabrous hand, dangling him as a child would dangle a puppet. Then he saw the bloodied hand dart forward towards the man's stomach. The nails pierced the flesh effortlessly and the leathery fingers closed around the archaeologist's intestines, pulling hard. Thick gouts of blood burst from the rent, followed by several sticky, bloated lengths of entrail which the abomination held before it like dripping trophies. Wallace could see that the innards were still pulsing like heavy veins. Blood sprayed everywhere, some of it splattering the policeman, who felt his stomach contract.

Blood filled Perry's mouth, his shrieks of agony gurgling through the crimson clots which filled his throat and surged upwards to cascade over his lips.

Morrigan lowered him a foot or two, his body already beginning to spasm. The monstrosity glared at him. With one lightning movement, it jabbed the needle-sharp claws into his right eye, carving through the soft flesh of the lids, scooping the bulging orb free of the socket and into the palm of its hand where it studied this new prize for a second before shoving it into the gaping maw of its mouth. As the jaws came together the eye burst, a gush of clear fluid and blood spilling down Morrigan's chin. The monster chewed for a second then swallowed the pulped orb.

Wallace could hold back no longer. He bent double and vomited violently, staggering past as the beast dug out Perry's other eye and devoured it, dragging him closer, allowing a wolfish, tumefied tongue to probe deep inside the bleeding sockets, sucking out the clotted blood and other matter which remained inside. Then, with a roar, Morrigan flung the body to one side and set off after Wallace.

He ran as he'd never run before, his head spinning, his breath drawn in great racking gasps. Aware only of the monstrous creature that chased him, moving sure-footedly in the gloom which was its home.

He slammed into a rock wall, bounced off and carried on running, not knowing how far he had to go to reach the shaft.

Or the children.

Dear Christ, the children . . .

They were just ahead of him. He could see them in the light from the torch. He flicked it behind him and Morrigan was illuminated in the beam, a vision of such monstrous corruption that Wallace began to fear for his sanity.

And she was gaining on him.

The ground before him suddenly erupted, a shower of dirt and stones spraying up into the tunnel. All around, the stonework began to crack.

The rumbling grew louder until it filled his ears.

Even the wild roars of the pursuing creature and the high-pitched screams of the children were lost to him now as more earth showered down.

The tunnel was collapsing.

Wallace threw himself forward as on his left another portion of the tunnel floor exploded upwards as if punched by some massive fist.

Was this the end? Was it to be as Perry had described it?

Wallace could see nothing but he could feel the life being sucked from him, his will draining away as the entity known

263

as Dagda began to rise. He knew, in that split second, what he must do.

There was a child close to him, one of the two boys.

Wallace made a grab for him but, before he could seize the fleeing child, he felt strong hands tearing at his back and he knew that Morrigan was upon him.

The claws cut effortlessly through his jacket and quickly found his flesh, reducing the skin on his back to bloodied tatters. Wallace rolled over, despairingly driving one foot into the creature's face, feeling bones splinter beneath the impact. He gripped the torch and used it like a club, bringing it down with bone-crushing force on her head. Blood gushed from the wound but Morrigan did not cease her attack.

Wallace put up an arm to shield his face and felt his forearm torn open by the claws. He drove his fist towards her face but one powerful hand clutched his wrist, squeezing tighter until much worse pain shot up his arm and the bones began to splinter. Wallace roared in pain and rage and drove a powerful backhand swipe into the monster's face. To his horror, it gripped his other wrist too, lifting him into the air with a strength that belied its size.

He felt mind-numbing agony sweep through him, then Morrigan hurled him against the wall of the tunnel. His head snapped back and a sharp piece of rock sliced open his scalp. But as he slid downward he used his one good hand to clutch a lump of the stone. He used it as a bludgeon, crashing it into the face of his attacker, feeling the nose disintegrate under the impact. Morrigan picked him up and hurled him to one side. He hit the ground hard and rolled, finding that he was close to the bottom of the shaft.

The children were there, waiting for him, screaming and crying with new shock as first Wallace, then Morrigan, emerged from the tunnel.

The ground burst open again, and now the entire complex of tunnels was beginning to rumble and shake as Wallace felt the air growing colder.

He struggled to his feet, searching for a weapon, knowing that time had already run out for him.

264

And for those above.

He snatched up a broken sword from the floor of the shaft and hefted it before him. The pain from his broken wrist was excruciating, but he gripped the sword as tightly as he could, bracing himself as Morrigan, Queen of Demons, came hurtling towards him.

Seventy

Broken though it was, the sword was still almost two feet long and it put sufficient distance between Wallace and his attacker. As she ran at him he swung the blade in a downward arc and it sheared through her puffy skin, opening her arm from shoulder to elbow.

A mixture of blood and blackened pus spurted from the wound, bringing with it a choking stench. Wallace ignored this, almost shouting with triumph when he saw the creature stumble.

He struck again.

Morrigan raised an arm to protect herself, but Wallace was driven on now by a mixture of fear and desperation which seemed to increase his strength.

The blade scythed through her arm just below the elbow, shattered the bone and carved swiftly through the remaining muscle, severing the limb, which fell to the ground twitching wildly. Morrigan roared and leapt at Wallace, using her remaining arm to seize him by the throat. The severed stump of the other spewed reeking fluid onto the policeman as he was pushed back against the wall of the shaft, the beast's claws cutting into his neck, drawing blood in several places.

His eyes bulged and he felt as if someone were filling his

head with air. The fetid stench of the creature's breath combined with the even more noxious odour of the blood and pus almost caused Wallace to be sick again.

He found himself staring straight into the demon's blood-flecked white orbs, seeing nothing there but blind hatred and something like triumph.

The ground all around them seemed to be bubbling. Small geysers of earth rose and fell rapidly as the pressure beneath grew to an intolerable level. Wallace knew he had lost, unless . . .

With a despairing moan he managed to push the creature away, smashing it across the face with the flat of the sword.

It staggered, momentarily stunned, and in that split second Wallace struck.

Gripping the sword in both hands he swung it with all his strength.

The blade caught Morrigan just below the jaw, carving through bone and muscle with ease.

The head rose on a thick arc of blood, screaming its defiance even though it had been severed. The mouth yawned open in a last roar of rage, then the head thudded to the ground on the stump of the neck.

Wallace fell back, not prepared for what happened next.

Morrigan's body remained upright, like a beheaded chicken, staggering back and forth for interminable moments. Then it seemed to swell up, muscles bulging outwards as if pumped by air. Bloated, replete with corruption, it burst like one massive boil.

The entire body exploded in a welter of blood and pus. A great stinking eruption of it seemed to fill the shaft, showering Wallace and the children. Great twisted lengths of intestine spiralled upwards like uncoiling springs coated in glutinous red muck. Nails burst from the swollen finger tips even as they flew through the air with the other sickening debris. Wallace screamed despairingly as the vile mixture covered him, matting his hair, lathering his face with reeking red foam.

Even the severed head erupted, greyish-pink gobbets of brain propelled from the riven skull which cracked open to reveal its sticky contents. The eyes burst in their sockets, viscous fluid from the obscene spheres mingling with the blood and pus.

Wallace staggered towards the children, one of whom had fainted.

He saw that two of them had already begun to climb.

'No,' he screamed, his voice drowned as the ground near him split open, the fissure shooting close to his feet.

Beneath him something huge, something loathsome, moved.

He looked down at the little girl, tears now coursing down his cheeks, cutting a path through the gore which coated his face.

He had no choice. He had to do it.

The girl moved closer to him, as if for protection, and as he tried to push her away he noticed that she too was crying.

'Oh Jesus, God forgive me,' he roared and brought the blade down on her head.

Such was the power of the blow that her skull practically split in two. A greyish slop of brain splattered him as she fell, her body twitching slightly.

'No. No!' Wallace shrieked, looking down at the body, at the fissures which were opening up in the earth. Then he turned back towards the tunnel entrance.

'There's your fucking sacrifice,' he screamed. 'Your damned offering.'

But his voice was swallowed up by the groan of parting earth, some of which clattered down around him as the shaft itself began to cave in. Massive lumps of debris thudded down like chunks of shrapnel.

'Stop it,' he wailed. 'Stop it!'

He dragged the unconscious boy to his feet and ran the sword into the lad's throat, holding the body for a moment before letting it fall beside the girl.

'You bastard,' he roared. 'You've had your offering. How many more? How many more, you dirty fucker? Take me instead.'

He turned and grabbed the rope ladder, jamming the sword into his belt, hurrying up the rungs in pursuit of the other two children. One more, he thought, one more. There had to be three sacrifices.

Just one more and it would all end.

He was close to them now, he could see the little girl ahead of him, about to swing herself out of the shaft.

He saw other figures too.

Policemen.

He drew closer, his hand reaching for the girl. He pulled her down, steadying the sword as he rolled her over.

Wallace found himself looking into the tear-stained face of Clare Nichols.

'Please don't hurt me,' she cried, and for precious seconds he hesitated. He couldn't hold onto her. She was pulled free and he found that men in uniforms were backing away from him, shielding the children from him.

Wallace hauled himself up and stood, sword in hand, his mad eyes flicking from one figure to another.

'Give the children to me,' he shouted.

The ground to his right was rippling, dirt and stones flying up in a series of tiny explosions. Elsewhere, huge rifts had scarred the earth. Men were running back and forth.

He saw a car topple into a large fissure, the driver screaming for help as the vehicle disappeared, then exploded in a sheet of flame as the earth contracted around it.

'Give them to me,' Wallace roared, his voice drowned by the shouts of his former colleagues, the roaring flames, and now, a low but growing cry which built to a terrifying crescendo. Beginning like a strong wind, it increased in ferocity until the sound was unbearable. Men nearby screamed and covered their ears, feeling blood burst from them as the onslaught grew worse, reaching an incredible pitch, forming into one monstrous obscene bellow of triumph.

Wallace looked up to see the sky turning red. Redder than a thousand sunsets, as if it had been drenched in the blood of millions. Then, against that redness, he saw a black outline. A shape so huge, so enormous that it stretched up into and beyond the clouds.

The shape was unmistakably humanoid, but grotesque beyond description. And it was still growing.

Wallace clapped his hands over his hears. Inside his head he could hear his own laughter.

The laughter of the mad?

Of the damned?

And all the time that loathsome black shape expanded, its monstrous roar filling the night as it stretched across the boiling skies. Its hideous form blotting out those blood-soaked clouds, filling the heavens.

Then there was only darkness.